Scorpion's Reach

Dedicated to the brave people of both the armed
forces and the Police who keep our streets safe,
Thank you for the safety we enjoy.

If you would like to know more about the author and
the stories, then join me through the following link
lawrence'sletters@wordress.com

Scorpion's Reach

Chapter 1

The tide had turned, but the wind hadn't. It was picking up, causing the waves to grow as they came in on the beach. The two vehicles raced across the sand to the meeting point. The sea wasn't too rough, but it was choppy, and not a night to be out.

"They should be coming in over there," the man in the passenger seat of the lead vehicle, a black Ford Ranger spoke. They were here to meet someone, or something, being brought in by helicopter; they had no idea who they were meeting, apart from 'They must be important'. The passenger pointed to a slight outcrop. "We need to set the HLS up over there, by the flat piece of the beach" he pointed to where the beach was at its widest.

"Bloody idiots must be nuts trying to land in this damn wind" the driver, a big man probably in his late thirties with dark leathery skin and a beer paunch replied, "I mean, it must be a bloody crosswind of thirty miles an hour. What the hell's the rush?" he hated these kinds of jobs. Just "Be there at this time and keep your trap shut" kind of thing, "And don't ask what you're unloading" etc was the rule and a damn good idea to stick to it, which stifled the next question he had.

"I know what you're thinking" the passenger a slightly older man in his early forties with lighter skin and a scar on the left cheek just below the ear. "Don't go there, and I've no idea anyway!" he scanned the skies for signs of the aircraft they were supposed to be meeting. "Not here yet, pull over and kill the lights" they did so, the vehicle behind did the same.

As soon as they stopped and the lights were off the man in the vehicle behind got out, took a moment, moved forward lighting a cigarette and sauntered forward like he hadn't a care in the world, in reality he was scanning everything, making sure no one was watching, he stopped at the driver's side, then pulled two other cigarettes out and offered them one each.

"These things will kill you!" Sam, the driver spoke as he took the cigarette and lit it, they all smiled.

"At least these will take a while to do that" he replied, "This job can do it in seconds, and without bloody warning." They all gave a small chuckle. "Any ideas what this is about?" he stopped for a moment; knowing he shouldn't really be asking, but it wasn't as if they were going to tell the bosses: they'd all be in the shit if anyone did.

"Not a sodding clue bro," the passenger who went by the name of big Jake replied. He was their leader, "The last shipment was only a couple of days ago, so I doubt it's a shipment; unless the dumbass trendy set in Auckland have been buying up large" that brought a chuckle from the others, but he carried on scanning the horizon, "But must be important if they want it, or them, delivered this quick!"

"Come on, let's get these damn things out and set up so they come into the wind" the older man spoke to the other two as they headed round to the back of the first Ranger, he unlocked and opened the back hatch, they had five lights for the Tee and another special one that would guide the aircraft down, all ex-military surplus, designed to give an instant landing pad for a helicopter but with the advantage that unless the 'aircraft' came in on the exact bearing the lights couldn't be seen, and the other advantage of using these was that the one coming in wouldn't need any landing lights.

They set the lights out in the form of a 'T', with the long part running east to west along the beach, each light about three meters apart. Only small perforations on one side where the light would shine through, unless you were almost directly in front of them there's no way you could see the lights, they were designed for landing a helicopter when you don't want people to know you're coming, or don't want people like the local authorities to find you, not so good if you're looking for the hele landing site without knowing what bearing you need to approach on. That's why the bearing and information were so important.

Next, Big Jake took another box that looked like it had a torch welded to the top and flicked the switch, that one would give the pilot his/her height as they came in a simple red, yellow and green system. If the light was red the pilot was too low, if it was yellow they were too high, but in the middle was the green that as the pilot stayed in the green by the time they got close to the light they'd see the beach coming up to meet them and be literally about four feet from them right at the end, and all without landing lights!

"All set?" Jake looked up and spoke just loud enough to be heard by the others who were heading back to the vehicles.

"Yep, all done" the one who'd driven the second vehicle, a younger guy with gang tattoos on his right cheek spoke up, "Just getting my stuff from the Ranger"

"Okay, I'll send the text" Jake spoke up again. He took a small mobile phone out of his pocket, one tap and the screen came alive, two more taps and he was putting the phone away, the message sent. "Now we wait" was all he said after that.

The 'text' was a simple set of letters and numbers. The receiver was wired into the pilot's console in the aircraft; a Bell Jetranger that right at that moment was approaching the coast further up North East.

The pilot was flying by instinct with all his external lights off and the lights in the cockpit dimmed as much as he could get away with to minimize the effect it had on his eyesight, the more light in the cab the less he'd see outside. He also knew he was only about fifty feet above the top of the waves (one hundred feet above sea level), one slight twitch, and they'd been 'in the drink' and sinking so fast that even a life jacket was useless, they'd be pulled under still clipped into the chopper and blades still spinning above them, ready to chop everything and everyone in half who tried to 'bale out' choppers aren't that good for 'ditching' like that.

He could see the coast ahead and was heading for the beach when he heard a beeping, it was the message coming through.

"Message for you" a voice spoke into his headset, it was the computer in the phone he'd wired into the system, one of the latest iPhones with a few little extras added.

"Read" he spoke back to the phone, the passenger he was carrying gave him a quizzical look, then, realizing that he wasn't actually talking to him turned and carried on ignoring him, he was just the 'delivery boy' after all.

"Charlie, Bravo, two four zero, ten, one hundred" the voice, a female voice devoid of all feeling came back, it was meant to be functional, but also not the kind of voice you'd expect in a machine so that it forced you to pay attention to what it was saying.

He understood the message perfectly, it was his directions to the landing site telling him "At the coast turn bearing two forty degrees for ten miles, stay at a height of one hundred feet" he knew that using the lights they were using for landing he'd see the red 'guide light' first telling him he was too low, he'd see that from about five miles away but keep going and the others would come into sight.

Eventually, the light will turn green, and that's when to begin the descent, the rest was simple. Just slow down and stay in the green and the lights will do the rest;

he'll feel the skids touch the sand and that's the time say goodbye to the passenger, that wouldn't be too hard as this passenger hadn't been the most talkative he'd had.

"If you're in the red, you'll soon be dead" he mumbled to himself, 'What's the rest of the saying? Yellow so high you need a Halo, Green you'll be seen and come in mean! Something like that anyway' he finished the thought off in his head.

"Any ideas when this clown's supposed to show?" Sam asked for the second time that night, they'd gone through two cigarettes each and were fast running out of smokes because 'as usual' he was the only one who brought any, and as soon as the work was done they all wanted one.

"Told you" Jake replied, "No idea bro, and don't ask questions, they can get you seriously hurt with these people!"

"So?" Sam stubbed his cigarette out in the ashtray in the back door, "when are these clowns going to show up do you think?"

"Everyone's a clown to you" Henry, the other one in the trio shot back, "you've got to be careful saying things like that" he stubbed his cigarette out too, "saying it to the wrong person could get you kissing the barrel of a 9 millimetre!"

"And who'd they get to do this crap with you lot?" Sam replied laughing. "Some other poor sod fresh out of stir and no prospects for any meaningful employment!"

That was the 'top and bottom of it. One stupid mistake as a teenager and no one wants to help out. Been to prison? Forget a decent job or income, they just aren't going to come your way and that's a fact, the only ones want to know you are the ones who got you into trouble in the first place,

"Anyway, less of the bitching about life's choices and let's get this job done looks like the chopper's about to arrive!" Henry spoke as he opened the Ranger's door and got ready to climb in, they could hear the faint but constant whine of a Gas turbine engine along with the constant but distant 'thwack' that the rotors made as the two blades sliced through the air violently pushing the air out of the way.

"Come on boys" Henry spoke loudly as he finished climbing into of the vehicle, "Let's get this over with, then we can all go home and 'lament' the lack of good jobs for us as those pricks head off to their offices and dead-end jobs and we count the grand that we got for being here and doing 'sweet Fanny Adams' if you know what I mean!"

"True" Big Jake chuckled, "Does kind of beat working doesn't it?"

"Yeah" Sam joined, "Just don't ask stupid questions, or you might find yourself with an extra ventilation hole or two, know what I mean!"

"Oh I dunno" Henry chipped in, "I love work, I can watch people doing it all day long" that brought a few more chuckles from the others.

"What's it sodding well matter as long as they pay well?" Jake was laughing, but getting a little impatient.

"Okay" Sam came back, "I'll drop it, for now." They all knew that they were going to have the same conversation all over again the next time they got to do a pickup.

The helicopter was about a hundred yards away when Jake spoke up. "Time for us to make ourselves scarce" he reached down and pressed the starter, she started the first time. The instructions had been very clear, wait until the 'chopper' is inbound then leave and don't look back, you'll be told in a few days where to pick the vehicle and lights up."

He put the Ranger into gear and began to pull away as the helicopter began its final approach, whatever or more like whoever was arriving, the bosses, whoever they were didn't want anyone to know about, that was fine as the three of them had no intention of thinking about finding out.

"The ground party are on their way" the passenger spoke with a slight Eastern European accent, his voice devoid of all emotion, he sounded more mechanical than Human. "You can land now" it felt like an order, and Carlos wasn't too good at taking orders normally, this time was different though.

As soon as the passenger got in the aircraft the temperature in it dropped, it was as if death itself was riding with him, and he just wanted this guy gone, so if that meant keeping his mouth shut until the job was done then that's what he'd do. He got the impression that guy wasn't into talking that much anyway.

The whole forty-five minutes of the flight they were the first words he'd spoken, not even a greeting at the beginning, even the drug mules taking the shipments ashore, as hyped as they usually were still at least gave a greeting; as if to steady their nerves. They never really knew what was waiting for them at the other end, but this guy was a whole different kettle of fish.

It wasn't that he was wary, or at least didn't seem that way, to him it just seemed as if he was going to a regular job, he just gave the impression that to ask what that job was, might be more than your life was worth. Carlos was glad he was getting rid of the 'package' and good riddance.

The Helicopter's skids touched the sand, the passenger hit the release button on his five-point harness, he opened the door, with his left hand and climbed out, closing the door, he opened the back and took out a heavy suitcase. As soon as he had the case he closed the door and without even looking to the pilot to get the 'OK' he just headed out forwards from under the rotor blades.

As soon as he was clear he headed for the Ranger and opened the driver's door looking for the electronic key that would open the back of the Ranger.

"Arrogant prick," Carlos thought to himself as he lifted back off the ground, "Not even acknowledging the ride!" He was angry but knew there was no point making any noise about it. They paid well and didn't give a shit what you thought of them. Just as long as he delivered the good when they told him to.

And money was what he needed. A struggling business and a willingness to, do anything that helps pay the bills was what got him the job, at first it seemed like a good job to have, ferrying a few things around so the cops didn't know where they were, a few plants and stuff, then it got slowly more serious until they had him 'by the balls,' and he was carting the hard stuff for them. Always at a moment's notice. He'd get a call and would have to drop anything that was planned to get the job done, asking questions wasn't an option.

As soon as Carlos was airborne he turned on a fresh bearing that would take him out to sea, ten minutes would see him fifteen miles offshore, then he'd be able to climb to five hundred feet and come back onto the radar for the little charade that fitted with his flight plan.

On the beach the lone passenger watched the Helicopter depart, he was glad to be alone and not having to deal with the stupid vermin that he often had to deal with in his profession, these people weren't particularly any worse than the others, they all annoyed him, but the pay was good and as soon as he'd got this job done he could disappear, until they needed his special skills again. Back to his own little world where he was left in peace and the rest of the world didn't intrude.

As soon as he got to the vehicle he went to the driver's door and opened it, the keyless ignition and door sensor were on the seat; he reached in and scooped them up. Pressing the button for the rear door he heard the click as the door opened. He put the suitcase on the rear seat but still opened the rear hatch, the pickup, or 'Ute' as they called them here, had a covered back tray.

As soon as the helicopter was gone he walked round to each of the lights in turn, turned them off and picked them up, carrying them to the ute (Short for 'utility vehicle') he put them in the back in the special container they'd come from, he didn't bother to wipe the sand off them or to wipe them down from the moisture, the 'minions' could do that when they got them back in a few days.

Five minutes later everything was packed up and he was ready to roll, he climbed into the driver's seat and reaching inside his coat he took a plain manila envelope out,

The envelope had nothing written on the outside, but he knew from previous experience that all the details he would need were in the envelope including the passport he'd be using to leave the country and the route they'll want him to take after the job was done, but most importantly for this stage there were the details of the passwords to access the encrypted files he'd already got on his laptop in his suitcase, all he knew was the target was in Auckland and he had a seven-hour drive ahead.

He pressed the starter, she started up first time, putting the vehicle into gear he set off, there was no need to worry about tyre tracks as the sea was almost up to the vehicle by now, within the hour the sea would cover the landing site and all trace of tonight's meeting would be lost.

Chapter 2

The scenery took his breath away, rather it took most of it, and what the scenery didn't take the ride did.

Joey still wasn't fully back to his best after Iran, the wounds had left him in hospital unable to do much for nearly a month, then the Doc had told him "No exercise for at least another month" and Sandy had insisted on making sure that he obeyed fully, she'd taken it on herself to make sure he 'did it' right, she'd become his own 'personal nurse.'

Not that he was complaining, he was actually over the moon about it, but he'd never even dream of letting on.

"Come on slow coach" Sandy turned and shouted over her right shoulder as she approached the next bend in the road, the hills weren't big, but they were constant, and besides the scenery to the left was the kind that if you caught a glimpse, it would stop you dead in your tracks as you tried to take it in, Joey wasn't a religious person, but seeing this scenery was almost a 'spiritual experience'

The mountains weren't tall enough to be snow-capped, but the rocky peaks surrounded by emerald green forests that hadn't been touched by man, and cascaded down the slopes until they suddenly dropped onto beaches, not 'pristine white' beaches but messy untouched and littered with driftwood, the things that the sea herself deposits on beaches, the kind of things that say "Man's not been here. And he better not touch me."

For Joey, coming from a place that's teeming with people and you can't see the beaches for deck chairs and stuff, seeing such untouched beauty was stunning, he hadn't really believed that such places still existed, but here they were, and they were everywhere on this Island.

The beaches themselves were sided by steep cliffs on one side and a turquoise sea that in places actually bubbled as the earth's crust was so thin that it warmed the water in places, at one point the other day they'd actually taken a hot bath in seawater on the beach!

There were four of them altogether; Joey and Sandy along with Sandy's sister Helen and her husband Kevin, a 'good kiwi bloke' as he loved to say. Straight after the hospital, Joey and the team had a meeting with Sir Michael who basically said, "You're too valuable to go back to your old regiment so we're transferring you to M.I.6 as soon as Joey's well enough to carry on."

That was it, Joey's days in the Army were over, the days as "Bond, James Bond" as he tried to say in a pathetic Scottish accent were just beginning.

"First order of the day" Sir Michael had continued, "Phoenix is wounded, but they're not finished, they want blood. AND WE MEAN YOURS" he'd looked around the room at the team. "Apparently they want your heads served up on a silver platter and preferably severed from your bodies, they're willing to pay a high price for them!"

"That along with the unholy political row that Iran caused" he went on. "Means we need you folks out of the way for a while" he shifted in his seat as he said the words, the rest of the team just looked at each other not sure whether they were liking what they heard, moving to M.I.6 was a huge pay increase and they'd get to play with a lot more 'cool gadgets' but the Army was all most of the team had ever wanted, taking it away like this seemed a bit cruel.

"Jacko" Sir Michael continued, "You and Mac are going to Canberra, the Aussie SAS would like to learn a few things from you, officially still with the Regiment, but at my beck and call" he didn't even pause as he turned to Smithy, "You're going to Burnham down in New Zealand, the Defence force there want a sniper instructor"

"What about us sir?" Joey'd stopped him in his tracks and was somewhat impatient.

"We're going on Holiday" it was Sandy that replied, "Don't argue!" she looked Joey in the eye, she knew he'd want to get back into the thick of things. "You need to recover some more, and besides I haven't said where yet, New Zealand, to see my sister and her husband"

"Oh" was all he could say, not sure how to take the 'meet the family' routine.

"You'll love it," Sandy replied. "They're the real outdoors people, just the kind you love"

The road that runs around the coast of New Zealand is known as the Pacific Highway. In places, near the big cities it's a wide open road, sometimes with dual carriageways, at other times, near the smaller places it's just a single carriageway around the Island, and in some of the more remote places, it isn't even a mettled road, just a gravel road; often clinging to the cliffs with sheer drops into the ocean.

Just north of Thames, on the Coromandel peninsular it's a single carriageway, but go too far and she gives way to a gravel road. They were still on the single carriageway, just south of Coromandel township, a small settlement near the northern end of the peninsula, a winding road at the best of times.

The rest of them were up at the hairpin bend, admiring the view, Joey wasn't that far behind, and besides, he could have easily kept up with them, but Sandy had explained that part of the job was not telling folks what you did, and being 'too fit' after a serious accident (that was the story) would kind of give the game away a little, it would have people a bit too suspicious, so he'd play along with it and was taking his time, but being called a 'slowcoach' was pushing it even if it was his beloved saying it.

The other three were on the small grass verge as he got to the bend, Kevin a born naturalist and ardent conservationist was explaining something to the two girls, Joey couldn't quite hear what he was saying but he followed their gaze to the creatures frolicking in the bay, there were a group of large black and white creatures swimming and diving in the water between the islands in the bay, the closest of them was probably only about two hundred yards off the shore.

"Are they?" Joey began, and then it dawned on him what they were watching. "That's a pod of Orcas!" was more a statement than a question, the only time Joey'd ever seen Orcas was on TV. "I thought they lived in the Arctic?"

"They do in the Arctic summer" Kevin replied. "And in southern Ocean in the Southern Summer, the Hauraki Gulf is a stopping off point on their journey, kind of a whale's refuelling station, they're stopping off for a feed in the bay"

They were mesmerized, watching a pod of creatures as majestic as the Orca is something special, even in New Zealand you could spend hundreds of dollars paying to go out beyond the horizon 'whale watching' and still not see a sight as amazing as twenty to thirty Orcas just feeding in the bay, what made it even more special was that just a little further away was another pod, but this one was Dolphins, and the two didn't seem to be bothering each other.

"Do the Orcas feed on Dolphins?" It was Helen asked the question that all wanted to know.

"Sometimes" Kevin replied, "But these seem to not be bothering with the Dolphins as they tend to fight back as a group"

"Kind of a don't screw with us then?" Joey asked cheekily. He was fascinated that the Dolphins would band together and protect each other.

"Put it this way" Kevin replied, "If they did feed on Dolphins, they wouldn't be welcome here! The Dolphins keep sharks away and they're probably Hector's dolphins, they're only found in New Zealand waters"

"Yeah" Helen agreed, "Dolphin's hunt Sharks don't they?" she asked.

"Not just that" Kevin continued, "but if anyone's in danger from sharks, the dolphins will come in and attack the shark, often driving it off and saving the people"

That bit was a bit too much, both Joey and Sandy broke out into a disbelieving smile, but neither said anything for fear of offending their hosts, Kevin saw it and jumped back in with 'proof' "I'll show the articles on the net when we get back" he spoke up, "Where people were swimming and the dolphins protected them! By the way, Orcas think sharks are tasty!"

James Cavell was an arrogant prick and not only did he know it, he really didn't give a damn what people thought of him, not even his boss at the Bank!

'When you make people tons of money' he thought to himself often 'They really don't give a toss what you're like' and he was making them bucket loads of cash, so he really didn't give a damn what people thought of him.

He'd been with the Bank just two years and in that time he'd made them a whole bundle of money that is if you didn't look too closely at the clients and some of the things they got up to.

But that was 'work' and right now he just couldn't care less about it. The sun was shining, the road was quiet, a gorgeous blonde in the passenger seat.

He knew she too only wanted his money, she wasn't an 'escort' or whatever they called themselves, but the only thing she wanted was his dough.

Truth was that was okay, he'd spend a little on her over the weekend, and maybe one or two more weekends then it'll be the old 'heave ho' and find another, that's the way he lived his life, and he loved it.

The weekend they'd got planned was a simple 'romantic weekend' away from the city at his place overlooking the bay north of Coromandel Township. The bay was one of the most magical ones you could imagine with emerald islands set in turquoise seas where amazing sea life can be seen.

"Snorkelling and sex" was all that was on his mind, and not necessarily in that order, the blonde was 'hot' after all and well, he just might not be able to hold himself back from sampling the delights of what she was offering! The road was the last thing on his mind.

Then again in a McLaren P1, you didn't need to do too much thinking about the road, the car did the thinking for you.

A formula one engine accelerates you from zero to sixty miles an hour or one hundred kilometres an hour in just under three seconds, the speed topping out at just over two hundred miles an hour making it a true 'supercar'

The traction control system keeps the car literally glued to the road as if with superglue, and human control is just too slow so it's all controlled by computer, yet just enough is left to the human that it feels as if the car is under the driver's control making it not just a good drive but a whole new amazing experience for anyone lucky enough to amass so much wealth.

The road from Auckland to the town of Thames had been reasonably busy with the cops patrolling and people keeping their speed down, still, it had only taken about two hours for the hundred-mile trip, but most of the traffic was turning right just before there and heading to Whitianga or Whangamata. 'Where the wannabes go' he thought to himself.

Cavell had a place in a secluded spot right on the beach halfway between Coromandel Township and Colville. A million dollar plus a place that, well probably better the bank didn't know about it as they might get worried just what he was doing with the clients' money.

The McLaren was cruising along just in second gear at the one hundred kilometres or sixty miles an hour speed limit. Frustration was beginning to show, he just wanted the chance to 'open her up.' That would come just after Thames, followed by hairpins and enjoyable roads as he tore along scaring the life out of anything he would meet on that road.

They pulled up at the last set of lights in town, right next to a Porsche 911 Cayman, the other driver gave a look that clearly meant "not impressed" and revved the engine, it wasn't even a contest. The Porsche can do standing start to sixty in just over three seconds, the McLaren does it in two and a half!

They stayed behind the Porsche until they got around the first bend, the other driver must have thought he had them beat; but on the long straight stretch, Cavell let her loose. The McLaren growled with delight, wheels spinning she blew past the other car as if it was parked, the long face and dropped jaw on the other driver said it all. She was flying. Cavell eased off the accelerator but she kept accelerating faster and faster as if the foot was to the floor, eating up the road like a ravenous beast devouring prey; He tried the brake, really sluggish, something wasn't right, they should have responded well. He tried again, even worse. Pumping the brake nothing happened, the brakes failed and the throttle stuck open, not good.

"Not good at all" he was beginning to panic

"James" Denise, the girl with him was looking worried. "Don't you think you should slow down?"

"I'm trying" he wanted to shout, it didn't come out as a shout though, more like a whisper he was concentrating so hard, he grabbed for the handbrake and began pulling, they'd reached a hundred and ten miles an hour and she was still accelerating, a slight right hand bend fast approaching, crashing the car crossed his mind except one side was rock and the other a twenty foot drop, neither were good options

"The accelerator's stuck" was all he could say, he was pumping the pedals as hard as he could, nothing was happening, "and the brakes aren't working"

"What?" she looked across at him worried.

The car was doing over a hundred and twenty miles an hour now and still accelerating hard. There was no way they were going to make the hairpin that was coming up, the only hope they had was for him to try and 'drift' the car round the bend, but with the traction control still engaged the chances of drifting were much reduced, there were people at the bend that he was probably going to hit, there was nothing he could do about it, it was either him or them and he knew whom he'd choose. The bend was fast approaching. He swung the steering wheel hard to the right to try and make the bend, still pumping the brakes to try and get the last ounces of fluid to apply the brakes just enough to get them round the bend, there was no time to worry about what next.

The car turned and slid sideways, the McLaren was so low on the ground and the centre of balance was so low that there was no way it was going to roll, but centrifugal force did take over and the car instead of going forward was now moving sideways; tyres squealing, rubber burning and sliding forward, but every inch forward meant a foot sideways with the crash barrier fast getting closer.

The four people at the bend were trying to dive out of the way as the passenger side of the car slammed into the crash barrier with a force that ripped the crash barrier clean off the support posts like tearing through a paper barrier and kept going; airbags deployed instantly but the force of the impact still threw them violently sideways almost snapping their necks.

Denise bore the full impact of the crash, the door moving back into her body and breaking every rib, two of them puncturing her left lung and a third going straight through her heart, she was killed instantly. Cavell wasn't so lucky; he was still alive when someone found him.

The vehicle came to a stop on its roof at the bottom of the incline. Cavell wasn't sure how long he was 'out for' only that when he came too he was upside down, held firmly in place by the four-point harness that was the vehicle seat belt, a proper racing harness similar to those used in racing cars.

There was blood on just about every surface inside the vehicle, He tried to open his eyes, but only one obeyed, a misty red scene awaited him as he tried to look around, searing pain in his lower abdomen told him there was probably some serious internal damage, he could feel his feet, but not move them, he was trapped.

Out of his good eye, he could see Denise, she was a mess, blood covering most of her face, and she was clearly dead. As he looked at her he saw another moving around the vehicle, a man wearing all black. He didn't get a clear view as the man seemed to be keeping his face out of sight, what he did see was a very slight build that seemed to move with grace and purpose around the vehicle.

"Help" Cavell tried to shout, but all that came out was a whisper, he looked for his 'Angel' to see what he was doing. He felt strong hands moving around his neck. "Checking my injuries," he thought to himself.

His sense of relief turned to alarm as those hands grasped a firm vice-like grip on his neck and gave a violent twist severing his spinal column at the base of the brain. The last thought he would ever have didn't have time to form before oblivion descended forever.

Chapter 3

Joey saw or rather heard the car approaching and something just didn't seem right. It sounded like the engine was screaming, almost like whoever the idiot was driving it, were they trying to blow the engine? Something just didn't sound right. He stopped and looked behind, he saw it didn't look right either, careering round the bends at breakneck speed, then it tried to take the hairpin and drifted.

"Everyone out the way NOW" he screamed and dived for Sandy to knock her out of the way, he'd felt the air disturbance as the car passed, Sandy was knocked into the crash barriers but he couldn't help that, 'she's gonna be pissed with me' he thought, but there wasn't anything he could do, he had to get her out of harm's way!

They landed hard on the tarmac, he stayed conscious, but hurting from just about every joint in his body, the aftermath of wounds not completely healed, yet being called on again to 'lay it on the line' but not for Queen and country this time. "You okay?" he asked as soon as he saw movement from Sandy, she was stirring and shaking her head.

"Think so" Sandy replied as she came round, "Apart from a whacking great headache, what about you?" she turned and looked over in his direction, he could see she wasn't quite focusing yet, "and what the hell were you doing?"

"Didn't exactly help my healing if that's what you mean" he replied, "But otherwise we just about got out of the way in time"

"What the hell happened?"

"Didn't you see the Sportscar behind us?" he asked, "I think it was a McLaren."

"No" Sandy replied, is that what it was?" she asked pointing to where the car had gone through the barrier, they could see it, on its roof away down the bank, wheels still spinning."

"Yeah" Joey replied, "looked like they lost control, but they were going at a hell of a speed, bloody crazy trying to take that bend at that speed!" he'd finished checking himself for injuries and started scanning Sandy, "Anywhere you hurt?" it was important they make sure they weren't injured before they started looking for Helen and Kevin. 'Try moving your toes"

Sandy brought each leg up and set them down again, she also wiggled her toes so they could see them moving in the shoes. "Nah, nothing broken" she replied,

"Just going to have one hell of a bruise". She went to turn over and tried to move her left arm, "Shit, that HURT" she almost shouted as she nursed the limp arm.

Joey did a quick examination, " be a break or a dislocation" he said. "Let's get it in a sling" he started looking for something to use.

"Find Helen and Kevin" She ordered, "I'll sort out a sling, but can you go look for them please?" she changed her tone slightly; feeling special that he was paying so much attention to her, but there were others needed help, and she really didn't want to get into the 'ordering her man about' scenario.

"Okay, but first call the Ambulance" Joey reached for the mobile he was carrying in his pocket, he handed it to Sandy, it had some interesting features on the phone, for one thing it was constantly monitored by M.I.6 and they both knew that Sir Michael would know of the accident before they got off the phone, it really was an emergency phone where they could be contacted at all times.

"I, I'm okay". Sandy was a little shaky, Joey wanted to stay with her but knew what was coming next. "You need to go check the others, see if they're okay, please" she grimaced clearly in pain, but a steely determined look he'd learned to recognize and not argue with came onto her face.

The first rule in accident first aid is 'triage' or in other words, find and treat the most serious patients first, Sandy was injured but nowhere near the most serious injury; the others would be worse.

"Give me the phone and get a move on!" Sandy was taking charge, "I'll call the ambulance" he pulled the phone out, tapped the emergency number and handed it to her as soon as the operator came on the line.

"Which service do you require?"

Joey was already moving when he heard Sandy say "Ambulance" truth was they were going to need all three, but the comms centres for all three were linked, as soon as one got the call, the others would pick it up and prioritize with the fatalities and injuries putting them right up there at the top. He could hear her giving details as he moved away.

The car had taken a ten-meter section of the crash barrier with it as it went down the incline. There was a gaping hole right there, and only the empty posts at the end of the section. He could see where the barriers had been ripped from the posts with the force of the car's momentum, he took a quick look down the incline, the sight that met his eyes was gruesome.

Kevin had been next to them, with Helen a little further along, he could see Kevin, at least what was left of him and it was horrible.

Joey'd seen some pretty rough things in his time, but this was 'right up there' with the worst of them. The car had been travelling at speed and had trapped him between the car and the crash barrier literally slicing him almost completely in two. Kevin's torso and legs lay at an angle that even if the spine was broken there's no way they could twist that way and still be connected to the body.

"Guess that answers that one" Joey said quietly to himself. "Better concentrate on finding the living" he began looking again, first scanning the incline to check if she was there.

He found her at the other end of where the crash barrier re-started. She'd been hit a glancing blow and thrown over the barrier, she wasn't breathing.

Normally you'd make sure not to move an injured person as you might do more damage and could end up paralysing them for life, the only exception is when they're not breathing, you have to get them breathing again and that means doing CPR or 'Cardiopulmonary Resuscitation'. Joey got straight into it without even thinking.

The first thing he did was check the mouth to make sure there was nothing blocking the airway, a quick visual check and a poke around with his fingers cleared the mouth of the two teeth that had been knocked out.

He was careful, tilting the head back trying really hard not to move her head too far so that he didn't move the spine any more than he absolutely had to then he pinched the nose and took a deep breath, then leaning over 'mouth to mouth' he breathed into her mouth.

"Six breaths and massage the heart" was his thought as he lay the head down and moved to the chest, one hand above the other he pushed hard and reasonably fast on her sternum, six hard quick pushes and he was back to the breaths. He kept going alternating between the two until he heard the sound of sirens.

Joey's senses were in overdrive. He was working giving Helen the CPR but at the same time his brain was taking everything in and noting where everything was, the threat assessment part of his training had kicked in big time.

There were no immediate threats to him and Sandy but it was the little things his brain was noticing as he worked on Helen, noticing yet not actively looking. Noticing tyre tracks down on the beach, they were new and looked like 4x4 tracks, then a man seemingly clad in black walking away from the McLaren. Joey wanted to yell to the guy but something stopped him, he didn't think much of it at the time and he had enough to do so he just 'filed the information' to talk to the cops about when they took his statement.

"I'll take over now sir" he half looked up as a fireman threw himself down beside him and motioned him to move over, he gladly gave the job over and almost collapsed on the ground, another fireman came up carrying a defibrillator, but Helen was already beginning to breathe on her own. They started first aid for the other injuries.

The Ambulance was the next to arrive, the Fire brigade and Ambulance people were all volunteers and it'd taken time to get from their regular jobs to the vehicles, they took one look at Helen's injuries and called for the rescue Helicopter from Hamilton.

"You'll be taken to the Hospital in Thames," the Ambulance officer told Sandy. "The other, the more serious injury will be taken down to Hamilton, that's where the spinal and neurological unit is"

"How bad is she?" Sandy was worried.

"Fractured Vertebrae in the neck, I can't say if the spinal column has been affected yet" the ambulance officer, a young girl with a ponytail and gentle manner replied. Sandy was impressed with this girl as she seemed younger than her but was taking all this carnage 'in her stride' yet able to care for those still needing the care. "Then there's a couple of fractured ribs, broken pelvis and two broken legs" the girl had finished her examination of Sandy and apart from the dislocated shoulder, a few deep bruises that had originally had them thinking 'internal bleeding' and a sprained ankle that would need binding up for a couple of days she was 'good to go'

The Police had been the last of the three to show up, the operator had mobilized the three services in the order they would be needed with the Fire brigade first, then the Ambulance and lastly the Police to take statements and take over 'traffic management.' The Police was one 'copper', a senior constable (by the looks of the rank insignia on the uniform) who headed straight down to the McLaren, just as he got there another two squad cars arrived and began setting up a traffic cordon, they were going to close the road until the McLaren was recovered, and a scene examination was done, a tow truck was on the way.

Joey'd made his way back to Sandy who was getting first aid by a very attentive fireman, that is until Joey showed up, and then he became a little more 'businesslike'.

He sat down beside Sandy and put his arm around her, she was in shock and looked totally numb.

The St John's Ambulance staff had taken over the treatment for the three of them, Helen had been stabilized and the rescue helicopter was on its way. "It's ten minutes away" the paramedic treating Sandy had said, she was a quiet and efficient worker, Joey wondered what she did in her normal job. 'Probably a helpful sales assistant' he thought to himself.

They'd been given thermal blankets to wrap around themselves, Joey gave his up and wrapped it around Sandy, she didn't seem to notice, all he could hear from her was "I'm sorry, I'm so sorry"

"Hey" Joey spoke softly to her. "It wasn't your fault!" She just looked at him as he gently put his arm around her. Sandy wasn't one to show emotions, she usually kept them bottled up inside, afraid that if they got out people would think less of her, but somehow it was just different with Joey. Around him, she felt safe. She felt she could show her true self even with the emotional baggage. Instead of pulling away as she'd do with anyone else she turned and moved closer into him feeling safe.

The dam that was her emotions and had withstood so much in the past would have ruptured, flooding everything in its path, but she'd found one with whom she could open the 'sluice gates' of emotion and relieve the pressure; the dam would not break while Joey was there to turn to. She simply turned towards him and the tears quietly began to come.

It was a full five minutes before he heard those tears subside, he didn't interrupt or say anything, the truth was he had no idea what to say anyway, he just sat there quietly trying to think of something to say, yet knowing whatever he said just wouldn't be adequate. Finally, as the tears subsided he heard Sandy's voice quietly say "Thank you"

He almost asked "What for?" as he'd no idea what he should be doing or saying, yet it seemed the right thing to do, instead, he just said, "You're welcome."

They were still holding each other when one of the police approached, he was fairly young looking. 'Probably not long out of Police College' was their initial reaction. Black hair, brown eyes, muscular build standing about five nine in height 'rugby build Joey guessed. "Which one, union or league?" He asked.

"Huh" the cop was a bit thrown by the question, he was meant to be the one asking questions. "League" he replied. "How'd you work that out?"

"Sorry, just very observant" Joey replied in an almost apologetic tone, the last thing he wanted was to annoy this guy; he was only here to take statements after all.

"Thank you for your patience" the cop began, "I'm officer" he began, it wasn't like they were going anywhere, but at least he was being polite, just trying to help what he must have thought were two shattered and terrified tourists, Sandy still had a bit of a vacant look about her but Joey was quietly watching everything, taking all the details in. "My name's officer Kingi and I'll be starting your statements, just the basics then the senior constable will 'run through them with you later when you've had time to compose yourselves, did either of you see the car before the crash?"

"Oh" they both replied almost in unison, it was odd as police normally like to get the statements properly at the start and only go over them if there's a discrepancy, at least that's what the movies show. It was almost as if the sergeant was saying "I don't trust you" at the start.

"I saw everything." It was Joey spoke up. "The car came round the corner doing at least a hundred," he began.

"Kilometres?" Officer Kingi asked.

"No, miles" Joey replied, "Take a look at the tyre tracks on the road, you'll see they're way bigger than they'd be for someone doing a mere sixty miles an hour" he pointed to the skid marks they could see from where they were sat. "He was still accelerating, but trying like crazy to stop which was nuts, he was bricking himself" Joey saw the cop look confused, "I mean scared shitless"

'Never heard that one before" the cop replied, glancing up from his notes," but point taken now"

The next ten minutes was taken up with Joey recounting the encounter in graphic detail, he noticed that the copper was wearing a name badge saying 'Hene', his full name was 'Hene Kingi,' Joey filed that information away in his brain for 'future use' but the copper was having problems accepting all that Joey was telling him, it's well known that people can make things up so they seem more important than they really are in an investigation, he wondered if Joey was doing that.

"You seem pretty sure of what happened" Hene began, "are you sure of what you're telling me?"

"Absolutely" Joey replied without any hint of offence, "I'm used to dealing with high-stress situations"

"This is a little more than just as 'high' stress situation" Hene started to reply, 'Fatal crashes usually"

"Are usually the worst" Joey finished the reply. "In my line of work I'm used to dealing with them, and often dealing with fatalities as well"

Just as they were wrapping the statements up one of the Ambulance crew came back towards them, they'd managed to carry Helen down a little way and two of the crew along with the Doctor and Paramedic from the Helicopter rescue unit were busy strapping her into the back of the helicopter, as soon as she was strapped in the doctor and paramedic climbed into the back, the engine pitch changed and the vessel began to rise as soon as the door was closed.

"They're taking the Lady to Waikato Hospital" the crew person, the petite blonde who'd treated them earlier explained. "We'll take you to Thames for treatment, and then arrange for transport for you to get to her"

"Thank you" Sandy was grateful. She didn't really want to be separate from her sister right at this moment, but there was no way they'd all fit into the machine, and Helen really needed the urgent attention. "There's no need though, just point us to where we can hire a car for a little while"

It was just then that Sandy's phone buzzed, they'd forgotten that when she called the Ambulance someone else had listened in to the call, it was them texting now, the message was simple and said: "Report in ASAP!"

Chapter 4

The mobile phone is actually a miniature radio capable of transmitting messages over vast distances. We don't notice it because the frequency they use is too powerful to stay near the earth's surface and heads off into space in a straight line. Put a 'rebroadcast station' in the line of sight though and you can transmit incredible distances.

The way the telecom networks get around it is put another receiver/transmitter out into space to rebroadcast the signal to earth, we call them satellites. One such picked up Sandy's call, a small piece of computer code built into the phone and transmitted, told the satellite someone else needed to know about the call so it was recorded and sent to both locations.

Twelve thousand miles from them and after a journey twenty-six thousand miles a computer picked the information up and an alarm went off, and it wasn't a silent one.

"What the?" Sir Michael was wrenched into waking. He propped himself up and looked at his clock, it said 3.45am, but it wasn't the clock alarm, he reached for his phone and looked at the number. He recognized it straight away, GCHQ Cheltenham. The top-secret branch of the government responsible for eavesdropping on whomever they need to.

Reaching for the phone he hit the 'answer' icon and without identifying himself simply said, "at 3.45am! This better be important"

"Sorry for waking you Sir Michael" the male voice on the end of the line didn't sound sorry at all, he sounded businesslike and got straight to the point. "You requested we monitor a number of mobile phones, one of them just placed a call you might be"

"Good God man, can't this wait?" He hadn't meant every damn call for heaven's sake! 'are these people thick?' was his thought.

"It was to the emergency services sir" the operator continued, "reporting a car accident, with multiple fatalities sir!"

That got his attention. He sat bolt upright "When?"

"Call just came through the satellite link sir" the operator replied, "we're listening to the Police and

Ambulance system now, its agent Little calling for the emergency services.

By now he was out of bed and already heading for the door to his private study, he'd need coffee to help him think this through. Was this an attempt on them or was it just a 'fluke?' He was a spy and didn't accept the idea of just dumb luck! You always treated everything as 'suspicious' until you'd nailed every reason as to why it wasn't, it was that simple.

"As far as we can tell" the operator came back on the line, "Both our operatives are still alive, though one of them may be injured, the Fire brigade are already 'on scene' and they're reporting that the deceased are two in the car and one cyclist, but not our operatives" he emphasised the last part.

"Send everything you have to my personal file" he reached out to turn his desktop on, it took a couple of seconds for the system to 'boot up' then went to the GCHQ website, entering his own personal password he accessed the system and began searching for the files he needed, they'd just 'arrived' and he began to listen to the recordings.

This was a nightmare, that was putting it mildly, he'd only just got the team out of the country, and to the safest places he could think of, now, as usual, the proverbial had hit the fan., had they been compromised? That was the first thing he thought of, he'd have to get onto it and have answers before anyone else found out.

Listening to the recordings didn't take long, more arrived as he was listening; it was clearly still 'happening' as he was listening.

Working remotely meant that he didn't have access to the equipment making the live recordings and as such was at the mercy of the operator, but this was to prevent the 'live system' being hacked or hijacked, they could get access (in theory) to the recordings, stored for other operatives and government bodies to listen to, but not to the originals which are stored on separate systems and have to be manually transferred to be sent to whomever requests them.

"Was this a breach in security?" that was the big question. Had the 'mole' found them? The same mole that had passed information as to who was stealing the drug money from the drugs barons and had got Steve Chambers taken. Their retaliation had been swift by sending Scorpion team into Iran to get him back, from then on they knew there was a price on the heads of each of the team, that is until they found out who was passing the information.

Splitting the team up and giving different people part of the information as to the whereabouts of various members seemed the best way forward, that way they'd be able to work out where the 'leak' was. Was this the 'mole' showing themselves?

The system was simple; it was also slow, inefficient (so other senior department heads told him) and belonged in the dark ages. Sir Michael's reply was "yes" to all of them, but it was secure and because of that it's damn well staying!

The computers gave you a letter and number. Follow them until they intersect and that gives you the password. Every time you go to it the computer asks for a different one, simple, easy and unbreakable code. Every week the card was changed and the old ones burned. They're known as 'one-time ciphers ' and spies love them because they're unbreakable.

Accessing the system from within Vauxhall house was easy, and seamless. With no 'hoops' to jump through, everything was there, behind all the firewalls and protected. It was coming in from the outside like he was doing now that was the issue. Yes, the computers recognized his machine and even the ISP address but they never knew if, or what malware might be trying to get through, especially since the issue with Oxford University and their servers that were hacked by the Chinese came to light!

All he was after this time was phone logs, he knew who knew about Joey and Sandy's travel plans. Each team member's travel plan had been 'compartmentalized', and only he knew all the details of everyone, so tracking the mole was simply a case of waiting to see if anything happened, and depending on who it happened to would tell them whom it was. However, first, he needed to make sure it was the 'mole' and not a fluke.

Spies don't believe in 'flukes' or 'luck' but they do believe in checking the facts, and that's what he needed to do. It was the only place to start, but first, he needed to find out what was going on in New Zealand and what kind of shape Sandy and Joey were in. The first point of call on the computer was the network where he accessed their phone number and fired off a very simple message, "Report in ASAP"

Chapter 5

As soon as he was treated, Joey got out of the hospital and went looking for a rental car. Just over an hour later he was back at the hospital, ready to pick Sandy up in a late model Toyota station wagon. It had plenty of room for anything they might need, it was also the first car that he'd been able to find and he really didn't give a damn, all he cared about was that his girlfriend's sister was in surgery after a serious accident, his girlfriend was worried and they needed to get there.

It turned out that Sandy's injury wasn't that serious, just a bad bruise that the nurses dealt with by strapping her up. The bandages felt a bit tight, but she'd get used to it.

The Toyota had a GPS unit, he was going to programme it, but Sandy stopped him.

"No need," She said as she got into the car, "I've already got 'Uncle Google telling me which way to go, and how long it's going to take to get there!"

Sandy mounted her phone into the holder the car had, and connected the charging unit through the USB port they all seem to have nowadays. Now they'd be able to use the phone as much as they needed to and not have to worry about flattening the battery.

The programmed the destination was 'Waikato Hospital' in and he was pleasantly surprised when it came up with a reading in Kilometres and an ETA (estimated time of arrival). There was a Bluetooth facility in the car so he programmed the phone to be able to take 'hands free' calling using the car's speakers as they made calls, the first one was the worst.

The female voice from Google started giving directions as soon as they left the car park.

"Have you called your Mum and Dad yet?" he was thinking of the difficulty she'd have making that horrible call, he chanced a glance at her, she was looking vacant, not really with him right at the moment, not surprising really considering the situation, but some things can't wait and the worst thing he could think of was the family finding out through the TV instead of a family member. "Want me to call them?"

Sandy didn't reply, she just nodded.

"Phone" Joey spoke in a commanding voice; the phone had verbal command facility. "Call Sandy's parents"

There was a slight pause as the phone worked its way through the programme then a quiet musical tone as the phone called the number told him that they were connecting, Sandy was quiet but tears were coming, he pulled the car over ready for the phone call, the last thing he wanted was to be trying to speak as they were driving.

The phone came to life as a female voice came on the line. "Little household," it said, "How can I help?"

A lump came in the throat as he started to speak. "Mrs Little, I'm Joey Metcalfe"

"Oh hello, Joey" the voice came back. "Sandy's told me about you; to what do I owe the pleasure"

"Mrs Little," Joey spoke again, "I'm really sorry but I've got some tragic news for you, is Mr Little there?"

"Yes, he is" she came back, "Hold on a moment while I put you on speaker" the phone went quiet for a moment, then a slightly fainter male voice came on the line, he sounded worried. "You're on speaker Joey, please what's the problem?"

"Mr Little" Joey began, he really hated to do this, but Sandy was in no shape to do it, she was silently sobbing. "Mr Little, there's been an accident earlier today, Sandy's okay slightly injured but okay, however, Helen's been seriously hurt"

"Good God" was all he heard on the other end, he really hoped they were sitting down, "I take it you're sure of this err 'Joey is it?"

"My proper name's Joseph if you like" Joey replied, "but friends call me Joey, yes we were with them at the time. I'm really sorry to tell you this, but Helen's husband Kevin was killed in the accident!"

The phone went really quiet for a good two minutes, so much so that it was only the lack of tone that told him that the phone wasn't 'hung up' Joey finally spoke up and said "We're on our way to the Waikato hospital at the moment, we'll be there in about an hour, we can keep you informed if you like?"

Mr Little was the one that came back on the line, "Thank you Joseph, err Joey, we'd very much appreciate that, we'll get a flight and be there as soon as we possibly can, do you have our mobile number?"

It took about two minutes to confirm the number and they were very thankful that Joey was thoughtful enough to call them and not leave it to the police or the TV stations. As he hung up he saw a slight smile on Sandy's face, she simply mouthed the words "Thank you"

He'd tried to work out Sandy's accent from the moment they got out of Iraq and hadn't been able to place it until she told him where they were going, then it twigged, Sandy wasn't actually English! She had British parents and as such qualified for a British passport, but she was actually 'born and bred' in Christchurch on the South Island of New Zealand. That's where they were flying up from.

"That's one important call made" Joey clicked the phone off, "are you ready for the next one?" he looked at Sandy not sure what she'd say. Someone had to tell Kevin's parents and it really shouldn't be the poor cop who turns up at the door not knowing the family.

Sandy was wiping the tears away, she looked frail but there was a look of grim determination on her face. "We need to call them." She spoke to the phone. "Call" she reeled the number off, Helen and Kevin lived on his parents' farm just outside Te Kuiti in the King country of the North Island, the phone connected immediately and mostly Joey did the same again. He left the gory details out.

"Are you sure he's dead?" Was the only question they had, that was after a while of crying and silence in that order.

"I'm really sorry Mr Smith" Joey replied, he wasn't sure their last name but seemed to remember it was Smith. "The ambulance crew said he died quickly and probably didn't feel any pain" there was no need to add the gory details as funeral directors would make sure the coffin was sealed when the family got it, there's no way they'd want the family to see the mess, 'better to remember him as he was in life' was the thought.

"Thank you" was all they could say, and then Mr Smith asked, "Where have they taken him?"

"As far as I'm aware they took him to Auckland as a matter of protocol" Sandy replied, "It was an accident and there'll be a bit of an investigation, but that shouldn't take more than a few days"

"Then we'll arrange to get him back" it was Joey jumped in, he knew the family would be in no state to arrange things. "I've still got to talk to the Police so I'll make a request for them to transport him down"

As soon as the call was finished Joey put the car into drive and set off, they knew they should call Sir Michael, 'he can wait' was the thought on both their minds, Sandy did however dictate a message to the phone to go as a text that simply said. "Both OK will report more fully at 0700 GMT"

The phone was sending the message as she spoke up next, "That'll give us about three hours before we need to call." She looked at the GPS, it was estimating their arrival at the hospital in just over an hour.

"We'll find out the situation with Helen, then I'll leave you at the hospital and go make the call" Joey glanced over at her; he was quietly amazed at how well she was handling things. Yes, agents get training in how to handle high-stress situations, but they don't usually involve immediate family members and triple fatalities, like today.

"Thanks" Sandy replied "But I probably should be there for the call"

"You're probably right" Joey replied, "But that's not going to happen, you need to be with Helen and be there when the family arrive, I can deal with the office, you need to be there for family"

Sandy wasn't going to argue, she knew Joey was right but didn't really want to think much about it. Letting him deal with London would be fine.

They arrived and found a park in the multi-storey car park at the hospital, the light had already gone and darkness was fast falling when they found the A and E department, Sandy approached the desk, "excuse me" she began, "but we're looking for my sister, she was brought here by helicopter earlier"

The nurse on the desk looked up, "Do you have a name? One that I can look up for you that is"

"Her name's Helen" Sandy replied. "Helen Smith, she was brought in about half an hour ago by helicopter" she looked hopeful.

The nurse started tapping on the computer keyboard, the screen changed as she worked through the system looking for the name she'd said. "Ah, here we are, she looked intently at the screen, it looks like she's still in surgery" she looked up. "If you like I can find out how the surgery is going?"

"Yes please" they both replied in unison. Then Sandy spoke up. "Is it possible we can wait somewhere?"

"We've got a waiting room just around the corner" the nurse replied paging a porter, "Give us a moment and I'll get someone to show you where and then they'll go find out for you"

"Thank you"

A couple of minutes later they were shown a small room that had a couple of chairs and a couch, there was a waist height table that ran the length of most of the room with a small kettle and tea making equipment in the middle. As soon as they were in there the porter disappeared saying that he was going for a doctor to find out how things were going on.

As soon as he was out of the room Joey turned to Sandy, "are you going to be okay, or do you want me to stay?"

"No, I'll be okay" Sandy replied, "You really need to call the office and let them know what's going on"

"He CAN wait you know," Joey replied he wasn't totally sure that Sandy was ready to be left alone.

"No, you go and make the call" Sandy replied. "Mum and Dad will be here in the next few hours, I'm going to need you then"

There's a lake not too far from the Hospital, he'd seen it from the windows in the stairwell on the car park as they were entering the main building, Joey headed outside and made his way towards where the lake should be, he soon found it and was pleasantly surprised to find it had a walking path that encircled it.

The path wasn't all that well lit which made it perfect for what Joey wanted, he didn't really need people coming along listening in to the phone call, he looked at his watch, five minutes to the appointed time, he found a bench and waited.

As soon s the five minutes were up he was pressing buttons, the call was connected almost instantly, a slightly gruff voice came on the line, the tone wasn't Sir Michael's usual one, but it was him. "What happened?" there was no need for pleasantries.

"We were hit by a car" Joey began. "Biking on the Coromandel peninsular."

"Hit and run?"

"No boss" Joey cut him off, "The car was a write-off, it was also a McLaren" Joey replied. "It lost control on a bend and ploughed into us"

There was an audible sigh of relief. "So it was an accident then?" was half statement and half question, Joey wasn't sure which.

"Not sure I'd say that just yet boss" he responded. "I saw the driver; he was fighting the car, almost as if he wasn't in charge if you know what I mean"

Sir Michael knew exactly what he meant, some of the latest cars on the roads were so advanced they had 'driverless' features that were supposed to mean the car was capable of driving itself, but also meant they could be 'hacked' and driven remotely making them a new very frightening and deadly weapon. "You think the car was hacked then?"

"Boss" Joey wasn't sure how Sir Michael was going to take this, but he had to say it. "I saw the driver; I saw the terror on his face and the way he was fighting for control, I'm bloody sure he wasn't the one in control, I just don't know why they'd choose a McLaren as a murder weapon if we were the targets." Joey went on, "I mean, if that was the case it was one bloody expensive murder weapon!"

"Explain yourself" Sir Mike was curious, 'Why would Joey say that?' he thought

"Remember a couple of years ago boss, Rowan Atkinson pranged his McLaren, an F1, cost the insurance company an arm and a leg literally, probably the most expensive auto repair job ever! Damn things are worth tens of millions, and I'm talking pounds"

"And"

"That was an F1 boss, a nineties model, this was a brand new P1, they go for a couple of million pounds new! Ain't no way anyone would use them as a murder weapon for a grunt like me, much better to put a bullet through my thick skull." Joey was very businesslike. Almost cold and detached, but he was right.

'This boy's very perceptive' Sir Michael thought, he'd said nothing to any of the team about his suspicions about the mole, but it sounded as if Joey at least had worked a few things out. "Do you think you were the target?" he asked.

"Not totally sure boss" Joey was truthful, "We made a hell of a mess in Iran, and I'm pretty sure they're still pissed off at us, but getting this far out? All I can say is what I saw!"

"And to you, it seems suspicious?"

"There is something else boss, that's bothering me a bit"

"Oh what's that?" suspicious minds were ticking over.

"The cops" Joey replied. "They took a statement sort of, at least the rookie cop at the scene did, but the senior cop was only really interested in the car wreck! We were a bit far away, but I'm sure I saw him put something into the car which is bloody odd if you ask me!"

"I've had a couple of people listening in on their frequencies, they did say the cops reported finding a half-empty bottle of booze in the car, are you saying he planted it?"

"Like I said boss, I was a bit too far away to be certain" Joey replied. "There's no harm in checking out who was the driver of the car though is there?"

"I'm already ahead of you on that one" Sir Michael replied, "and with it being a McLaren I've got a couple of friends there who'd be very interested to find out what went wrong, they take their car building and safety to extremes over there at McLaren, I got the registration number from satellite photos and have been running it against the NZ database, I'll check it against McLaren's own information about the car owner, I should have the details in a few minutes, I'll email them to you"

Joey was impressed, he'd thought they'd need to wait at least a couple of days for the information, and then he'd have to go through 'official channels' to get them. "Thanks, boss" was all he said.

"Don't worry" Sir Michael replied, "It's all above board and legit," he continued. "By the way, while we're talking, just to let you know no one in NZ knows what Sandy does, as far as they're concerned she works for Sun Alliance insurance, and so do you right now, have you got that?"

"Understood boss"

"The McLaren Company is also with Sun Alliance so you won't have a problem getting a look at the car if you need to, they'll insist on it, but it'll be after any Serious Crash Unit investigation, I'll email you any credentials you need." Michael continued, "I'll also get them to let the NZ subsidiary know you're the one dealing with it, Let me know if you need anything else" and with that he hung up.

Joey sat there stunned for a few moments, he'd expected to just report in that they were okay, he wasn't really expecting Sir Michael to take his suspicions as seriously as he seemed to, then again Iran had caused a real shit storm to break loose and there were more than a few wanting blood from the fallout, and they weren't all people on the wrong side of the law.

He got back to Sandy just as Kevin's parents arrived, the first thing they did was give both of them a huge hug, not sure who needed the hug most Joey heard silent weeping as he was embracing the pair of them, it just felt right to keep the embrace until they were ready to let go.

Chapter 6

Hene was furious. It just wasn't right and he knew it, but Murray was his boss and getting on the wrong side of him could finish his career before it's even begun, but still, it just wasn't right.

He brooded over it for the rest of the morning, but then came to a decision. He could delete the statement but still save the original on a thumb drive. He was going to Hamilton later in the week, he'd still have the original, so he could talk it through with one of the detectives there, they might be able to give him some advice, it might also let them know that something just wasn't right here, but he'd have to be careful that it wasn't just some rookie 'probationer copper' trying to get 'one up' on his boss, then again, what was he supposed to do?

It had been three days since the accident and still the Police hadn't been in contact, not even a 'follow up' call from victim support or any of the groups like that, that seemed odd to everyone, not least to Sandy.

"Are you sure the cop got our right address?" Sandy asked for the third time that day, "I mean it's damned odd that they haven't been in touch" she was slowly getting more and more movement back into the shoulder, Helen was off the critical list but was still in intensive care, so the family were staying pretty close to Hamilton. Sandy's parents were at the Hospital with Helen, but the rest of them were at the farm Kevin had shared with his parents. They were sat around the kitchen table discussing things.

"He got our address right" Joey replied with a hint of frustration, "I made him repeat it a couple of times"

"That would have been amusing" it was Mr Smith spoke up. Joey was confused why that would be, Mr Smith continued. "An Englishman trying to tell a Maori how a Maori name should be pronounced" It was actually good to see the small smile on his face, it'd been a while since he had anything to smile about.

"Gave him my phone number as well" Joey replied. "Actually, I've got his so maybe I'll call and find out what's going on" He stood up and made his way outside. The conversation around the table turned to where Joey and Sandy had met, she told them he was a work colleague whom she'd 'taken a shine to' and they 'went from there.' Joey'd already told them that he was ex-Army, that went down really well with both sets of parents and a couple of invites to the local Returned Services Association had been extended, so far Joey'd managed to pass on both of them.

He came in a couple of minutes later looking a little confused, Sandy saw it before the others and managed to get him to one side before the others noticed.

"What is it?" She virtually demanded as they stepped into the living room.

"I got through to Officer Kingi" Joey replied, "He said he put the statements in but got a strip tore off him by his boss who wants him to rewrite everything."

"Well?" Sandy asked it was obvious Joey wasn't telling anything.

"I told Sir Michael I saw one of the cops walking down to the crash site with an empty bottle of booze!"

"You're sure of that?" she asked.

"Absolutely" Joey replied. "I can't tell you what it was exactly, but I'm sure it was either Beefeater Gin or Whiskey, the bottle was that shape!"

"And he's looking at putting it down to excess alcohol?" She asked no one in particular, "still, they've got the Crash Unit's scene and car examination yet" she carried on the thought, "But it does sound strange, almost like you want them to find things that way."

"Oh, Officer Kingi's been told not to speak to us unless he wants to lose his job" Joey continued.

"What?" that was just too far, Joey had to be joking.

"Nah, I'm not" Joey could see what she was thinking. "Apparently this 'constable Murray' is a bit of a power freak. But Officer Kingi is afraid for his job at the moment"

"But that doesn't make sense"

"Tell me about it" Joey replied. "The whole bloody lot isn't making sense; they want this "brushed under the carpet"

Sandy was looking directly into Joey's eyes, there was a steely look in her eyes that just made her look all that more sexy than normal. "I think we need to know a little more of what's going on!"

"We are meant to be on holiday, remember?"

"So, we just let something like this lie? Even when we know somebody's hiding something?" Sandy replied asking the question knowing full well it wouldn't sit well with the awkward Englishman.

Joey was in agreement with Sandy, he didn't need to say anything, but she knew she'd hit a nerve, however, he still needed to hear it from her. "So, what do you want us to do?"

She stopped for a moment, "I think we need to find out why they didn't want statements, and who exactly was in the car?"

"Speaking of which that reminds me," Joey interjected. "Sir Michael said he was going to get us some paperwork for checking the car itself out, that should answer if it was really an accident!"

"Sounds like someone's already been scheming!"

"No more than usual!" he replied, "You didn't think we'd be dropping it altogether, did you?"

"First let's find out where the car was taken," she headed back in, the rest of the family were drinking tea. Their laptop that was there on the kitchen bench, closed up, she took the laptop and headed back to the lounge, "Sorry folks, got some things I need to do, won't be long." She mouthed to Joey to wait there with the rest of the family as she headed off.

"So, how did you folks actually meet?"

Joey sat down back at the table, he relaxed and allowed a slight smile to come, they'd been waiting for these questions for the last few days, but now, it was a sign of a family desperately trying to find something, anything that would take their minds off the reality of the horror they were going through. They'd been through a lot in the last few hours and they deserved the break. "We met at work" Joey replied without letting too much out, "Sandy got into a bit of a fix with a client and me and a couple of buddies got the chance to help out"

"Really?" That family were a bit surprised, "Then again, if Sandy's anything like Helen then no wonder!"

"She's got a habit of getting into 'pickles' then?" that brought a few laughs, the tension was slowly dissipating.

"You could say that" it was Mrs Smith that replied, "Ever see that programme, what's it called Jack?" she turned to her husband. "Farmer wants a what is it?"

'Jack' her husband was smiling, he had a huge smile, "Farmer wants a wife?" he replied, "it's an Aussie programme originally, but this was the New Zealand version"

"What reality TV?" Joey was laughing, really surprised at the revelations.

"No" he replied "Not TV, it was run at the last Fieldays event, about nine months ago, they both entered the competition and she's loved it ever since"

Somehow Joey'd turned the question time round and was finding out more about the family than he was telling, but he had to give a bit more.

"I work in the security side of the business." He came back into the conversation, "Sandy was getting a bit of grief from a client whose security wasn't as up to scratch as it should have been, me and a couple of mates showed them where the problems were"

Just then Sandy came back into the room, they were all talking animatedly and laughing, she wondered just what Joey had been telling them, she looked over at him, he just smiled back and gave a 'don't worry' signal, she began to relax, "Okay, what have you been telling them about us?" she half-joked.

"Oh only that we're madly in love and you're just like your sister" Joey came straight back, "always getting in deeper than you can deal with" she almost kicked him under the table for that. But it did seem to have relaxed the situation dramatically, besides she hadn't heard Joey actually say those kinds of words before and they sounded really good coming off his lips, even if they were 'half in jest'

It was a couple of hours later that Sandy and Helen's parents Peter and Joanne arrived back from the hospital, they look absolutely shattered but needed to talk a little if only to unwind so they'd be able to sleep.

"Helen's doing better" that was the first thing they said as they sat around the kitchen table, "She's out of the coma and the doctors think she's going to be okay" it was Peter spoke up for the two of them, "though they say it might be a while before they know if she'll walk again" he almost broke down in front of them, Sandy stepped forward and hugged her dad, Joey also stepped forward and gave Joanne a gentle hug, both Mr and Mrs Smith also stepped up, despite the agony they were going through with a son that wasn't going to come home, they put that aside and were simply there for the other family

If you ever want to see how a real family functions then look at one that's going through hell on earth! Some will pull apart and try the 'I'm an Island routine' totally destined to fail and do so spectacularly! It may not happen immediately, it might even take years to happen, but it will as each one comes to the conclusion that there really is no one there for them when they've pushed everyone away.

It's the family that pulls together and at times buries their differences that are the one that comes out stronger. Joey and Sandy both felt a little strange, a little on the 'cheap' side as there were some things they couldn't tell these amazing people, yet they were pulling together even though they hardly knew each other, they were becoming a 'family' where the bonds will not break!

It also gave them the drive to find out what the hell happened on that road, and how anyone could attempt to tear such precious bonds apart.

"That was no accident" Joey was adamant, "I'm bloody sure of it" they'd waited until everyone else had finally gone to try at least to sleep, Sandy was still awake and had something she wanted to say.

"We got a message from London while you lot were talking" she started. "Mike started checking out the car, apparently it was bought new and brought into the country by a 'James Cavell' a banker"

"Kind of explains stuff a bit," Joey said, "I mean they've usually got lots of the old ready cash" he rubbed his thumb and fingers together in the age-old sign.

"What are you two talking about?" A voice quietly spoke up from the back if the room, it was Peter, Sandy's dad, he was stood in the doorway, just observing.

"How long have you been there?" Sandy was disturbed she hadn't noticed him.

"Two minutes" it was Joey replied, turning towards Peter he commented. "I saw you heading for the toilet about ten minutes ago, then the toilet flushed five minutes ago, two or three minutes to wash hands, so I figure two minutes right?"

"Very perceptive" Peter had been leaning against the frame, now he stood upright and came towards the table, he took a chair and sat down. "She's not as good at hiding things as she thinks she is you know!"

"Dad!" was all she could say.

"What?" He replied looking up and shrugging. "I'm an old 'Copper' what else do you expect?" He carried on. "I've not told your Mum" he carried on. "But I knew as soon as I saw the way you two were acting, there are things you aren't telling us, what are they?"

"That obvious eh" Joey muttered. "Okay here goes, I don't think it was an accident, how does that sound?"

"Got any proof?"

"None, apart from what I saw" Joey replied.

Sandy made a fresh pot of tea; she served them both a cup. "Joey's not one to panic under stress dad" she turned to Joey, "I think I'd better explain, Dad's a retired police inspector, with the Criminal Investigation Branch, that right dad?"

"Never said he was, and yep that's right" Peter replied lifting the cup and taking a sip, she'd remembered just how he liked it. "But why not leave it to the police? That is their job after all"

"Cos it's been three days and the cops haven't been back to take our statements" Joey replied.

"And before you say anything dad" Sandy picked up it, "Just before you and Mum got here earlier, we checked with the cop who did talk to us, they've already closed the case"

"That's not unusual." Peter replied, "once they've got the facts, they do that"

"Without the accident investigation report?" Sandy asked knowing the answer.

"That can't be right" Peter replied. "They don't"

"Do they do it knowing they haven't got all the pieces? and kicking the one cop who did file a report from us to the kerb? And Sandy's already said they haven't done the accident report yet" Joey asked. "I don't know why, but someone doesn't want people asking questions!"

"Does sound strange I'll admit." Peter shook his head slightly, "but you're accusing cops of corruption, that's pretty serious"

"No, we're not accusing anyone" Sandy replied, "least not without proof"

"Glad to hear that" he looked accusingly at his daughter, it's hard when someone, even your own family accuse an institution you worked many years for and trusted for many years of wrongdoing, even if it just might be one single member of it. There was silence for a while minute, one pregnant with tension, they all knew something was building.

"That's why we tracked down where the car is" Sandy broke the silence. "The company wants us to repossessed it once the cops have finished with it"

"What?" Peter was shocked, "you can't, you were involved, and which company?"

"McLaren, they're insured by our company" Joey answered. "And as the only representatives in the country they've sent us the paperwork for taking possession of the car and doing a thorough examination before sending it back to England"

"You're sending scrap back to England?"

"It's a McLaren" Joey replied, "even as scrap they're worth millions of pounds! They do it all the time, and they really want to know what failed, the cops shouldn't have a problem with it!" he took a long swig of the mug of tea Sandy had put next to him.

"So, we're sending a crashed car back to the manufacturer so they can find out what went wrong!" Joey went on, "and let's not forget these things cost a couple of million pounds each, even the engines are worth about a million, naturally want to make sure it's not a defect that's going to kill someone else, even when they're driving in a stupid and imbecilic way!"

Chapter 7

"So glad you could make it" Sir Michael rose to meet his distinguished guest, he indicated the gentleman to take a seat, it pays to be nice most of the time' he thought to himself, 'especially when you want something.'

"Thank you for inviting me to your club Sir Michael" the gentleman spoke with a soft, but slightly Latin accent, just hinting at his Argentinian origins, something that along with his very German sounding name of Bauer managed to throw the average businessman a 'curveball' that he loved to take advantage of, "I do believe it's the first time I've been here." he looked round approvingly, "Very hospitable I see" there was a waiter was waiting for him to order something.

"I'll have my usual, it's Martin, isn't it?" Sir Michael ordered for them, "and a glass of beer for my guest, Herforder Pils I believe" he turned and looked at his guest.

"Yes Sir, will that be all?" Martin, the waiter asked.

"Can we also have a plate of sandwiches?" he turned to his guest, "Hope you don't mind, but it's been a long day"

"Not at all, I might ask you to make sure it's enough for two though, if you don't mind" he turned to Martin, "If you don't mind that is?"

"I'll get right on it sir" Martin replied and briskly walked away.

As soon as he was out of earshot the guest, Herr Bauer broke the silence, "I take it this isn't really a 'catch up' call is it?"

Sir Michael smiled, he knew that an old university friend like Manfred would pick up that some things don't happen by chance, the call from the head of M.I.6 always caused question, and Manfred wasn't dumb enough to think for a minute that he just wanted to 'catch up', they'd been good 'chums' at Oxford, but 'sorry, it just doesn't happen' he thought to himself. "I'm afraid you're right" he replied.

The waiter brought the sandwiches back, along with the two drinks, "I'm surprised you remembered, about the beer that is!" Manfred said.

"Old habit" Sir Michael replied, there wasn't any point in trying to hide what he did, it was a matter of public record, "Old spies are good at remembering things you know." he picked a sandwich up, they both chuckled a little at that, truth was they both knew Sir Michael had a near perfect memory. "But let's cut to the chase, I heard there was an accident involving one of your cars, over in New Zealand, I'd like to help"

"I heard about that" Manfred replied, "not much to worry about really, by the sounds of things, the police are saying alcohol and speed!"

"Already? You sure about that?" sir Michael asked raising the drink, he took a sip.

"What do you mean?"

"From what I heard, on my grapevine" Sir Michael went on, "The police may have decided before they even investigated, and if I remember rightly, the cops usually get told to piss off by your company if they try and investigate, you like to know the real reasons, isn't that right?"

"Not anymore" Manfred replied, " we don't get away with those kind of things anymore, not when there's fatalities involved, but anyway, we've no one in New Zealand at the moment, so we'll have to just 'go with the flow' and see what they say"

"And end up with egg on the face when people find out the report was a total whitewash" Sir Michael interjected.

"What are you getting at?" Manfred was getting a little uncomfortable.

"Just that I've got some people over there at the moment who'd love to get a look at that car" Sir Michael replied, "and make sure they get to the truth.

"And you'd like my help?"

"All I need" he picked his drink up and took the first swig, "is a letter authorizing a 'representative' from Sun Alliances' UK office to deal with the salvage and shipping of the car, after all, the engines alone are worth millions, and your engine supplier really wouldn't like it's secrets to fall into the competitions hands would they?"

It took a good two minutes for Manfred to process what he'd just been told, he knew it wasn't a threat, but his bosses, the people he 'advised' had shares in both McLaren and Mercedes Benz who supplied the engines, there were things in those engines that they really didn't want to get to the competition. "Okay" he finally said, "I'll draft you a letter, let me have the details you want in it!"

"They'll be in your inbox within the hour" Sir Michael held up the drinks that Martin had just delivered, "Prost"

"Excuse me" Sandy spoke to the waitress who brought their coffees, "but I noticed you have free Wifi, could I get the password please?"

"Sure, no worries" the waitress, a young girl with a ponytail replied smiling, "just give me a minute or two." She put the two drinks down and headed back to the counter, neither Joey or Sandy spoke while they waited.

She was back within the minute, "here you are" she handed a piece of paper to Sandy, "it'll give you an hour access, if you need more just let me know."

"Thanks" Sandy replied, "that should be enough, just got important email to deal with" which was half true, an email from Sir Michael made it 'clear as daylight' he wanted the car checked, AND NOT BY THE COPS!!

It took her about fifteen minutes to find what she was looking for, and another couple of minutes to access the incident reports, they were all there, but the witness reports seemed a lot briefer than they remembered giving.

"The car's in the Thames compound" Sandy glanced up from the device she was using, it looked just like an iphone, but way more powerful, and directly linked to '6's servers, "according to the log the serious crash unit hasn't processed it yet, they're planning to do that tomorrow."

Joey sipped the coffee, it was good coffee, "Sounds like we need to get our 'skates on' then" he downed the rest of the drink,"how far is Thames from here?"

Hold on there cowboy" Sandy gave him a frustrated look, " before you go barging in let's check the security."

A couple of minutes later they had all they needed, the password protection on the security clearance hadn't been much of a problem, though Sandy was impressed it took the servers fifteen seconds to break the code, that doesn't sound a lot, but when you realise they were bombarding them with half a million bits of information a second, that's a hell of a lot of combinations. They once broke the Metropolitan police computers in ten seconds, so fifteen was pretty respectable.

"Looks like they've got four cameras on the garage floor, and two monitoring the outside, all watched from the police station"

"Any chance we can get in without being seen?" Joey asked as they stood up.

"No need" Sandy reached for her bag as she replied, "maintenance is booked for this afternoon, I just booked it in the system"

Most people would need at least a week to get over the trauma of the accident, they didn't have that luxury, with killers possibly right on their 'tail' they needed to stay ahead, and the only way that could happen was find out what happened with the car, what caused the crash:

"Afternoon officer" Joey, dressed in the overalls of a technician, greeted the desk officer, "here for some scheduled maintenance on your security system for the compound and yard" he plonked a heavy toolbox on the ground, the thunk reverberated round the reception area of the station.

"Hold on a minute" the duty cop looked up from the computer, "let's just check the system" he tapped a few keys on the computer keyboard.

Joey just stood there, impassive; just as if nothing was happening, absolutely no sign of nerves at the fact that only a half hour before he and Sandy had hacked into the police database to insert the 'backstory' for their fake 'technician'.

The screen came alive with a picture of Joey, but the name was slightly different, a 'Jimmy Metcalfe' and enough of the truth there that if he was asked a question he could easily get away with it, there was also a set of fingerprints.

The officer reached down and took what looked like an electronic fingerprint pad from under the desk, it had a cable coming out of the end which he inserted into a USB port on the desk computer, he looked over at Joey.

"Oh shit" Joey exclaimed as if in shock at suddenly remembering something, "Left my bloody ID badge at home, SHIT!" he almost shouted as he began running through pockets, "Damn, sorry officer, I'll have to come back tomorrow SHIT!"

"Hold on a moment buddy" The officer smiled, "Even if you had it, we wouldn't care, not without the fingerprint scanner confirming who you are, put your right hand on there" he pointed to the scanner, "If that confirms then you can carry on and we won't mention the ID badge!"

"Oh, Cheers bro" Joey gave a good Kiwi impersonation, he did as he was told, the machine was silent for a moment.

"ID confirmed" the officer more or less read off the screen, he looked up at Joey, making eye contact "you know where the junction boxes are?"

"Pretty much" Joey replied, "do I need an escort?"

"If you'll wait a couple of minutes sir, I'll get someone to take you through" the officer said as he reached for the internal phone

They were there a total of twenty minutes, just enough time to let the cops think they were checking the camera feeds, they were, but to Sandy's laptop. The idea was she'd record ten minutes footage, then when Joey was ready to go in they'd play that footage in a 'loop' giving him ten minutes to get in, check the car over, retrieve anything interesting and get out, all without giving any indication anyone had been there.

It was dark around nine, the town was beginning to 'party'. That meant a busy night for the station: Cops would be coming and going all night.

That was good, at least for Joey and Sandy it was, it meant people moving around, it was good cover for the little escapade they had planned.

The only hassle they had was that the recordings had been done in daylight, but they were doing this at night, they'd managed to compensate for it some, but they were still relying on a 'busy station' and overworked cops, a vigilant cop might just catch the switch, if they were watching the screens right at that moment in time.

The compound had a back way in, it was pretty secure, with Chubb locks and a burglar alarm wired directly to the front desk

"Loop's running" Sandy spoke through the earphones, she was in their car, with the engine running, the laptop was plugged into the cigarette lighter. "I've bypassed the alarm, you're good to go"

"Cool" Joey replied as he worked the first lock, "see you in ten" as the lock popped open.

There were two other vehicles in the compound, all of them had their own space, plastic sheeting creating separate spaces, keeping them apart, so one didn't contaminate the other.

He found the McLaren in the end space. Everything from the crash was there, even photos of the scene, and detailed notes of where each and every piece of debris was found, basically they could rebuild the scene down to the nearest millimetre with the notes.

"Two gone" Sandy's voice came into his earpiece, "eight left."

Joey took his time, about five minutes in he spoke up. "I'll need longer", he was starting with the obvious places, under the car.

"How much longer?" She couldn't hide the concern.

"Couple of hours" Joey suggested. He knew she couldn't see the smile on his face, he just couldn't resist the teasing.

"What?" She was so loud he almost removed the piece, "that's not what we"

"Just kidding" Joey tried to calm things down, "but possibly another ten, that possible?"

"At a stretch" Sandy replied, "not found anything?"

"Oh I've found it alright" he sounded like he was concentrating, "it's just going to take me a little longer to disarm it!"

"Disarm what?" She almost deafened him again, "what have you found, a bomb?"

"Yeah, some kind of incendiary device," Joey replied, "don't worry, I've got this under"

"Joey, get out of there, NOW"

"I told you, I've got under control" Joey hissed so strongly it made her jump, he'd never used that tone with her before, "it looks like a timer on it, I'd say whoever did this, planned all of it, even this but"

"Blowing a bloody police station up?" Sandy was incredulous.

"Perfect way to get rid of evidence" Joey sounded almost blase, like it was 'nothing really', "think about it, the car's been here what, a day or so?" He was still working, "ah here it is, I've found the timer, it's not a bomb as such, more like an incendiary, kind of like a flare."

"Two minutes left Joey" Sandy couldn't think of anything else to say.

Two cylinders, that's what it was. Both plastic, but the lower one was much bigger than the top one, it also had a glass inner, all the evidence said whatever had been in there had been extremely corrosive, probably an acid concentration of some kind. The brake pipes looked like they'd been eaten by an acid, and damn quickly.

'I bet the top is white phosphorus' Joey thought to himself, 'If it is I'm in deep shit' he thought as he began assessing the situation.

The second cylinder had a valve like fitting, the valve looked like it had a small motor and wires leading to it.

'I see what gives' he talked to himself, not quite loud enough for Sandy to make out what he was saying.

"What?" She asked, "never mind, resetting the loop, give me twenty seconds", "there, done"

"I just worked it out," Joey spoke again, "it's white phosphorus, timed to expose and ignite in about an hour, I can disarm and remove the device, that's what I'm going to do"

He slid from under the car, he needed some duct tape, he'd seen a roll of it just before climbing under the car. Reaching for it he sild back under and began peeling it off.

"But if it goes off" Sandy began, "wouldn't that alert the cops that something wasn't right?"

"And injure a whole heap of 'em" Joey replied, "they'll look at what was going on here today, put two and two together and come up with five, and we'll have one hell of a manhunt on our tails, they'll be coming for us, not the real villains!" he explained, "Besides, I've figured it out, and I can stop a whole lot of innocents getting hurt"

"By putting yourself in harm's way?" Sandy knew the reply, but she had to say it.

"It's what I do honey" Joey replied, his voice was soft, almost asking for understanding, like he couldn't help what he did."Besides" he started again, "This way the cops carry on unawares, but the bad guys get a message, one that's loud and clear, someone's onto them, it's not the cops, and as the movie says, be afraid, be very afraid"

"And that's good because?"

"Cops play by rules" Joey replied, "we don't!"

Placing the end of the duct tape over the valve he began wrapping it round tightly, three or four times round the cylinder and it was secure, even if the timer went off, the valve wouldn't release now. Next he cut the wires, they were spring loaded and and he saw the valve try to open, but the tape held it firm. Lastly he cut the tape.

Three bolts held the cylinders in place, they took a few seconds to undo.

"Okay Kid" he said to himself, "Let's get the hell out of Dodge!"

"Here the bitch is" Joey almost shouted as he held up what looked like a small box.

"What?" Sandy was taken by surprise, she'd never heard Joey use that kind of language before, and it took a moment for her to realize he wasn't insulting anyone, he was talking about the device he found

"What've you found?"

"Take a look." they were in the car about to make their way back to the house, he held a strange device up for her to look at. Sandy was in the driver's seat, but they'd pulled into a layby just outside Paeroa.

It looked like two small cylinders strapped together, each one was about three inches long and a half inch in diameter, one had a hole in the bottom, but the other didn't. "Looks like a brake cylinder" Sandy observed, "But it's not, what is it?"

"My guess" Joey replied, "It's a murder weapon!" he went on, "Careful with it, the open one's still got acid around it"

"Acid?"

"Yep acid" Joey replied, "It's just like an old world war 2 detonator I remember reading about, except this one's been adapted a bit to release acid not blow things up!"

"What ARE you on about?"

"Ever heard of a place called St Nazaire?" Joey asked.

"It's a place in France" Sandy replied. "In Normandy"

"Back in world war two the allies needed to make sure the Germans couldn't use their Big Battleships in the Atlantic; St Nazaire was the only place that had a dry dock big enough to take the Bismarck and the Tirpitz. The Allies had to come up with a way to destroy the dry dock without losing too many people"

"Yeah, I'm following so far" Sandy replied though she was totally confused as to how this related to the little contraption they'd found. "But do I really need a history lesson?"

"The only way they could do it was using an old rust-bucket of a destroyer, to make sure they could get off in time they needed a delayed action fuse" he held up the cylinders. "Just like this!"

"Is that what it is?" Sandy asked.

"Only difference is this one was filled with an acid, my guess is sulphuric acid" he pointed to the cylinder that had the hole. "The acid dripped out and dissolved the brake pipes, making things look natural, but this one here" he pointed to the other cylinder. "Misfired, this one was supposed to dissolve too, and in there I bet there's phosphorous, nasty stuff that burns on contact with air and meant to destroy the evidence!"

"By the way" Joey carried on, "The world war two one misfired too, went up five hours after it was supposed to, killed an extra three hundred Germans who were 'treasure hunting' not realizing they were walking on a floating bomb!"

"Okay" Sandy brought things back to the present. "That explains the brakes, but what about the accelerator?" she asked.

"That one's easy" Joey picked up the other thing he'd brought out with him, take a look at the carpet, I cut this from behind the accelerator pedal, by the way, I'm not sure how they're going to see the missing accelerator pedal, maybe they'll realize someone has been playing with their 'scene' but I needed you and Sir Mike to see it!"

Sandy leaned over and grabbed the pedal from him, she tugged. "It won't budge" she said!

"Try harder" he encouraged her.

She tried but it still wouldn't move. Then she saw a thin film of something. "Okay she said, superglue! Very effective"

"A tube in a thin plastic bag behind the pedal wouldn't be noticed until you put the foot hard on the pedal, look here," he pointed to what looked like a small pin behind the pedal. " you aren't going to notice right until the pedal sticks to the floor, it'd take about five seconds to set then you've got real problems. You've got an eight litre V8 racing engine running at full throttle, automatic gearbox and no brakes! With little or no evidence to suggest foul play"

"Throw in a cop willing to muddy the waters" Sandy carried the thought on, and you've got a perfect murder, or almost any way!"

"You really think that's what's going on though?" Joey asked, he knew he'd had the first suspicions, but couldn't really get his head around the idea, it might just be going a bit too far.

"Only one way to find out!" Sandy replied as she looked over the two cylinders, question is why he didn't make sure the device went off."

"That I can answer."Joey replied. "It's a primitive timing device, wasn't meant to go off then, the car bursting into flames would be too suspicious." he relaxed into the seat as Sandy put the car into drive. "Better for the device to trigger a day or so later, but before anyone got suspicious and did a thorough check."

Peter was waiting for them when they got back, they'd already discussed a lot on the way, and Joey wasn't happy that Sandy didn't want to say anything to the family, he thought they should at least tell them something..

"So" Peter started, "Been gallivanting around then?" he half joked with them, he knew they'd gone to get answers, but wasn't sure he wanted to know them.

"Take a look for yourself Peter" Joey indicated for Sandy to pass the device over. "Simple, but effective, and take a look at the timing device"

"And?"

"You're not going to like this" Joey replied, but it was timed to go off in about an hour, "Right when the cops would be knocking off from the night shift, and day shift coming on duty, probably take out the whole impound compound with it, not to mention any cops unlucky enough to be in the back of the station in Thames"

"What the?" Peter was almost speechless, he wasn't sure what he was seeing, "What is it?"

"Simple incendiary device" Joey cut in, "Designed to ignite and destroy evidence, the car probably still had a full fuel tank, or near enough, imagine that causing a fire and the fuel tank getting in on the act!"

Slowly it dawned on him, just what Joey was talking about, and if he was right, just how much trouble they were in, not just the 'tampering with evidence, but the fact that whoever it was, could be brazen enough to burn a police station down, and Joey still thought a cop might be involved. He was angry, and let it show.

"So" he asked them, "What is it you're not telling us?" Peter found a chair and sat down, they were still on the front porch.

"What do you mean, not telling you?" Joey asked trying to sound casual, "we've told you all we know"

Peter actually began to laugh, not a hearty belly laugh, but a nervous I'm' worried and I don't know why laugh'. He reached out for something, anything would do. Something to take his mind off the worry. "Don't Bullshit me" he shot back, "first we get the call there's been an accident and Helen's seriously hurt, then you folks tell us, rather tell me that the police aren't doing things right" he went on. "Then you tell me you're the people responsible to ship the car back to England, now I hear you've been under the damn thing pulling bits off. AND THAT'S WHILE IT'S STILL IN THE POLICE COMPOUND!!"

He turned and looked directly at Sandy. "So, what aren't you telling us?"

"Dad" Sandy began."I'm not sure you've worked out what I do." She began

"Even I know the 'insurance' bit is a ruse" he cut her off. "Who is it M.I.5?"

"Mr Little" it was Joey took it up. "We can't actually say suffice it to say we're the good guys" he went on.

"Yes" he twirled the stick he'd found, it was only small, about a quarter inch think and four inches long, "but we're the good guys"

"And I'm the pope!" Peter shot back clearly angry, "You're telling me half with a big But with a capital 'B', now what's that 'But'?"

"It's not easy to say, Mr Little" Joey replied. "You're probably not going to"

"Please Joey," he turned to face him. "It's Peter or Pete okay" the 'formality' was nice at first, but it was beginning to wear thin.

"And this was no accident err Pete" Joey continued. "And before you ask" he threw the cylinders to him, "here, take a look"

It took him a full five minutes to explain everything. Joey was surprised at how calm Pete became, considering what he'd just been told, or was it shock at finding out your daughter might be a target for something so hideously evil, either way he was impressed. 'Maybe it's the cop side of him kicking in' he thought.

"What you're telling me" Peter was getting frustrated, it was clear that neither side was listening to each other; he began to try and explain what he was thinking. They weren't listening.

"What we're telling you dad" Sandy interrupted, "is it might be safer if you take everyone else down South as soon as the funeral's over, and we mean everyone."

"Stop right there" he exploded, sheer frustration pouring out. "You're asking me to pack up and 'run off' with one daughter in Hospital, another son in law freshly in the ground and all on your say so" he looked directly at Joey. "Sorry buddy, but that isn't going to happen! Not without at least some form of explanation, and if my suspicions are right about whom it is you actually work for, that's something else that isn't going to happen" he paused to look at the two. "Now I'm not as stupid as you think I am"

"We never thought you" Sandy began.

"Shut up Sandy" Peter cut her off with a ferocity she'd never heard from him before, it really surprised her. "I'm not stupid, and this is coming because it's either M.I.5 or '6' that's pulling the strings, you're not going to say which, and I'm not going to tell either way but let's not kid each other about this okay? We're not moving and I'm not asking Kevin's family to 'run off' from the only home they've known just on your say so!"

"But Dad" Sandy began. "It's dangerous staying here, we can't say what these people will do next when they find out, and they will, in about an hour"

"Then why not let the thing go off?"

"You're not seriously thinking that are you?" Joey asked, "Think of all the innocents that would have been hurt!"

"I don't know what I'm thinking!" Peter shot back, he was angry, hurt and scared, and he didn't know which one was coming out, but then again the old police training was kicking in that said "Find the S.O.Bs and make 'em pay." he finished with."Then you better make sure they don't find out where you are then, but I'm not forcing people to move on the say so of people who won't tell us why and whom they work for, so either you find a way to make sure they don't find out where you are, or you find a way to protect us, but we're not moving and leaving Helen without the support she needs, have you got that?"

"But Helen can be moved with you" Joey butted in.

"And that'll tell whoever you're afraid of where we are" Peter replied, "It's NOT happening!"

The three of them were silent for a full two minutes before Sandy spoke again. "You know," she said, "there may be a way forward." She looked at Joey, it dawned on him what she was thinking.

Chapter 8

They'd driven all the way up to Auckland in silence, after the uncomfortable confrontation that took place with Peter, Joey still thought they needed to say something, but he respected both Peter and Sandy's wishes, it just didn't sit well with him and he'd been brooding about it.

"Can we talk some" Sandy asked as they pulled into the carpark of the coffee place just before the Bombay hills, they were only half an hour away from the city, they needed to get some things sorted out.

"Yeah" Joey spoke softly.

They were still in the car park, she turned and looked at him, "I think I've worked a way round it, but we'll need to convince some people about the plan"

That sounded intriguing, was Sandy talking about having another go at persuading her dad to take the family back to Christchurch?

"Okay" Joey looked her in the eye, "fill me in"

"We've got to report in at the consulate" she began, "Sir Michael wants a video conference, apparently he's got some things he wants to give us an update on"

"And we've got an update or two for him." Joey held the cylinders up to emphasize the point. "Should be an interesting briefing to say the least"

The British consulate is right in the centre of the city, it took them just over an hour to get there. Finding parking wasn't a problem as the consulate has its own secure facility, but persuading the parking staff to let these two strangers in was another story. The parking entrance had two booths for entry, one was key card entry, but the other was for visiting embassy staff and controlled by remote. Cameras were watching both entrances.

"Miss Little and Mr Metcalfe here for a conference call" Sandy spoke through the intercom as soon as they'd pulled up.

"One moment please" a disembodied voice came back, "no, there's no one at the consulate by those names" the reply came back.

"No." Sandy came back, "that's because we're in the car, but we're expected for a video conference call with London, she paused so they could check any paperwork, "check your logs!"

"One moment please" the disembodied voice spoke again. "No, we have no information on a video call happening today."

"Please check that with the consul general" Sandy replied, "She was notified three hours ago. This is urgent!" She added for emphasis.

"Please wait a moment." This time they were kept waiting.

"What are the odds someone forgot to tell the security staff?" Joey asked half joking.

"Bloody good" Sandy replied with a hint of frustration, she was one who liked to be organized and hated it when things weren't as well run as she liked. Joey'd learned the hard way that sometimes the Army isn't as well organized as people thought, especially with some officers that as Spike Milligan the comedian once put it "Shouldn't be trusted with a water pistol!"

It took a full ten minutes before the voice came back, "Sorry for the delay, consular staff will be with you presently," the barrier arm lifted and they proceeded in.

They parked the car as a sheepish looking staff member came out of a side door, he went straight to the front of the car. "What's the odds he's the one forgot to pass the message?" Sandy asked Joey just before she opened her door..

"Dead certain" Joey replied smiling as the young man approached, he was probably late twenties; slightly overweight, but not by much, one of those who thought he was fit. He extended his hand to Sandy "Paul Smith," he greeted them both but his eyes were fixed on Sandy, clearly thinking he'd make a good impression.

Joey wondered if the guy actually knew what he was doing! 'This should be good' he thought to himself. It took him a moment to remember that while the guy clearly 'had the hots' for Sandy he'd followed protocol as she officially worked for the government where he was a 'consultant'. He smiled to himself.

Sandy wasn't so impressed. "Just point us to the secure conference room, get us coffee and some breakfast" she didn't even add a "please".

'Paul Smith's face was as red as a beetroot, obviously not expecting to be 'blown off' and put so thoroughly in his place, a part of Joey had really enjoyed seeing the way Sandy had done it.

He led them without another word to the elevators; they went straight to the fourth floor of the building. "The conference room's in the third," he explained, "but the elevators only stop at the fourth, security reasons" he carried on explaining.

"We get the picture" Joey cut him off, "just show us the way, and don't forget the food." He sounded just like an NCO barking out an order, which is just the effect he wanted. The elevator doors were fully open now, they stepped out into a light coloured reception area complete with bespectacled receptionist busy typing away at her keyboard, phones going off in the distance, and full length portrait of the Queen sitting regally on her throne, draped in the full regalia of monarchy, there just in case you forgot this was the British Consulate.

"Just at the end of the corridor there's a door leading to a flight of steps" Paul Smith spoke up, "the conference room, is at the bottom on the left" he pointed off to the right where the corridor was, "I'll have someone bring breakfast down for you" he made to leave but was stopped by Joey's voice.

"You'll need to bring it" Joey wasn't 'barking' the order' anymore, they'd begun to 'soften up' a bit as the staffer had probably had enough punishment for one day, so he spoke a little more softly, "The less people who see us here the better!" He didn't explain.

"Oh" that took the consulate staffer back a bit, "Who exactly are you calling?"

"Actually" it was Sandy replied. "We're not doing the calling, he's calling us, and you better not ask, then we won't have to lie!"

Strange people turning up at the consulate, wanting as few people as possible to know about it, and then admitting they'd lie about who they were, now he really was curious, but something about them made him decide not to push it, it was a wise choice.

They found the room, it was pretty plain, no windows and only the bare minimum of functional furniture, only the absolute minimum for its function as a secure conference facility, which amounted to a table, a computer, a couple of large screens and a few leather chairs, there was another table against the wall, clearly a sign that a coffee pot visited that spot from time to time.

Every Embassy, and some consulates have these rooms, usually not on any of the 'official' plans for the building, but hidden as an extra large 'broom closet' of something like that, some strange soundproofing and interesting electronic devices built in, this room had all that, along with plain carpet and a huge hardwood (Sandy thought it looked like Rimu) table with two large leather office chairs. There was a laptop on the conference table connected to the large screens, Sandy booted the laptop up and opened Skype. Then taking a flash drive out of her bag she installed a few things they were going to need.

"Feels more like an episode of 'Star Trek' than a bloody room in an Embassy" Joey commented as they 'booted the system up'. "Just waiting for Captain Kirk to show up!"

"That's not a nice way to talk about our new friend" Sandy was laughing a little as she replied.

"What him?" Joey shot back, "He's a green blooded Alien, and I don't mean Mr Spock! Spock's too intelligent!"

As soon as the system was 'up and running' Sandy typed in a series of commands, then they waited. A few moments later the screen came alive with a picture of a conference room with two men sat at the conference table, just as the picture came on there was a tap on their door, Joey got up and went to it, a few seconds later he was back with a big pot of coffee, a plate of Croissants, butter and Jam.

"I can see you've got your priorities right then!" one of the men on the screen spoke, it was Sir Michael.

"Sorry" it was Sandy spoke up, "We've been on the go since four am this morning, this is the first chance for a 'refuel' we've had" she took a croissant, cut it in half, she wasn't going to tell him about the little stop at the

Bombays, that had been more of a 'get things straight' type of stop anyway, they could see the heat rising off the pastry, the aroma was wonderful, she spread a 'noggin' of butter on one half, then taking the Jam (it was Strawberry, her favourite) she put a big dollop onto the other half then put the two together. Coffee and croissants, it was heaven, but they were here for a reason. "We were kind of expecting them to bring this after the conference call sir." She lied.

"You called for a conference Sir Michael; we've got quite a bit to report" Joey jumped in to carry on. "Here we are" he was pouring the coffee.

Sir Michael smiled a little, "So have we, I've called on Steve for some forensic accounting help looking into the car driver's accounts.

"Good to see you two again" the 'Steve' was Steve Chambers, the guy they'd gone into Iran to rescue in the first mission. "Though you ARE supposed to be on holiday you know!" he wisecracked a little, he knew them both pretty well and knew they had the sense of humour that would appreciate it, "I guess someone forgot to tell you"

"Well, it was great, while it lasted." Joey replied. "That is until the accident!" he carried on, "anyway, we've got a few things that might throw some light on things."

"First of all" Sandy interrupted, "The car is going through it's serious crash inspection as we speak" she saw Sir Michael begin to interrupt, she cut him off with a holding up of the hand, "They're not going to find anything, other than a few smudges in the brake pipes, we got there first, then it's on its way back to England, it should be leaving the country within a few days, all the paperwork has been filed."

"What did you find then?" Sir Michael wasn't known for 'beating about the bush'.

"Take a look for yourself" Joey replied as he lifted the device onto the table, he plonked it right in front of the camera, "Can you see it clearly?"

"Looks like a Bomb of some sort?" it was more a question than anything, and it was Chambers asked the question.

"Yes, and no" Joey replied. "The first part wasn't, that was this cylinder" he pointed to the one of the left, "filled with acid of some kind, probably Sulphuric, activated by a timer like so" he gave a demonstration. "This bit here," Joey pointed to a small valve on the end of the first cylinder, "is the control mechanism, open it and the acid pours out."

"How long would it take to work?" Chambers asked the question.

"It was right above the brake master cylinder," Joey carried on. "Probably no more than a couple of minutes before the first holes, about ten minutes and you've got catastrophic failure!"
That explains the brakes." Sir Michael spoke up, but wasn't the car accelerating?"

"Yep, she was" Joey replied, he reached down and pulled what looked like a rectangular rubber tile out of the bag, "hope the McLaren boys and girls don't mind we kept this back" he placed on the table, "it's the accelerator pedal, SUPERGLUED TO THE CARPET!!" She waited a moment for the statement to sink in. "Crude but works every time!"

" I don't want to know how you know that!" Sir Michael shot back, "Back to the original question, "How'd you get your hands on this, if it was supposed to be in the police compound?"

"Oh it is in the compound boss" Joey replied, " and the cops still have one, that wasn't part of the killer's plan, take a look here" he pointed to the second cylinder, "Filled with white phosphorus, that was timed to rupture a couple of hours ago, while the car was in the compound."

"And don't tell me" Sir Michael cut in, "above the brake cylinder, brake fluid is chiefly alcohol based which ignites, that starts to burn, which in turn reaches the fuel tank right?"

"And you have a very crude, but effective bomb levelling most of the station" Joey finished off. "Not to mention how many cops hurt in the blast, last thing they'll be thinking about is what caused it! Least not for weeks."

"The killer knew Cavell wouldn't be able to 'floor it's until he got to Thames, then he wouldn't be able to resist" Sandy broke in. "Thus he knew roughly where it was going to happen" she took another croissant, cut the pastry and spread a thin layer of butter then Jam on it and took another bite, she went on. "It was planned down to the last detail"

"So" Chambers spoke again, "We're all pretty convinced that you weren't the target, that sort of fits with what we've found out at this end." He brought the meeting 'back to the point'

"Hold on" Sandy spoke up, she tapped a few keys on the laptop, "I've just sent you an enlarged picture of what he's talking about." She nodded slightly in Joey's direction.

Joey continued running through the details of the device, but that didn't answer the big questions. It was Sir Michael asked the obvious, he hadn't spoken much to Chambers beforehand.

"But it doesn't tell us why though?"

"I think I can help a bit with that," Steve spoke up, he pulled out a small keyboard from the desk he sat at, Joey and Sandy's second screen came alive, one half showing the two men, the other showing an 'employee identity badge from Barclays Bank. "Meet junior exec James Cavell" he went on. "Remember about three years ago Barclays got stung for a billion pounds in fines for screwing the mortgage rates?"

"I remember that" all three said it almost at the same time, it was Sir Michael continued. "Old Bob Diamond resigned over it, if I remember correctly"

"Yes sir he did," Chambers glanced over at Sir Michael, "we gave him an ultimatum 'resign' or face jail time!" He let that sink in, "anyway it wasn't the only shady dealings going on, we couldn't prove things, but there was a strong link with some unsavoury characters at the time and one name kept cropping up!"

"Don't tell me he was involved there" Sir Michael didn't like this, he was the one had pushed for letting Diamond walk away with just a resignation.

"Unfortunately that's exactly what I was going to tell you sir" Chambers continued, he half turned to Sir

Michael and carried on, "at the time there wasn't enough evidence to bring it to anyone's attention, let alone try and prosecute, just little rumours and suggestions at the time, mostly linking to the Yakuza and the Triads, but nothing concrete!"

"You folks really know how to 'mix things up don't you?" Joey almost forgot where he was and whom he was talking to, "I mean probably the two worst criminal elements there are, and you happen to 'forget' that he was in league with them! Jesus, what else?"

"As I said" Chambers shot back, "There was no evidence, and when he moved on a few months later they seemed to disappear, so we didn't follow up!"

"And now it's come back to bite us" Joey couldn't resist the comment. "In the arse and big time!"

"There was no evidence, as I said" Chambers was starting to get impatient, 'But the rumours we heard were disturbing enough that if anyone found out it was a powder keg waiting to explode, we'd told Barclays themselves so when they let Cavell move with a glowing reference we figured they'd checked them out." He tapped his screen, the part with the ID photo changed to what looked like a statement. "Here's what they found" they were a series of figures.

"They look like a series of bank transfers to me," Sandy spoke up, as much to diffuse the situation as anything, she could feel Joey tensing up as if he was getting frustrated at not being told the whole picture, "Money between banks"

"You're right there Sandy" Chambers replied, "but notice the discrepancy between the figures on the left and right, the one on the right" he highlighted the figures on the right, "is smaller by a significant amount, we estimate about five million American dollars"

"Could it be just that they didn't use the money yet?" Sir Michael asked, he hadn't seen this information before.

"No sir" Chambers replied, "This is the money that neither Barclays nor our own forensic accounts people can find! It simply seemed to vanish, though we've got a clue as to some of it's path"

"Secret Swiss bank accounts? Or is it the Caymans?" Sandy asked.

"Right idea, wrong locations" Chambers replied with a slight smile, he was beginning to relax after the near confrontation with Joey, "Try the Channel Islands!"

"What?" Sir Michael had been taking a sip of a glass of water when that last statement came out, he nearly choked, "How the hell are they pulling this right under our bloody noses?" he was angry, the Channel Islands were a tax haven, but they were also part of the British Isles, anything involving them also involved Britain and he thought he knew everything about what went on there.

"The money coming in to the Barclays account often came from some of the Banks in the Channel Islands, we think they were using the Channel Islands to 'clean the money' from dubious sources abroad like Chinese and Russian Banks, but a small amount went back to the Channel Islands and that's the amount we can't find!" Chambers replied, "about five million dollars"

"And you think the Yakuza or Triads found out about it!" Joey was putting it together now, "Kind of makes sense"

"If we put it together then they could have too! We only started looking when the 'body appeared' they've been looking for two years or so!" Chamber's logic was frustratingly right on the money.

"So, we've got Yakuza and Triads after this money," Joey spoke silently but with a grim determination, they were 'in the shit' but there wasn't time to feel sorry for it. "What do you want to do boss?" he looked directly at Sir Michael, he could feel Sandy doing the same, they'd killed a member of her extended family, and injured her sister who was one of her best friends, he knew she'd want blood, but at the same time they couldn't go doing things 'off their own bat'

"If this gets out" Sir Michael began, "just knowing that we were suspicious and did nothing could cause some serious trouble, hell there'll be questions in parliament, not to mention a diplomatic row between Britain and New Zealand, something we really don't need right now." He shifted in his seat, then continued "We need to know where that money went! I want you to find where Cavell might have hidden the information and find that bloody money!"

"We've got his address both here in Auckland and on the Coromandel boss" Joey replied, "we'll get right on it" and with that he leaned forward clicking the button that cancelled the connection, they both sat there stunned for a good couple of minutes, a 'family holiday' had gone from a great break to horrendous accident and was now transforming into a dangerous mission with little backup. "Oh well, nothing new" he thought as he disconnected the feed.

"Some holiday" was all Sandy said.

As soon as Joey'd disconnected the feed Sir Michael reached over and flicked a switch, the screens came back to life, this time they showed two slightly older people and while they were in conference rooms like his own they one was across the Thames in New Zealand house and the other far away in Wellington.

"Jerry, glad you could join us for this, you too Mildred" he turned and addressed the two screens in turn. Gerald Jones was the resident agent from the New Zealand Secret Intelligence Service in London responsible for dealing with the likes of M.I.6 and the C.I.A and stuff, 'Mildred' was his boss over in Wellington, both were probably in their late middle age and looking forward to a great retirement, after what they'd just heard they both wished it'd already started. This was going to be one hell of a mess! "As you can see" Sir Michael carried on, "This wasn't something we went looking for! Our agents were actually on holiday when the whole thing blew up in their faces"

"From the likes of what I've heard" it was Jerry who spoke up, "It seems to happen wherever these two go! Weren't they involved in the Iran fiasco?"

"They were" Sir Michael shot back, "and Iran wasn't a fiasco from our point of view, the politicians can call it what they want but we got our man back!" he carried on, "the important thing is this is happening in your backyard and we need to keep you in the loop"

"Sometimes I wish you didn't have to!" Mildred replied with a hint of a smile, "it's much easier to be pissed off at you than to act like it when the thing blows up like it's going to!"

"But at least with the foreknowledge" Sir Michael replied, "You can prepare the politicians for the fallout!"

'Mildred' wasn't her real name, it was more a code, or 'handle' that she went by. Some appointments in the intelligence community are done by politicians, and as such everyone knows whom they are, Sir Michael had been appointed by a previous Prime minister, and as such everyone knew who he was and what he did. In New Zealand the Prime Minister is also the 'minister for intelligence gathering, in other words, they keep the 'top job' but that means their 'deputies' have the advantage they can 'work in the shadows' hence they didn't need to use their real names, and 'Mildred' was her 'handle' so her real name wasn't known, kind of like 'M' in the Bond movies.

"Murder linked to a corrupt Banker and suspicious Bank accounts spanning the globe, and it's all being covered up by corrupt cops here in New Zealand," she carried on uninterrupted. "You are aware that we had a Banker for Prime Minister aren't you? He only just resigned. The opposition will be asking the ex PM if he knew him!"

"Mildred" Sir Michael replied quietly, "I realize you only just got the file, but I can assure you as far as we're aware there's no connection apart from them dealing in the same industry! And Jerry before you ask, I'd stake my life on the information being correct, Chambers here was the man they got out of Iraq so his life was staked on these two!"

He stopped for a moment, then quietly he phrased the question that he needed to ask, "we uncovered this, and we came to you as it's your 'backyard' if you tell us to back off we will, but I need to ask you if you'll let us run with this and see what we can shake loose?"

Mildred stopped for a moment, it was mid morning where she was, she took the cup of coffee that was on her desk and took a sip, more to give her a moment to think than because she needed the coffee, in her government she was Sir Michael's equal and as such she'd be the one explaining to the PM what the hell was going on and her 'arse in the sling' if it all went pear shaped!

"I'll need to brief the PM on it pretty much right away" she replied. "But we can make it 'his eyes only' and we'll need to be kept in the loop all the way is that agreed?"

"Absolutely"

"Can we get one of our own in there with them?"

"Actually that's another thing I need to mention" Sir Michael said. "One of the team is in the South Island now, teaching at the Sniper school, the other two are in Canberra, if this thing turns the way we think it might we'll need to get that team together pretty quick and they may need backup!"

"So that's a no on our own people apart from the SAS from Papakura right?"

"The team are on first name terms with most of the boys and girls there" Chambers chipped in.

"Then it doesn't look like I've got much of a bloody choice then does it?" Mildred fumed quietly, "knowing you Mike, you'll go ahead and do the bloody thing anyway!"

Sir Michael tried really hard to hide the smile, he wasn't totally successful, she was right, he would without any hesitation, he'd been tempted to anyway, it was the threat of "Any more stunts like the one you pulled with my predecessor" from the New PM that reminded him not to!

"Very well" Mildred said finally, "But we want full disclosure, and I want Jerry in the loop all the way!" and with that she reached over and killed the connection.

"Jerry" Sir Michael spoke to the remaining figure, there's a pass downstairs for you when you get here, nothing about this op will leave this floor of my building, you'll be able to report everything to Wellington from here, it's nearly ten now, you can come over now if you want, otherwise you can start tomorrow"

"Tomorrow's fine" Jerry replied, I'll need to tell the High Commissioner I'm not going to be around for awhile, I'll tell him it's a security exercise we're running in light of a Royal visit, I'll see you around eight then you can leave me with the files to catch up" and with that he killed his connection.

Chapter 9

Auckland is one of those places where the property market is constantly 'on steroids' and if you want to get a place with a prime view you're going to have to pay 'through the nose'.

Cavell had a salary of about a quarter of a million dollars. He should have had a place out in one of the nicer suburbs, but, not in the most expensive area, he didn't! His was 'prime waterfront right down by the 'viaduct' or 'party central' as it was known locally, every time New Zealand has a celebration of any kind there's always a huge party down by the viaduct. There even the smallest place will fetch a million dollars, Cavell's place wasn't small, and was in a building that had its own security!

The apartment building was a twelve storey affair with a glass security door on the ground level allowing access, a silver fern was engraved on each of the two glass panels, they added style to an otherwise plain doorway.

To the left of the door was a panel with all the residents names, along with intercom buttons, the speaker and mike were just about head height, Cavell's place was on the tenth floor. Sandy walked up casually and pressed a button on the third floor.

"Hello?" A female voice came over the intercom.

"Oh, er sorry about this" Sandy began, "My boyfriend and I are staying with a friend up on the tenth floor" she lied "and we've forgotten our door key, can you buzz us in?"

"You're the second lot today!" The voice sounded frustrated, "how many parties is he going to have?" There was a pause then a click as the door opened, the voice came back on, "please make this the last time." There was a click as the line went dead.

As they reached the elevators Sandy was about to call them, Joey held out his hand, "See the two outside?"

"The two trying to look interested in the newspaper? Yep, I figure they've arranged a reception for us." she replied as Joey pushed the button pushed the button then, he carried on, "wait for my text, then send it to eleven then call it back, we'll play a little game with them. I'll see you up there" he turned and headed for the stairs.

Nine steps per flight, two flights of steps per storey and ten storeys totals one hundred and eighty steps, a normal person wouldn't even think of it, Joey didn't think twice! It had to be done and he was used to this kind of stuff.

Part of the final test for firefighters working in London is they have to carry a full load of equipment while wearing the heavy firefighters clothing and breathing apparatus weighing about eighty pounds in heat up to two or three hundred degrees to simulate a real fire where there's only a narrow stairwell to get to the fire, Joey and the SAS often trained in the same building under similar circumstances, but with different purposes, and with a different kind of 'heat'.

He took less than two minutes to reach the tenth floor, just as he passed the ninth there was a fire extinguisher and a broom cupboard, he opened the cupboard and took a broom handle out. Next he undid the clips fastening the fire extinguisher and took it with him, 'they'll come in useful' he thought to himself.

As soon as he got to the door, he took a few moments to get his breath back; reaching into his pocket he took the phone out and sent the text, it said simply "SEND IT" and waited.

The lifts were about fifteen feet to the left of the stairwell. He heard the motors on the lifts start as Sandy sent the first elevator to the eleventh floor, there was a second elevator, the motor started on that one as she sent that skyward, panic began to break out as the intruders began to prepare for their unwanted guests, there were two that he could see, but he was sure there was at least one more in the apartment searching.

It was almost amusing to see the panic as the lift started its ascent and they got ready for whatever was coming up, he realized they were 'semi professional' at best as both of them tensed up waiting for the lift door to open, they both drew weapons, "Glock 19s from this angle" he thought as he saw the weapons. 'Good, reliable and easy to get hold of' he thought, 'Standard Police issue all over the world' but from their stances they'd watched too many cop movies where Bruce Willis turns the weapon sideways, truth is if you try and fire the thing that way it's going to break your wrist and you can forget hitting what you're aiming at!

The lift opened and he half expected them to fill the air with lead as the doors slid back, but they showed remarkable restraint for two whose nerves were 'on edge'

Nothing in the elevator, that got them really panicking especially as the door closed and it continued on its way, the second one stopped on the eleventh, Sandy must have pressed the button for it to stop there, one of the goons started running at full pelt for the stairs, heading Joey's way, he was ready.

The guy burst through the door heading for the stairs and straight into Joey's outstretched broom handle, flying arse over tit he crashed down the first flight of stairs landing in a heap. Joey was on him in an instant; he didn't hesitate but clubbed the guy with the extinguisher knocking him out cold, damn near killing him in the process, not that Joey was too worried.

A quick search gave up the guy's wallet and phone as well as another clip for the Glock, Joey was wearing Army issue combat gloves that were perfect for this kind of stuff as they had padded knuckles that meant you delivered a devastating punch but didn't leave any DNA behind, they weren't even leather which was even better.

Next he took the guy's belt off and used it to secure the wrists, finally before moving on he pulled the man's pants down and wrapped part of the belt around the crotch of the pants effectively trussing the guy up like a chicken, this one was out and staying that way. Now for number two.

Sandy waited the two minutes impatiently, she wanted to be there and get involved with this, but at the same time knew the best thing she could do was stay down here and send the elevators as Joey'd virtually commanded her to. She hated taking orders from him, but at the same time even though she was pretty good at this, Joey and the team were in a league of their own. 'Better to stay and do as he says' she thought.

Two minutes passed before the signal came, as soon as it did she sent the elevator on its way, and called the other one, she decided to send both of them to different floors. That way the people upstairs would have no idea which way they were coming from, she really wished she could see the faces as the trap was sprung!

It was a further three minutes before Joey sent the 'ALL CLEAR' text meaning she could come up, three frustrating and slightly worrying minutes as things could go wrong.

As soon as the door opened she was through them and there was nothing! Where the hell was he? Then a voice came from the room down the hall, "There were three" it was Joey, "And they're sleeping like babies" he popped his head round the corner. "Any idea what we might be looking for?" he asked. "Though with the mess these clowns made, I don't think they've got it, whatever it is!"

"My guess is either a computer or a flash drive," she replied, "and I don't mean a fancy car!"

"Damn" he shot back, "and I thought I was getting a Ferrari!" they both laughed a little, tension relief was needed somewhat.

She stepped into the room, and over the three prone figures trussed up like Christmas Turkeys with their pants down around their ankles. "Joey really" she said in a slightly mocking tone, "You know I'm a modest girl, I mean really, did you have to arrange a show like that!" she pointed at the three men.

"Only way I could think of" he replied honestly shrugging his shoulders, "But you're right, they're not much to look at" one of them was just starting to come round, Joey knocked him out again, "anyway let's get to it" he began searching through the piles of discarded possessions they'd left strewn around.

Sandy stopped for a moment and thought, then she headed straight for a room that looked like it'd been a home office.

The apartment was minimalist, all except for the office room, that looked as if it was transported straight out of the eighteenth century with beautiful portrait paintings on the wall, perfect for hiding a safe behind, but right in the middle was an amazingly ornate writing desk complete with gold leaf legs and felt top, it was amazing looking, she stopped and stared at it.

"Not really got time for admiring the furniture." Joey spoke softly, 'maybe the cogs in that incredible brain of hers were working on something' he thought. "We've got to get a move on before the clowns outside realize and call for backup"

"No, I'm just remembering something I learned watching the antiques roadshow once" she replied, "They often have pieces like this on, and often there's a" she was looking and running her finger along the back of the desk, he heard a faint click and the front of the desk opened fractionally where there hadn't even been a crack before, "There it is" she said with a note of triumph" there was a slight, barely audible click as she pressed something under the desk, a small spring released a panel in the bottom of one of the drawers, a hidden drawer revealed itself.

"Well I'll be" Joey exclaimed, "A secret bloody drawer"

"And" she reached in, pulling her hand out she clutched a small piece of technology no bigger than her thumbnail. "A flash drive" she took the laptop out of her bag and booted it up, "Don't worry" she said to Joey's concerned look, "I'm only going to check that there's actually stuff on here, not start fiddling with it right now" she powered up the laptop, as soon as it was on she plugged the drive in and went to the file manager. "Yep" she let out a small yelp, "We've got files here, and they look like the right kind" she slammed the laptop shut without taking the drive out, "Now let's put some distance between us and this mess!"

As soon as she said that Sandy went to pick up one of the weapons, there were three of them, all with silencers fitted, Joey reached out and stopped her. "No," he said quietly, but with a confident note, "we're leaving them for the cops to find!" He paused, then continued, "they'll shit huge bricks when they do.' He was almost laughing.

They still needed a plan for getting out of the building, and it sounded like he had one. Sandy trusted him even when the 'plan' was a 'half cocked hare brained scheme like jumping of a thousand foot cliff into the night wearing nothing but a piece of cloth, on second thoughts she hoped this one was better!

"Come on" Joey encouraged her as he headed for the door, the three Chinese were still trussed up but starting to come too, he figured they'd be fully conscious in a couple of minutes, then it'd take them another couple of minutes to sort themselves out, by that time the police will be breaking down the door on three armed men 'ransacking' the apartment of a guy killed in a 'car crash' if that doesn't set alarm bells off in the police nothing will!

"Which service do you require?" The operator asked.

"Police please, QUICKLY!" Joey tried to sound panicky but was smiling as they ran down the steps, he was slightly out of breath and that helped 'sell' the pitch. Another operator came on the line, "police what's your emergency?"

"My name's John Smith" Joey lied, "I live at 842 Queen Street, in the ninth floor, I think there are people trying to break into the apartment above" he stopped for a moment, giving the impression he was out of breath, "I think they're carrying guns!"

"Which apartment are they trying to break into sir?"

"Number 1014" Joey replied, "it's the one belonging to that guy killed the other day, Mr Cavell", please hurry, they're shouting in a foreign language!" He hung up, they were on the second floor. "Come on" he headed down the steps.

They didn't have long to wait, the first police cars showed up as soon as they got downstairs, they parked a couple of blocks away and effectively sealed the street off, next the New Zealand equivalent of a SWAT team, or the Armed Offenders Squad turned up in full gear, guns bristling, they were straight into the building

Joey stepped up to the first officer he saw as the guy came running through the hallway, "They're in apartment 1014" he started, "If you like I can show you the way" he volunteered though the voice that was coming out of his mouth was more like that of a scared civilian than what you'd expect from a member of an elite fighting unit, Sandy was surprised at how well Joey was playing the role, he was pretty convincing.

"No need sir" the police officer came back, she was clad from head to toe in body armour, so much so that it hid the fact she was a woman, that is until she spoke to them, "We've got all the information we need, if you'll go over the road there," she pointed to where a couple of uniformed police were gathering, "you can talk to the officer who'll relay any important information to us" and with that she turned and was gone up the stairs.

Chapter 10

"Chris" the voice was unmistakable. "What you got for me?" Samantha Hughes, all five eight, seventy five kilos, blonde hair blue eyes that beguiled many a criminal into thinking they could outsmart the cop behind them, eyes that have tricked many into long jail terms were climbing out of the big black Chevy, the red and blue lights still flashing in the windscreen.

"One of the strangest yet!" Chris Trent, fifteen years with the force and officer in charge of the Armed offenders squad replied as he exited the building.

Sam had parked opposite the building, she made her way over to him, he slung his weapon back so the muzzle was pointing towards the ground, "run me through it" she took out a notepad and started tapping the keypad.

"Best I actually show you!" He started walking back to the building, opening and holding the door open he let Sam through first.

"Anyway, where's Jack today?" He asked nonchalantly.

"Off sick" she replied, "so you've got the pleasure of my company" she gave him a dazzling yet half joking smile.

"And what a pleasure it is!" He shot back equally half jokingly.

Coming from anyone else Sam would have taken it as 'condescending' and put thcm in their place, but they had been mates for years, he'd been the cop who showed her the 'ropes' as a rookie.

Chris made for the stairs, "this way"

The stairs were pretty well lit, with safety lighting installed in recesses on every floor and halfway up each flight, the stairs themselves were concrete, but there was carpeting on each level, on the whole it looked every bit the expensive place it was.

"Won't the elevators be quicker?" Sam asked curious, she enjoyed exercise, but as a relaxation, not as necessity!

"Would be" he replied, "but you'd miss why we wanted a detective! You'd miss the fun bit"

"What fun bit? It was three men with guns right?"

"Sort of, you need to see for yourself"

"What do you mean 'SORT OF?' it either bloody well is or isn't!" She snapped back, they were on the fifth floor by now and could see the two people in white coveralls up ahead, "and what the hell is forensics doing out here? they were in the room weren't they?"

Chris was actually smiling; he'd taken an easy pace up the stairs, though Sam was starting to struggle. "They were when we found them." He replied.

"Meaning?" She asked, "you're not giving much away"

"I'm as confused as you are" Chris replied, "we found them in the room, but they were tied up, no make that trussed up like turkeys, and just coming round!"

"We're talking three armed men right?"

"Yep" Chris replied, almost chuckling. "Or at least they had guns with their prints on, but we need to show you something, and it starts just here!" they'd reached just below the tenth floor.

The two forensics people were busy working, they'd sprayed luminol to find where there was blood, now they were checking for fingerprints but you could tell they weren't holding much hope.

"I take it there's not much to work with then?" Sam asked the nearest white clad person who was dusting a banister.

"On the contrary" the second one spoke up, "bloody thing's covered with them, problem is there's too sodding many!" She stood up and walked over, "we're going to have to fingerprint everyone in the whole sodding place, just to rule the prints out!"

"How many?" Sam knew she probably shouldn't ask, but needed the information.

"Twelve levels, five apartments per level, that's sixty apartments, two or more per apartment, you do the math!"someone wasn't a happy camper.

"Don't mind Scott" Chris spoke up again. "He's just frustrated he can't solve the case in a one hour time slot" he joked, "you know, like CSI!"

"Har bloody har" Scott shot back disagreeing emphatically, "like you bloody clowns do better"

"Now now boys!" Sam knew the rivalry between these two, and it wasn't always amicable, fact was they didn't like each other ever since Chris took Scott's girlfriend off him about ten years before, the fact he married her and they were still happily together made things worse! "Tell me what this has to do with the three?"

"Follow me" Chris started through the door into the lobby, "we did find the men in the apartment, but it looks to us like whoever 'took them out' did the first one here, on the stairs"

"Sentry?" She asked.

"If he was there'd be bullet holes everywhere" Chris replied, "there aren't any, I think they had a lookout who told them someone was coming, that someone" he went on "had an accomplice who played with the lifts, sent number one scurrying for the stairs and he got ambushed there!"

"Weapons?" If you're going to take down armed thugs you're going to need them, that is normally.

"None" Chris replied, Sam's face was utter disbelief, only the totally insane or supremely confident, to the point of insanity would even attempt that, "Well, not the kind you'd expect anyway!"

"That means" Sam replied to the last comment, "Our attacker's got bags of confidence then!" There was more than a note of sarcasm in her voice.

"You haven't seen the best yet" Chris kept going, they were by the elevators now, he turned and faced the elevators. "Number two was here, ready for whatever came out, gun drawn," he took up the stance, "sees something out the corner of his eye" he started to turn towards the stairs, "and gets flattened by the attacker who somehow manages to break his nose, sternum and four ribs in two blows delivered at the same time!"

"How the hell? Flying kick to both the nose and chest?" She was stumped, "how'd they not injure themselves?"

Chris was amused, "I'd say whoever it was," he stopped for a moment and pointed to something on the floor, "used his target as a cushion for landing!"

"Wow. This one's full of tricks?" There was genuine admiration in her voice, it's not often you get to see a 'thug' with this much style. "Mixed martial?" Sam asked, there were three more forensics people working this scene and the chaos that was the apartment, one of them, an older woman with thick glasses stopped what she'd been doing, looked up and replied, "don't think so, too clinical!"

"What, the Martial arts?"

"No," the forensics lady stood up and held out a hand, "Sorry, I'm doctor Kate Shepherd from the forensics lab." Sam shook her hand and continued" who then, the assailant?"

"Oh yes" Kate replied, "this one knew exactly how to strike, and when to stop! He knew exactly what he was doing!"

"Doesn't that fit the bill for a Martial arts expert?"

"Only to some degree" Kate explained, "they don't get the practice for this kind of stuff, this guy's had lots of it!"

"What?"

"This one's had lots of practice at this kind of stuff; I believe that's what I said?"

"Yeah, I know" Sam replied, "but what or rather who the hell are we dealing with then?" She asked no one in particular, she was processing her thoughts, neither Chris nor Kate interrupted. "And why didn't they just shoot them once they were down, you know, neutralize the threat for good"

It was Kate replied, "I expect it's because he wanted us to investigate a few things!" She was slightly impatient, "after all, that's what the police do don't they?" she said with a hint of sarcasm.

"What about the rest of the scene?" Sam studiously ignored the barb.

"Only stuff there was done by the three bozos that got taken down" Kate stepped into the room, "CAREFUL" she half shouted as Sam went to follow her, "that's evidence!" she pointed to something on the floor, something Sam almost destroyed by standing on it. "Watch where you're walking girl!" Kate wasn't impressed. "You damn near contaminated the scene"

"Sorry" Sam felt like a chastised schoolgirl caught smoking behind the bike shed, "so, do we know anything about the assailant?"

"We know there were two!" Chris replied, "Though only one did the physical stuff, the other created the distraction"

"And one of them was female" Kate added

"How'd you get that?" Sam asked.

"Come, take a look" Kate turned to Sam, crooked her finger and headed into another room, "and bloody well be careful!"

'Yes ma'am' she felt like saying, but managed to bite her tongue enough to prevent further inflaming the older woman.

The room they stepped into was a revelation, it was like stepping into a time warp and emerging two hundred years earlier.

On one wall, a set of full length heavy drapes with gold embroidery covered most of the wall, they knew from the outside view that the doors onto the balcony were modern, but that didn't stop the effect the drapes had of fooling you into thinking it was an eighteenth century study complete with portrait paintings and study desk.

Kate headed for the desk. "Those three may be professional thugs, but they're rank amateurs at searching." She stopped and crouched down by the desk, "the assailants on the other hand knew exactly where to look!" She crouched down at the desk, then turning to Sam said, "Here take a look underneath"

Sam and Chris both crouched down by the desk, at first they saw nothing, then Sam noticed, "there's some kind of imprint, a hand maybe?" Fingerprints maybe?"

"I wish" Kate replied, "they were too smart for that, but look at the size of the marks, too small and delicate for an adult male, probably not hard enough to do the damage in there" she cocked her head towards the door, where the men had been found, "but they knew exactly where the release catch is" she pressed something under the desk, a very faint click and the concealed drawer opened a fraction, "my guess is it's all about what was in there, whatever it was?"

Sam's head was swimming, dead bankers, armed thugs beaten to pulp, apartments ransacked, something stolen but no flaming idea what because the one who could tell them was dead in a supposed 'accident'.

"Great, just flaming great" She cussed under her breath, "is there ANYTHING that can help us identify who attacked them?" she stood up. "Fingerprints, DNA, anything?" She almost pleaded, "what about security cameras?"

"All blacked out" Chris replied as he got up from the squat, compliments of the 'three stooges!"

"And what about those guys?" Sam barked getting more and more frustrated, "where are they now?"

"On the way to the prison hospital at Spring Hill" Chris replied, "there's no way I'm sending them to a regular hospital, they've got armed officers escorting them by the way"

"Shouldn't they be on the way to Middlemore?" Sam asked, "that is the closest A and E department?"

"They were armed" Chris reminded her, "There's no way I'm putting men like that in public hospitals, injured or not, I don't give a shit, they're not getting the chancc to escape!" he said it with some conviction, it's often too easy for wanted people to get away from police in hospital even when taken there after being arrested, then the arresting officer gets it in the neck from the public for 'putting them in danger'. Chris wasn't taking that chance. "By the way, I'm also running the serial numbers we recovered!"

"You mean they weren't smart enough to remove the serials from the weapons?" Sam smiled slightly, at least that was something.

"From the weapons they did" Chris replied, "but as usual they forgot the springs in the magazines! I'm running those as that'll tell us where the magazines have been if not the weapons themselves".

"And we're doing ballistics on the weapons," Kate added, "we'll check them internationally just in case!"

"Either way" Sam was thoughtful for a moment, "we'll have an answer as to who they are in a few hours" She turned to leave the room. "That'll be a start."

"That is if they're in the system" it was Kate that spoke, "then again with these clowns, they're thugs but not that good, they'll be in someone's system somewhere"

"And then" Sam carried on the thought that Kate was having, "we try and work out how the hell they turn up here in New Zealand trashing the apartment of a dead man, and what the hell is going on?"

"Good luck with that" Kate replied in a genuinely sympathetic manner, they all knew it wasn't going to be as easy as it sounded.

Chapter 11

"This has to be the best entertainment I've seen in a long time" Joey spoke quietly as he lifted his coffee and took a sip, they were only a hundred yards further up the street and watching the whole thing unfold, and both of them were enjoying every second of the mayhem they'd caused in the streets of Auckland.

The coffee shop owner was enjoying it too, but from a different perspective, the shop was packed with onlookers, all wanted to watch their tax dollars in action, curiosity was rife. More importantly for her, they were buying food and drink and that'll always make a business person happy.

Questions were being asked and answered by those who had no clue as to what was really going on, the latest story, and one that both Joey and Sandy were fuelling was the three men were armed robbers who'd been 'bested' by the eighty six year old lady with a walking stick. No one had any sympathy for them, but no one really believed the story.

"Hope they throw away the bloody key!" was the most common comment, along with "They should bring back hanging!" followed by, "Nah, Hanging's too good for them!"

It's amazing how people who normally don't believe in capital punishment suddenly change their view when it's a violent crime committed in their neighbourhood.

"You sure this is a good idea?" Sandy was a little nervous, but still enjoying the situation.

"If we leave too soon" Joey put the cup down and took a spoonful of the carrot cake they'd ordered, "we might get noticed, better to take our time, just like a tourist would do!"

"I thought they'd run a mile!" Sandy said in mock seriousness.

"Probably" he replied, "but this cake is too good to pass up!" he took another spoonful, it was as if he hadn't a care in the world, exactly what she loved about him, and what drove her nuts at the same time.

"We better make tracks and head on back" Sandy said as she finished the last of the carrot cake on her plate, they'd paid at the start and with cash so there wasn't any need to hang around.

"Yeah, we should," Joey agreed reaching for the bag that contained what they took from Cavell's place, "getting a look at that stuff's going to be interesting I'd say"

They finished up the coffee and cake they'd ordered and sauntered out of the shop just as the plain clothed police officer was coming out of the building, she didn't notice them and they didn't really pay much attention to her, this part was done, the police would be confused, but eventually they'd be looking in the right area.

"I need to do some things to the drive first" Sandy stood and picked up her purse, she took the car keys out, "you drive, I'll write email"

Joey's idea of parking the car a few streets away from the apartment paid off handsomely, the streets for about two blocks were snarled up, but the rest were relatively clear and more importantly there were no police.

"Okay" Joey replied, there wasn't any need for clarifying anything, Vauxhall house was going to be in a 'bit of a flap over this, so they may as well get it over with. "Make sure and ask 'em to find out who the three stooges were"

As soon as they got into the car Sandy went for her bag, taking out a long rectangular box she plugged a cord into one end, then clipped the cigarette lighter adapter onto the end of it.

Plugging the adapter into the cigarette lighter holder she powered up the little machine that was going to make a duplicate drive. The box had a flap at the opposite end to the cord. Sandy flipped it open to reveal two places for flash drives.

The device wasn't actually hers, so she was still figuring things out, it'd been given to her by a friend who was a computer genius, and one she figured was a bit of a 'black cap' or hacker. a while ago, but she'd never had the opportunity to try it out.

She figured the slot on the left was for the original, taking the flash drive out of the bag she checked it was the original and put it in the slot, straight away the machine started analyzing the files, including what encryption had been used for passwords and things.

"Standard commercial encryption software" she said softly to herself, "pretty high end though!"
Joey glanced over, by now they'd gotten out of the city and were at the on ramp for the motorway.

"That doesn't look 'like standard issue, is it legal?"

"It's not, so you're right." She replied leaning over to give him a peck on the cheek, "on both counts"

"Hey, steady in there" Joey tried to concentrate, "I'm driving"

"Just reminding you why we need to get back home" she spoke softly and seductively.
The distance flew by, but then the anticipation grew by the minute, so that made it feel like an eternity.

As soon as the machine had copied everything it transferred all the data to the new flash drive, but with one difference, it had already deciphered the codes so it did it 'in clear' ready for the next part.

As soon as that was done Sandy took the two flash drives out and shut the copier down, than placing the original back in the bag she took the laptop out and 'booted it up'

"Are we going to have time for that?" Joey asked, "it's only about an hour to the house."

"I'm only sending the email." Sandy replied, "that way they can start working on the data, and find out your new friends are!" She joked.

"Not my bloody friends" Joey played being grumpy.

"And anyway" Sandy went on, "I don't recall any martial arts like you used being taught anywhere!"

"And you won't" Joey replied, "compliments of a Korean roommate once at Hereford, there for some training in the killing house!"

Every SF operator learns how to take down a bunch of bad guys with hostages, preferably without injuring the hostages, but the SAS go one better with a special purpose built facility where they can go in with live hostages and live ammunition, it's usually the most junior gets to be the hostage and they hope like hell the boys aim isn't off, SAS don't believe in 'practice'! Every time (even in training) its for real!

"Still didn't look like any martial art taught" "That's cos it isn't" Joey replied. "Only Korea's 'White Tiger' brigade get this form of Tae Kwon Do, it's all lethal moves"

"And you 'just happen' to know someone right?" She said with a slight but playful tone.

"Me and the team" Joey replied. "It was Jacko set up our end of the deal!"

"And what was that?"

"Normally I'd say 'sorry, but official secrets act' but that isn't going to wash is it?"

"Not a chance" Sandy laughed, she was enthralled, and loving finding out about Joey.

"Hostage rescue from an oil rig" Joey began.

"Is that all?" She cut in.

"Using wing suits and landing on the pad at night" he added, that silenced her for a whole minute.

"Okay" she finally spoke up, "that was impressive, even if total BS"

"It's true!" He exclaimed, they were just at the edge of the city, a series of small hills known locally as the 'Bombays'. Back in the 1930s New Zealand took in hordes of farmers from India to work the land; many of them settled just outside Auckland, hence the name 'Bombays'

"You're telling me" Sandy was trying hard not to laugh, "you took a bunch of Koreans on a 'Sea Lord' op?"

"Next time you see Jacko ask him" Joey's brief but stern look said he wasn't lying.

"But come on!" Sandy continued, "those ops are top secret! Heck, even Parliament doesn't even know we do them!"

'OPERATION SEALORD' Britain's method of dealing with a terrorist attack on a North Sea oil rig, 90% of Britain's oil and gas comes from the North Sea, the threat is very real and the SAS train constantly in ways to get there and stop any problems.

"Yep" Joey replied, "just what I'm telling you, besides don't forget, the Koreans have the same issues in the seas around them!"

They drove on a little while, then Sandy said "pull over when you can, I'm ready to send the email and need the GPS unit for a bit."

G.P.S. or Global Positioning Software as the full title suggests is a computer based system that allows not only soldiers to track where they are, but also for their commanders who could be many miles away to know exactly where each 'asset' is at any given moment in time down to the last tenth of an inch.

The way it works is a soldier or vehicle transmits a signal on the ground that is picked up by overhead satellites, the satellites then interrogate each other (there has to be at least four of them) to find out how close the soldier or vehicle is to each of them and once they've triangulated the position they send the information both back to the soldier and back to the soldier's commander.

About five minutes after the satellite system going 'live' some bright spark came up with the idea that as the satellites are basically modified communication satellites, they can also be used to send two way communications back and forth, and depending where you put the antenna on the satellite they should be impossible for an enemy to either intercept or jam them.

A few months later someone forgot to tell MI6 not to 'tap into' the system, or at least that's the story.

"I'll get us some coffee," Joey said as he pulled into the car park to the service station at the top of the Bombays, he put the car in 'park', turned the engine off and got out.

Sandy fumbled a little with the back of the screen, found the connection she needed and hooked the laptop up through a slave lead.

The actual GPS unit isn't the screen you see, the real computer that does all the work is usually somewhere else, like in the boot or trunk of a vehicle or under the back seat.

It took about five seconds to send the information, as soon as it was finished a message flashed up on the laptop's screen, Sandy wasted no time disconnecting and returning everything back the way it should be.

The message travelled a total of sixty five thousand miles, twenty four thousand into space to the satellite, seventeen thousand between satellites (the message was accompanied by commands telling it which satellite to talk to, and exactly where in the sky it was). Using dish antennae you can direct where you want the radio signals to go, the narrower the dish the more control you have on who gets the signal, hence they can't be 'eavesdropped'.

The message, even travelling that great distance only took just over half a second to reach its destination, but it took another fifteen minutes to get to the person it was meant to, but that was due to the Human side of things.

Chapter 12

"Boss" Sam was thinking out loud, "something just isn't right here?" Sam had invited herself into inspector Mather's office; a poky little place that was only just bigger than the desk and solitary filing cabinet he kept there. Sam took a chair from the squad room, flipped it inside the door and plonked herself down opposite him.

The only other furniture (if you could call it that) was a small whiteboard above the two and as usual it was filled with details, all relating to a murder case he was working, Jimmy was supposed to be with her in the briefing, but as bloody usual he was off sick with something, she was getting a bit pissed of with it.

"I take it this incursion into my sanctuary has something to do with our Asian friends that turned up trussed up like turkeys then?"

"Not just 'something' boss" Sam made inverted commas sign with both hands, just like you do when you're quoting someone half sarcastically, "The whole bloody case, something just isn't right. It's not adding up!"

Danny Mather was an 'old school detective' in many ways and had a cigarette hanging from his mouth, he knew the building was supposed to be a 'no smoking zone's but he'd been a twenty a day guy for as long as he could remember and he wasn't changing now, "you don't like my smoking? Don't flaming well come in then!"He even told that to the station commander at least once.

He took the cigarette out and flicked the loose ash into the ashtray by the open window, his one compromise to the 'non smokers' and it only gets opened for those he respects, Sam was one of the few with that honour, "okay I'm listening," he leaned back in his chair, took another drag of the ciggie and blew the smoke out the window. "Run what you've got by me then."

"You've got the basics there" Sam pointed to the open file on the desk.

"Humour me" Danny replied, "run through it for me"

He was right, sometimes just verbalizing a problem can help you solve it, coming back to it a day or so later and talking through everything gives you a clear perspective you might not have seen the first time. "Okay" she began, "yesterday coms central get a call about three men with guns in an apartment block right?" She took a marker pen and wrote 'call at 1pm' on the whiteboard. "AOS and uniforms attend within ten minutes" she stops and writes 1.10 on the board, "instead of three armed men we get there men trussed up like turkeys, but with the crap beaten out of them," she wrote 'three armed men beaten' on the whiteboard, "but no sign of our caller!"

"So" Danny interrupted, "no one to give the bloody medal to then?" He was smiling, "so what's the problem, they had weapons didn't they?"

"Sure did boss" Sam said with a fake southern drawl, she was being as facetious back. "Glocks, and silencers."

"Expecting trouble?" He asked

"In the apartment of a dead man? Oh did I forget to mention the apartment was the one of that Banker who got himself killed in a car wreck last week, over on the Coromandel!"

"That does sound dodgy" Danny replied, "any hints of dodgy dealings at the Bank?"

"There's only me working this boss, remember?" she shot back, "But for your information, they've clammed up 'tighter than a ducks aresehole, they're not saying anything"

"In other words" he took another pull of the cigarette, "You betcha, but no proof!"

"At the moment" she came back, "I'm just working what I have, I'm not looking for a fight with the Banks and the like, We'll go there if we get more to go on!"

"Wise move" Danny replied, then looking round he asked, "Speaking of the lame and lazy, where is he?" everyone knew Danny didn't have a very high opinion of Jimmy, and he didn't help himself with the amount of time he took off.

"Who bloody knows?" Sam shrugged. "Yesterday it was one of the kids sick, anyway I haven't checked about the deceased as Thames said it was their case, their offices in Coromandel are coordinating everything."

"And now you've got an armed B and E at his place, what do you think? Any idea who dealt with the case?"

"The statement given was next to useless, by some rookie cop, but a 'constable Murray' was officer in charge at the scene!"

"Murray?" Danny started digging through the file, he found the scene report, "I remember a constable Murray, was with us for a few years, got pissed off at kept getting passed over for promotion, he transferred out, somewhere like Thames or something"

"Friend of yours boss?"

Danny seriously contemplated picking the ashtray up and throwing it at her, "he was here for a while" he began instead, "But he was pretty useless, that's why he got passed over so many times, I think it was at least a couple, you could say I showed him the door when he decided to 'move on' to greener pastures" He'd finished his ciggie and reached for the saucer of mints he had on his desk, "too many things went wrong then, when he moved on they stopped 'going pear shaped' if you get my drift!" he popped the mint in his mouth, "never could prove anything though." He paused for a moment, the continued, "what else?"

"That's just it boss" Sam replied, "No crash report from Serious Crash Unit yet, apparently that's scheduled for today, but it's not in the computer yet, no post mortem or anything! Just this Murray saying that it was due to high speed and excess alcohol! That doesn't sit right!"

"You're right there." Danny replied leaning forward and tapping the file, "especially if the SCU hasn't finished yet, still, what about these clowns though? How does that fit with the 'accident'?"

"That's what I'd like to bloody well know" Sam shot back, she was tossing the marker pen in her hand, thinking at the same time. "The three bozos were taken down by a professional that I'm sure of." The way she said the last part made it clear there was no doubting it in her mind.

"Why?"

"The force used!" she answered, "it was just enough to stop them and prevent them scarpering, but not enough to do any permanent damage!"

"Broken legs and arms aren't permanent?" he exclaimed with a mock surprise, "Remind me not to take you on!"

"Chris from the Armed Offenders Squad was there!" she explained, "Thats his assessment, not mine!"

They both knew Chris, and they both knew that he was an expert in the field of unarmed combat, just like their American counterparts in the SWAT teams the Armed Offenders Squad were trained in all kinds of specialist means of 'taking a bad guy down'. If they said the offender was 'professional' then that's what they were and that could not be good, even if the guy was 'on their side'

They both stopped talking, as if the last statement needed time to penetrate the armour that police put around themselves so that they can focus on getting to the truth of a matter, eventually it was Danny broke the silence.

"So, we've got a highly trained person or persons playing 'vigilante' on our turf and somehow" he picked up the photo of Cavell that was in the file, "This dipstick was linked in even though he's been dead a week!" he stopped and leaned back in his chair, then continued "Sounds like you need to take a trip over to the Coromandel and talk to some people" he finally finished the mint and thought long and hard about reaching for another ciggie. "Take the trip tomorrow, just you and try to keep things on the 'down low' if you know what I mean"

"Yeah" Sam sighed, truth was she was absolutely wasted and just wanted to sleep, she looked at her watch, "Shit, err sorry boss, but I had something lined up for tonight, guess I screwed that up!"

Danny started to chuckle, just about every cop does that on a regular basis, the job just takes over and the rest of 'life' gets put on hold. "Give him a call; tell him you were busy, If he's half decent he'll understand!"

"Did that ever work for you?"

"It's why I'm divorced!"

"Great advice then"

"Sod off, get out of here and drive over tomorrow, only make sure you don't call ahead" he was emphatic, "Don't give them any chance to get prepared!"

"Any other pearls of wisdom?" she asked as she headed for the door, there wasn't any need for him to tell her a second time to take the rest of the day off.

"Yes" He replied, "watch your back"

Chapter 13

The two families had some hard talking to do. What was going to happen to the farm now? With Kevin gone and Helen so badly injured, things were starting to look bleak.

Helen was in an induced coma as the hospital said the injuries were too severe to cope with at the moment, but they were hopeful that would change in the next couple of days.

"It's not just the funeral arrangements" Kevin's dad was as saying, he was almost breaking down "but we're going into the busy time of year, last thing the farm needs is to be a couple of experienced hands down, let alone our situation" Reality was with both of them gone the farm was going to struggle to survive.

"We can help some." Peter offered, truth was him and his wife would be glad to have something to do, even if just to take their minds off the situation.

"And I've got a couple of ex Army mates here on a working holiday" it was Joey, he and Sandy were just walking through the door, no one noticed the 'dagger like' look she gave him, "they'd be glad of the work, in exchange for beer of course!"

"What? why?" Kevin's dad asked, "there's no need to"

"Don't talk soft" Joey replied. "They'd love to help" he didn't even wince as Sandy dug him in the ribs hard.

"Let's talk" she spat out between clenched teeth and headed for the door.

As soon as they were outside she rounded on him. "Just what the hell was that?" She only just managed to keep her voice down, Joey was making promises he had no responsibility or authority for!

"What?" He gave a hard look back.

"You! You bloody idiot!" She shot back, "what the hell are you thinking?"

"Truth?" He asked, "this whole sodding lot is about to get really ugly, and I mean real fast! We need to be ready, bringing Jacko and the others in might just be the excuse we need"

"I know that, but Sir Michael will never go for it!"

"Probably, but I don't give a shit if he does!" Joey's face was as hard as flint, "we look after our own, and these folks have no idea what's coming! We tried sending them away; they refused, only other option is 'bring the mountain to Mohammed' as the saying goes"

"Despite the fact it'll blow our cover and tell people who we are?" Sandy replied just as strongly, "I know, it's my family and I want to make sure they're okay, but I still want a job at the end of it!"

Joey almost smiled, he could understand where she was coming from, but Sandy was missing a few things. "Sandy," he began. "Why do you think Sir Michael sent our team to Iran? And anyway, you really think your Dad doesn't know that we aren't insurance agents? He bloody well knows and I'll bet a hundred dollars your mum's worked it out as well, just she's got the good sense not to say anything"

"Because you were the best!"

"That" Joey was somewhat embarrassed, "and something else, he knew there was no way we'd obey the second part of the brief! He expected us to 'bend the rules' just like he's expecting it now!"

"Look" Sandy came back quietly, "I'm with you all the way, but there's got to be some other way?"

They were both thoughtful for a few minutes, finally it was Sandy broke the silence, "The best way" she began "would be to get him to"

"Think it's his idea!" Joey finished her line off, he turned and gave her the biggest hug he could muster, lifting her clean off her feet and swirling her round, "You're a genius, and I love you!" he stopped and let her slide down until their faces were fractions of an inch apart, then he slowly kissed her, she responded in kind, a full minute passed before they parted. "We tell them the truth, about the incident at the apartment, with just a little plausible embellishment" Joey continued, "they'll already be wary of anything happening, so anything we say will only nudge them into action"

"The last thing anyone wants is a bloodbath on foreign soil where it's innocents caught in the firing line" Sandy thought out loud.

"Especially when you could have stopped it" a voice spoke out from the darkness, it was Peter, Sandy's dad.

"How much did you hear?" Sandy was suddenly defensive.

"Not much" Peter replied, "But Joey's right, I didn't buy the insurance agent crap, but thought I'd go along with it as you must have had good reason!" He moved towards them, "by the way no one else knows, or if they do they aren't saying and preferring to believe the story you gave, also by the way Joey, I came out to tell you not to call your mates just yet as Jack says he wants to try for some local guys first," Peter said as he approached them, he was holding two cups of tea, offering them to Joey and Sandy he carried in talking and asking questions, "but just who are you folks? I mean yes, you're my daughter" he turned to Sandy, "but you've changed since you went to university, who are you? Or rather who do you work for?"

Sandy looked upset, she was keeping things from the family, she was having to, but it was beginning to tell on her.

It was Joey spoke up, "Mr Little," he began, "maybe it's time you and I took a walk" he waived indicating a walk down the farm track, "there's some things we can tell you, but some things we can't! Not because we don't want to but some things are dangerous to know"

"That's what I'm worried about!" Peter replied, she's my daughter.

"Don't" was all Joey said, "it's not danger for her or me we're talking about, it's dangerous for you, that's what we worry about!"

"What the hell do you mean?" Peter turned and looked at Joey, "just what in the good Lord's name is going on?"

"There's things I can"

"Don't give me that horseshit son!" Peter rounded on him, "I'm a copper remember!"

"I know" Joey remained calm as he replied, "what I was going to say is there's things I can tell you, and they'll have to be enough!"

Their little discussion and walk took fifteen minutes

Sandy was still outside on the porch when they got back, Joey could see as they approached she was still upset, not crying but showing frustrations in other ways. "How much did you tell him?" The question was almost an accusation.

"As much as a dad needs to know, "Joey replied, "but not as much as a copper wants to know!"

"What?"

"He's a cop and wants to know what cops want to know!" Joey explained, "told him that wasn't happening." He took her in his arms and gently stood her up, he looked into her eyes, "but a dad needs to know his daughter is safe and knows what she's gotten into, that I did tell him not to worry about,"

"Bet that went down well" Sandy cracked a small smile.

"I think he realized that once he knew we weren't going to tell" Joey replied, "He realized the 'dad' in him really didn't want to know, and the dad took over!"

Chapter 14

"When in Rome" was Murray's thoughts as he headed for the open sea, he'd got a few days off and as usual with the time off he'd headed to the marina in Whitianga where he kept his boat, loaded up the supplies and was off for the day fishing.

"Damn, can't they give it a bloody rest?" The phone was ringing, not the work one, but the other, the one that even he didn't like hearing from, the one with the Asian voice on the other end, he thought seriously about not answering, but the money on offer would be too good an offer to turn down, besides failure to answer might indicate to them that he wasn't interested anymore and that could not end well!

He picked the phone up, swiped the screen to 'answer' and spoke as calmly as he could, trying not to show the frustration he was feeling. "What's up?" he was abrupt.

"We have a problem" the Asian voice said in a very cold tone. It sent a shiver down his spine.

"What kind of problem?" it was more a statement than anything else, Murray was disowning any problem they'd try to shift onto him, that way they would pay more for 'clearing the problem up'

"The car" the Asian voice came back, "Something happened, the car is still in police compound" his english wasn't perfect, but Murray got the jist, the car was still in the compound, and it shouldn't be, at least his Chinese friend thinks it shouldn't be.

"Why's that a problem?" Murray had no idea what they'd planned, but it obviously wasn't good for someone.

"Someone tampered with the car!" the voice came back, "big problem, how they tamper?"

"What the hell? I thought you were someone to do that?" Murray was incredulous,"You're telling me, your boys or girls didn't and someone else got to it?"

"That's the problem" the voice cut him off, "The car was meant to be dealt with permanently, it should be a pile of molten scrap by now, it isn't, and we want to know why not?" the voice rose considerably with the last word, no mistaking what the voice meant, the car was meant to have either exploded or caught fire by now, and it didn't.

"What are you talking about?" Murray's voice got lower, almost as cold as ice, he was well and truly in the crap if anyone found out what they were doing, if the car had exploded, then dozens of cops would have been hurt, and no quarter given in the investigation, they would nail his arse to the wall, throw him in some deep dark cell and throw away the key!

"We arranged car explosion" the voice said again, "problem disappear, but car not explode someone knows, and that someone not Police!"

"So?" Murray asked again, "I did what you wanted, I thought you'd remove the evidence, didn't realize you'd be stupid enough to try destroy it, along with a flaming police station, you idiot, what the hell were you thinking?"

"Remember, you're in this too" the voice cut back, "Or how about we remove you as well?"

"You want me to find out who?" Murray asked, hoping they didn't think too much about the last part of what they said.

"Also we sent three of our men to an apartment in Auckland to 'retrieve' something for us" the voice continued. "They were intercepted and have been arrested"

"Then get a lawyer to get them out!" Murray was frustrated, this was a mundane issue that a lawyer could clear up, even if it was just getting them out on bail and then disappearing, "Don't bother me with stuff like this, I'll find out about the car, you deal with the rest." He clicked the phone off.

Within a second the phone rang again, as soon as he answered the voice came back on again. "That wasn't the smartest move constable!"

"Look, where's the problem that I need to get involved with?" Murray asked.

"Do whatever it takes," the voice came back, "You've shown pretty incompetent so far, so make this work, or else"

"And just what do you mean by that?" Murray asked through clenched teeth, "who're you calling incompetent?"

"You were told to make the death an accident!" The voice came back, cold and calculating, "if you'd done that my men would have retrieved what we need from Cavell's place and no one would know who'd been there!"

"But they'd still know someone had! How long do you think before someone figured it out?" Murray was amazed at how close arrogance sometimes is to stupidity!

"That's why we have people like you on the payroll!" The Asian came back, "someone got suspicious, and they showed up!"

"What did your people tell you?" Murray asked.

"Young, European looking male and female"

"Pictures?"

"In your email, find them and deal with the situation, and this time don't screw up!"

Murray swiped the phone off; he wasn't a 'happy camper' but there wasn't a lot he could do about it at the moment, he was out of range for the email to work and took a moment to think whether he should go back and put some things in place to deal with whoever was causing the problem, he'd a good idea it was that young idiot Metcalfe and his 'floozy' with the red hair, but he'd need to confirm that with the photos, "That can sodding well wait" he thought to himself as he pushed the throttle on the thirty foot Rayglass 2200 boat, she responded immediately, eager for the open water.

"Detective Sergeant Sam Hughes" Sam flashed her warrant card at the duty officer, a petite young female constable, she looked almost afraid behind the huge desk and bullet proof glass, Sam carried on. "I'm hoping to catch a senior constable Murray, is he around?"

"Err sorry" the young constable began, "But he called in sick today, I can put you through to the officer in the department if you like? A constable" she fumbled with the computer mouse as she brought up the right screen on the computer "Constable Hene Kingi" she looked up and straight at Sam.

"I did call ahead to make sure he was going to be here!" Sam was frustrated, and didn't mind too much that the desk officer felt the frustration, it was one of the desk officers, and maybe the same actual one that had told her it wasn't a problem and they'd make sure Murray was available. "I suppose Kingi will have to do, it's about the fatal accident they both attended last week"

"The one with the McLaren" the desk officer replied as she buzzed Sam in, "Down the corridor on the left, he's just finishing a shift, so he'll be in the locker room, I can send him up as soon as he's changed" she indicated the interview room where Sam was to wait, even the interview would be recorded. "I'll get you the files while you wait"

Sam sat down in the interview room and waited for the files, she didn't have to wait long, and the file wasn't all that big, a quick glance told her there wasn't anything more than she already knew in it.

The room itself was simple to the point of being spartan, no windows, a small table with a recording device built into a cabinet and secured into the table so that only the tapes can be accessed and preventing anyone from ripping the recorder out or smashing it. Four chairs for the two officers, the lawyer and the person being 'interviewed' were the sum total of the furniture.

"Not very comfortable are they?" A male voice came from behind, Sam swivelled in the chair, he was quite tall, 'maybe five ten, mid to late twenties' she thought. "They're not meant to be" she replied, "They're meant to put the interviewee on edge, but as a cop you'd know that"

"True" he replied, "I'm officer Kingi" he held out his hand, she was surprised, it was a confident handshake, not what the reports seemed to indicate by what she'd read about officer Kingi. "I'm just about to go get something to eat, care to join me?"

Sam couldn't believe it! He was 'hitting on her' at least that's what it felt like, "Thanks, but I'm only here to talk about the fatal crash you attended a couple of days ago, if you don't mind" she pointed to the seat opposite.

"I know you are" Kingi replied, "and I'll be happy to answer any questions, but I really need some food! Please, I'll buy." she didn't move, so he added, "People often talk better outside the interview room!"

Read that as 'I'm really uncomfortable with talking around people who might be Murray's friends' she thought, for some reason Officer Kingi wasn't comfortable with talking in place where what he said might get back to his 'mentor'.

This wasn't the 'insecure officer' she'd expected from the reports, and the way he was behaving about the station said something wasn't quite right, she just didn't know what yet.

"Besides" he continued, "It'll be best if I actually take you to the scene after we've eaten, that way you'll see what we talk about!"

"That sounds like a plan" Sam replied as she grabbed her bag off the floor, "lead the way"

They exited the station and headed across the street to a small cafe, this early in the morning there was a brisk trade, mostly tourists eating a quick breakfast before making the drive either up to Colville township, further up the peninsular, or towards Auckland, there were a couple of things worth seeing in Thames which was about an hour south of them,, but nothing that'd take more than a day.

"By the way, the name's Hene" the young officer turned to Sam, "want a coffee?" He took a piece of carrot cake from the cabinet; she was a little surprised as he'd said he was hungry.

"Cappuccino, with chocolate topping please" she turned and headed for a table.

A few moments later Hene joined her at the table, "I thought you were hungry?" She asked.

"Yeah, right" Hene was slightly hesitant with his reply, "sort of, but talking in the station's not always a good idea" he sat down, "you sure you don't want some? Kind of makes me feel guilty eating on my own!"

"Thanks but the coffee's enough" she replied. "Anyway I wanted to talk about the guy killed in the accident last week."

"There were two men killed in the accident" Hene reminded her, "which one?"

"Yeah right" she shifted slightly, the waitress arrived with the coffee, she put the chocolate top in front of Sam, and Hene had mocha.

"I'm talking the car driver" Sam replied, "what can you tell me?"

Hene took a packet of sugar, ripped the top open and poured it into the mocha, "Cavell I think his name was," he thought for a moment, then went on "some banker I think, killed on impact, I took witness statements, so I didn't actually see the deceased!"

"Witness statements?" Sam asked, "the reports said they weren't reliable enough, and none were taken" she sounded quizzical, "am I right"

"Right about the report" Hene replied, "Total BS about reliability though! These two were totally coherent, hell the guy saved one person's life doing CPR!"

"But you wrote that in YOUR report didn't you?" Sam replied pointing out that it was Hene's name on the report.

"I didn't write it!" Hene replied 'matter of factly' he took the mocha, took a sip and put it down, he went back to eating the carrot cake!

"But your name's on the report, so to all intents and purposes you wrote it!" Sam replied, she looked into his eyes, he wasn't lying, but there was a hint of frustration there, was it the questioning, or something else?

"Yeah, I know" he slowly, almost reluctantly replied, "I submitted a report, textbook with all the details, but Murray hit the roof with me!" he replied.

"Why?" The more she heard about this situation the more confused she became, why would a copper criticise another for doing his job properly? "What was wrong with it?"

"Nothing as far as I'm aware" Hene replied, he took a spoonful of the carrot cake, "I had all the details, all the information from the witnesses, including the detail about the mysterious character seen leaving the crash scene just after the impact."

"What? This wasn't in the report!" she replied taking her notebook out, Hene reached over and placing his hand on hers stopped her, "There's no need for taking notes," he said, then taking out a small flash drive he gave it to her, "It's all on here, the original report that I wrote before Murray had me take it down!"

"Are you telling me?" She began

"All I'm saying is I got my arse kicked for filing the report before Murray had a chance to sanitize it" Hene replied, "we had a huge argument over it, and I'm pretty sure he's looking for the first chance to 'can' me if you know what I mean" he gave a steely stare back, "I've been waiting until I went to Hamilton in a couple of days to talk to someone about this as I don't really trust anyone here! It's a pretty small station and most of 'em are Murray's mates"

"You realize what you're saying don't you?" Sam was concerned; it wasn't everyday you found stuff like this going on.

"I'm the 'newbie' here" he replied, stretching out and returning the cup back to the saucer, "maybe no one will listen, but I do have a duty to report it, I know that, meanwhile I'm the one who looks a total incompetent with a report like that one filed in my name!" Hene was angry, "anyway I wanted to take you to the scene so you could see for yourself, you'll see what I mention in the real report!"

Sandy couldn't sleep, something, she had no idea what but something was bothering her, "was it just that it's too quiet?" She was trying to sleep, but it was eluding her.

It would have been good, just to have Joey to snuggle up to, but with her parents in the same house, but it just didn't feel right, hence he was in one room and she was in the other.

Unable to sleep, she decided to get up and check on things, coming out of her room she went to turn the light in, nothing happened, she tried again, then a familiar voice spoke quietly.

"I took the bulbs out" it was Joey, he was sat in a corner, the curtains were open, he was silently watching the outside, on his knee was a shotgun.

"Joey" Sandy pointed to the gun, "something you're not telling me?" He was just sitting there watching the silhouettes on the outside, a couple of windows were open.

"It's from Jack's gun cabinet" he replied, "and yes, it was locked, but that wasn't much of a problem"

"Did you break the lock?" She asked, Joey wasn't known for being gentle.

"Give me some credit" Joey sounded slightly offended, "I HAVE BEEN WATCHING you know!" He paused, she was going to say something but he held his hand up, he was concentrating on the outside.

Sandy found a chair and sat down, it was totally silent, Joey had the windows open, but they were actually sat just inside the ranch slider which was closed, there were no lights, not even from street lights, the view was sensational, with the wide belt if the milky way stretching overhead meeting the darker silhouette of the forest, but even there shapes could be seen, something was moving, you could just see the movement in the shadow.

Things were just too quiet, that was when she noticed she couldn't hear the birds, at first she'd thought it was the windows closed, but Joey had two or three open, there wasn't a bird making any noise, it seemed almost eerie.

"So quiet" Sandy whispered, "Almost too quiet"

She reached out for a chair, her night vision was coming back slowly, she was beginning to see differences in the shades rather than just the silhouettes, she thought she saw things moving outside.

"You're right there!" Joey whispered, "sorry to say but I think things are about to 'turn to shit, and very quickly" he opened the gun chamber and started feeding cartridges in, the gun, a Remington 870 tactical wasn't quite the Bushmaster he was used to, but she was a good weapon in a tight spot, the seven cartridge magazine was slightly more than the average pump action, and she was real easy to reload! "Best get the folks up and to safety"

"The garage?" She asked.

"Yep, in the car, get ready to drive like a maniac!" he replied, then turned to her, she could see a slight smile, "Oh, and by the way, Sir Mike was slightly ahead of us, help's waiting at the end of the track" he said pointing to the second exit.

A 1956 Norton commando isn't just a bike; it's a statement, one that says, "I'm king of the road, and you, GET OUT OF MY WAY!" But then a 'Commando' isn't a 'big bike' but she's fast, built for the Isle of Man TT races, she's a bikers dream in many ways, and his nightmare in others, but once you've owned one, you'll never go back to the modern 'crap'

The 'commando' was leading the pack, then came two Harleys, bigger machines but nowhere near the same statement, the last guy was riding a Triumph Bonneville, all the bikes were fifties vintage, and all paid for dealing the hard stuff.

"That the place?" One of the Harley riders asked", pointing to the letterbox at the head of the drive, the drive itself looked pretty dark with trees lining the roadway, there was a left hand curve in the road up the drive that kept them hidden from the house.

"From the info we got it is!" 'Norton' replied, they had their mobiles wired into headsets and were using them like radios with the difference they could all talk at once. Norton continued on, "He said only to scare 'em, but if anyone gets hurt it's their problem not ours!"

There no lights on at the house, that was good, it meant the occupants were asleep, they were about to get a rude awakening!

Chapter 15

Steve had been working on the files since Sandy had sent them. They were encrypted using a commercial encryption program that the computers had identified within a couple of minutes, and taken another ten minutes or so to crack the program.

Normally M.I.6 would send the file to the people at GCHQ in Cheltenham to crack as they're the specialists at code-breaking, they're the people who listen in to every conversation on the phone and every email sent, they're the ones to track every means of electronic communication looking for Terrorists, Spies and Drug dealers and they have a good record in catching them!

But there's a mole in 'six' and they needed to know who that mole was? Was it someone here in Vauxhall house? Or someone somewhere else? Until they found out nothing dealing with Scorpion one left the building, and left the conference room in particular.

It was the early hours of the morning, he was tired, but the coffee pot had been working overtime and the third refill of the pot was waiting for him to take the coffee, he was too busy looking at the screen, he'd finally started to understand what he was seeing.

"This is bloody unreal" he was alone, but couldn't help speaking out loud, he paused for a moment, reached out and took the half full coffee cup, "So simple yet bloody ingenious!" he took a sip of the coffee, it was lukewarm, but he was concentrating on the screen so much that he hardly noticed.

"What have you got" Sir Michael asked as soon as he walked through the door. It was early morning; the sun was reluctantly beginning to show its face through the skyscrapers of Canary wharf to the east of Vauxhall Bridge. "I hope it's worth dragging me in at this ungodly hour!" He was somewhat grumpy both from the urgency of the email he got and the lack of sleep.

"Morning to you too boss," Steve glanced up from the screen, he'd set things up so that what he was working on showed up on one of the two big screens in the room. "Coffee's on the left, a fresh pot, and there's a couple of bagels in the toaster by the coffeepot, and can I strongly recommend you make it strong as you're probably going to both love and hate me after this!"

"That good then?" It was a question more than anything else.

"There's an abbreviated report been sent to the folks at the New Zealand High commission and Wellington, but the full report is there for you," Steve looked up from the screen, "you want me to 'walk' you through it Sir Michael, or just want to read the report?"

"Just the important stuff, and when's the conference for?" He replied reaching for a cup and sorting himself a coffee out, the toaster popped up with the toasted bagel. "Where'd you get the toaster from?"

"Brought it with me yesterday morning," Steve replied. "As soon as I saw the file from Sandy I kind of knew it was going to be a long day!"

"You got it past security?" Sir Michael wasn't sure if he was more surprised at the hours Steve had put in cracking the file, or the fact he'd gotten unauthorized equipment onto the premises, did he congratulate Steve for 'initiative'? Or fire the security team?

"As they say boss" Steve gave a mischievous smile, "it's not what you know, but who you know, besides the night shift and I did a deal, it's not allowed out of my sight, and night shift supply their own bagels!"

That brought a smile to his face, there were some pretty nice folks worked security on the night shift, and Sir Michael probably knew them as well, if not better than those on the day shift. He buttered the toasted bagel that had just popped up, put another in for Steve, took the coffee and bagel and made his way to other seat at the head of the table, the report was waiting for him there. "What time's the conference call?"

"Not until eight this morning" Steve replied, "about two hours"

"Thank the Lord for small mercies!" Sir Michael held his hands up in a 'theatrical' gesture, neither really smiled much, but the tension dissipated slightly, he settled into the chair, put the bagel down, picked up the report and began reading while sipping the coffee at the same time, that was a mistake.

The second paragraph knotted his gut so much he nearly choked on the drink, spluttering and cursing at the same time he turned to Steve. "Are you sure about this?" He demanded waiving the report about.

"If I wasn't" Steve replied almost blase about the situation, "I wouldn't have put it in there!"

"But the size of the thing?" He demanded, he'd put the coffee down, "I mean a global network? And no one's picked it up, come on, it can't be right?" It was more hopeful question than anything.

"From the data we've got now" Steve came back, "it's not complete, but it all points to being global, with Banks worldwide being the 'mules' for the network!"

"But" he began again, "the whole idea, I mean it's ludicrous!" Sir Michael, took a bite of the bagel, "and you're saying they're doing it without us, or anyone else for that matter, getting wind of what's going on? I mean come on"

"Ludicrous or not" Chambers cut him off, "it's happening, and by the way, it seems that someone did know, or at least suspected something was going on that wasn't totally 'kosher' remember what we found out about Barclays?"

They sat there in silence for a moment, it seemed like an hour, but neither spoke, too afraid to think about it, finally Steve plucked up the courage to continue. "What we've got is just a small piece, where Cavell's money came from, and some of where it's sitting now!"

"So what you're telling us" it was 'Mildred' spoke, "is the files are like the spokes of a wheel?"
"Pretty much," Steve replied, "Cavell was only really interested in the money he was getting, at least with this file"

"Is the money still in the accounts?"

"It's still in Cavell's accounts," Sir Michael replied, "chiefly because they haven't found it yet, it's probably what they were looking for at his apartment!"

"How much?"

"A little over four million pounds, seven million New Zealand dollars!" Steve replied. "In fifteen accounts scattered throughout various Banks around the globe"

"Is that all?" Mildred was slightly annoyed at the meeting, especially if it was only covering 'small sums'.

"That's just what Cavell had in HIS accounts on the day he died!" Steve was abrupt in his reply, "it doesn't account for the ten million he spent in the last twelve months, not all from the same account though, or what seems to have been going through the other accounts they've managed to move to 'safety'!" He made the classic quotation sign with both hands.

"What other accounts?" Jerry the intelligence officer from New Zealand house asked, "how many, and how much?"

"Possibly as many as fifty accounts around the globe." Sir Michael took that question, "it's in the report we sent you."

"Actually boss, I may have to revise that figure upwards," Steve butted in, "the fifty was what I knew of when I wrote the report, but further digging showed about twenty more, all with reasonable sums taken out" he moved his hand slightly, the mouse on his computer moved and they each saw a file open in their machines. "What you're seeing" he began again, "is the last transfer out of those accounts, as you're aware any amount over $10k without prior notice taking out over the counter triggers alarm bells, and they have to let the government of that particular country know right?" He looked directly into the camera that was transmitting, "what the Banks don't tell is they keep records of every transaction, big or small, physical or electronic, and they record where it goes to!" There was a moment's pause, "the last transactions shown here all happened after Cavell was killed and weren't on the flash drive we recovered, we got them off the Banks own servers, take a look at the size of them!"

There were seventy accounts on the screen; each of them showed three to five million dollars disappearing within minutes of each other.

"Half a billion dollars!" There simultaneous gasps from all three of the others.

"That's US dollars" Steve added, "and just the tip of the iceberg, I've only really accessed historic records for a couple of the accounts, and the picture is pretty staggering," he clicked the mouse, another screen came up on their computers, "take a look here" he pointed to the column on the left, "those are the dates of historic transfers for just one of the accounts, next to it is where the money went, and finally how much, the last one's what Cavell took for himself!"

"But" Mildred spoke up, "the one account shows fifteen million!"

"Yep" Steve replied, "and don't forget, that's American dollars not New Zealand ones!"
There was a stunned silence as each one absorbed the information, they only had part of the picture, but the bit they had was huge.

"Any chance these are clearing accounts?" It was Jerry spoke up.

"That's exactly what we think they are!" Sir Michael butted in, "but look, the reason for the call isn't just about where the money goes, we've also got a bit of a situation"

"Your assets on the ground!" Mildred butted in, "you want them out?"

"Not an option" Sir Michael replied firmly, "removing them now tells the opposition we know about this," he gestured to the file in front of him, "you can guarantee it'll disappear without a trace, and besides, they wouldn't listen anyway!"

That actually got a few laughs, but they all knew it to be true, men people from units like the SAS weren't exactly known for following orders when it put friends 'in the firing line '!

"No" he continued, "It's more to do with the family there, innocents, caught right in the middle of the whole thing."

"Any chance we can get them to relocate?"

"Our assets already tried suggesting that," Sir Michael replied, "didn't go down too well!"

"We could arrange them to go into protective custody or witness protection!" Was the next suggestion, but no one was too hopeful

"One cop for sure is with the drug gang!" Steve interrupted, he wanted to add 'there's no guarantee there aren't more' but instead he continued "if the gangs find out we know, you can kiss goodbye to all this." He gestured to the files, the meaning was clear as crystal, there was no way the families would even consider moving to safety with Helen still in the hospital, and she was still critical. That didn't leave many options.

"Okay ' it was 'Mildred' broke the silence. "Mike, I've never known you NOT have a plan," she'd been playing with a pencil the whole time; she slowly put it down, "care to enlighten us?"

Chapter 16

"Mum, Dad" Sandy whispered through the slightly open door of their room, "We've got a bit of an issue; we need to leave, NOW!"

"Okay" Peter replied, "We couldn't sleep anyway" he sort of propped himself up and reached for the light, he flicked the switch, nothing happened. "Damn, light must have blown" he began fumbling about.

"Fuses removed" Sandy replied, not adding much more." Look, wc've got to move, and no lights okay?" The last part was a 'don't argue ' kind of statement.

Peter was out of bed now, and getting dressed, Sandy's mum was also up and moving, "Where's my blouse? How the hell am I supposed to get dressed when I can't find my bloody clothes?" She was tired and grumpy, and everyone was going to know about it.

"Sorry mum" was all Sandy could think of, "but it's for your own safety!" She began.

"And if I trip over a bloody cord and break a leg, how's that safer than using the sodding lights?"

"At least you'll be alive to do it!" Sandy retorted giving more information than she intended.

"What's that meant to mean?" Both had found clothes and were getting dressed, not liking their daughter's tone.

"What I flaming well said!" Sandy was frustrated, "there's some people here meaning to do us some serious harm, now get a bloody move on and quit moaning!" She felt awful talking to her parents this way, but they needed to realize the danger they were in.

"Not the 'friends' you and Joey were talking about before are they?" Peter's voice reminded her of the way he used to speak when scolding her and Helen as kids, there was also a huge dollop of worry in the voice.

"Yep" She replied, "Haven't met them personally, but I don't want to either, now come one!"

Jack and his wife were already in the garage, Joey had woken them, they were whispering to each other.

They say you can smell fear, but what they never tell you is You can taste it too! It's the vile taste you get just before you want to vomit, that's what fear tastes like, the sickening sweet yet burning sensation you can taste in the back of the throat that's telling the stomach to leap out through whatever orifice will open!

She could feel the fear in the air, the dark hid some of it but she was sure the other two women were shaking they were so afraid.

Joey seemed not to be affected by it that was on the surface of things, "guy's got bloody ice for blood!" She heard her father say, she daren't say anything, she'd learned Joey's trick of 'channelling the fear.

"Hell, he even searched the house for weapons!" She thought, he had, and it turned up an old pump action shotgun (the Remington) with a broken trigger spring and a Ball Bearing gun, both of which were repaired, cleaned, oiled and in better working order than they'd ever been, even when new they didn't work as well as they do now.

Sandy had learned too, she'd spent the last few days mapping out the property and the escape routes, they'd called them 'bug routes' after the military term 'bug out' meaning 'run like hell, but in an orderly way!' They had 'bug one's through the main gate, 'bug two' down a disused and overgrown track at the back of the property, and 'bug three' was for if the shit really hit the fan, that one was really treacherous as it involved crossing open ground!

"They've come down 'bug one' " Joey whispered to Sandy, "take bug two" he turned to the rest of the group, "right folks, back of the Land Rover please, lie down in the back, that'll give more protection"

The Landrover was an old Mk1 that Kevin had restored, she was old, but as well as being the first ever four wheel drive they were still regarded as being among the best, if somewhat temperamental. Sandy slid into the driver's seat and checked everything, she turned the key and all the dash lights came on telling her the 'lannie' was ready as soon as she pushed the button.

Joey handed her the Remington, "last resort!" He said, "Five in the mag, one in the chamber, also there's bad news and good news!"

What can be worse than knowing there's people out there wanting to do you or your family some serious harm? "Give me the bad first!" Sandy replied.

"Apparently there's more showed up, a couple more at the head of bug one as we speak!"

"How'd you know?" Sandy asked hoping it was just a guess.

"That's the good news," Joey replied. "Jacko and Mac are waiting for you at the end of bug two, Smithy is watching the rest!"

She felt like launching herself at him, flinging her arms around his neck and kissing in such a way it'd make her parents blush, but that'd have to wait. How?" Was all that would come out. "How the hell did they get here?"

"As I said before" Joey whispered back. "Sir Mike was ahead of us on this one, but then again, who cares! They're here and waiting at the end of 'bug two' they've got orders not to interfere"

That was understandable, you don't just walk in on a position when all hell's about to break loose, the danger of friendly fire is just too great, and with Joey here they knew everything would be covered, traps would be everywhere and they'd be guaranteed to walk into one! "They'll take care of protecting the family" Joey was saying, she wasn't fully hearing. "Smithy's going to take care of any 'late arrivals' and make sure they don't interfere!"

"And make sure the others have no chance" she wanted to add, but didn't "What about you?" was all she could think to ask.

"I've got the four legged friends, and a few surprises set up" Joey replied, he began lifting the garage door slowly, they could see some movement in the distance as the bikes approached, they were still a couple of hundred yards away, trying in their own way to be quiet, but to be honest it was comical. "They've got no sodding idea, these clowns, look" he pointed to the headlights that were still on, they had no idea that Joey'd seen them a good kilometre and a half away.

Just as they were speaking they saw the others arrive, there were at least six now, six against one wasn't good odds, even when it was clowns like these out front, but Joey had an 'equalizer'. Rather he had four of them!

The first thing every shepherd needs is a good dog. Kevin and Helen owned a sheep station, that meant a pack of working dogs, and theirs were a variety of breeds, not all theirs were the 'nice' kind, mostly due to the fact Kevin had also liked to hunt the local wild pigs, he had a couple that were especially good at taking a two hundred pound wild pig down, and a couple of 'little helpers' who loved to chase anything, besides, they had a few things on the farm that were valuable, and needed a 'little extra; to protect them.

That 'little extra' was a pack of four dogs, Rufus, a Border Collie Rottweiler cross. He was the 'Alpha' and at nearly a hundred Kilograms of energy and intelligence nothing argued with him, his sidekick Brutus a Mastiff, Border collie cross (same mother different father) was only slightly more placid. Against them. Not even the biggest pigs stood a chance, Humans didn't 'have a prayer'. Next came the two terriers, a Jack Russell named Jack and a Cairn Terrier that Joey couldn't resist calling "Daniels" partly because of his golden colouring that reminded him of the famous Bourbon and partly because of his attitude. one that seemed to be 'game for anything, they loved to chase, and were even less afraid of things than the big dogs were! Joey figured that dogs so small didn't have room in their bodies for all that energy and fear as well!'

A variety of breeds maybe, but well traincd they were, and they'd accepted Joey as their 'pack leader', they did everything the pack leader wanted, and without argument. More to the point, they would defend the pack and it's leader with everything they had, their very lives if they had to.

Joey turned one last time to Sandy as she climbed into the Landrover, "Wait for the screams" he whispered then silently closed her door for her and made his way outside.

'What the hell was he meaning?' she thought, She shuddered to think, but there wasn't time to ask questions, 'Oh well, all will be revealed' she continued the thought. She reached down and checked the electrics, everything was ready, the dash lights were on and all that was needed was to 'hit the button'.

The bikes came to a stop about seventy yards from the house, there wasn't much cover between them and the house, but that wouldn't matter as they'd be 'in and out' before anything had time to register, the plan was to scare the inhabitants and get the information from them, not really to harm them, but if that happened then no big deal, just serve to teach these pricks not mess with the 'gangs' and leave the drug trade alone!

Least that's what they thought the message was, no one actually knew who ordered the hit, just their boss 'Chopper' got a call and he made a 'call'

"Got the kero?" Alex, the guy on the commando demanded.

"Yeah, relax, it's all under control!" One of the others replied.

"Don't give me that shit!" Alex shot back, "let's get this done and get the hell outta here!" He stood the bike on its stand, climbed off and went for the empty beer bottles he'd brought specially for the job. They'd been wiped down so there were no fingerprints on them, washed thoroughly so there wasn't any DNA trace, nothing to trace them back to the gang.

The most effective way to deliberately start a fire uses three ingredients, empty beer bottles, kerosene and a piece of cloth.

They parked the bikes and switched off the engines. Alex took a half dozen of the bottles and stood them upright, one of the other bikers, a big guy with dirty long hair, two days stubble and a scar across his left cheek, went to his 'saddle compartment', took out a funnel and a gallon can of kerosene, he placed the funnel in the first bottle, popped the lid on the kerosene and began to pour. He stopped as soon as the bottle was a third full, then moved on to the next until all six were ready.

One of the others had brought some old rags, they stuffed the rags into the bottles and passed them out, one each.

Most people would soak the rags in Kerosene, but then most would end up with third degree burns all the way up their arms and spend the next six months in intensive care!

When you light the thing it's not the kerosene that burns, it's the fumes! As soon as you pour you've got fumes, light it and you get a fireball that'll engulf your arm, light the dry rag and you've got maybe a minute before the fireball, by the way the fireball will be about three feet across, but the trick is just to get literally 'a smell' on the rag, but that's easy, just let it soak from the bottom, then it acts like the wick on the Kerosene lamps you see in the old movies.

As soon as they were ready Alex checked everyone, a couple of the gang had sawn off twelve gauge shotguns, they were loaded and ready.

They began walking towards the house. 'No lights' he thought, he began to grin, not that anyone could see it, he was going to enjoy this. "Get ready boys" he spoke quietly.

Clothesline can come in really handy, not just for hanging clothes, but used right it can make a great trip wire or wire for pulleys, and Joey'd rigged a pulley of sorts for something else he'd rigged to a couple of hundred watt spot lamps he'd rigged into the system, all it needed was a foot in the right place.

They walked slowly across the gravel driveway, almost cautiously, the two with the shotguns spreading out, checking the guns and cocking them, clearly a little more planned than just 'scaring' them!

Fishing line makes great trip wire, and it's perfect for booby traps. Joey's was simple, a trip wire or two across the driveway linked to the switch for the lights, and the blankets covering the dogs cages. The dogs were restless, but the blankets blocking out any light was keeping them subdued enough, not that it mattered too much, a farm without dogs would be a strange place indeed!

The bikers stopped, Alex took out his lighter and lit the Molotov, he began a run forward, all hell broke loose.

He never saw the trip wire, but he did see the light, It damn near blinded him.

"Take the bloody lights out!" He screamed covering his eyes with the free hand, the fuse was burning; he began to run forward, that was a mistake.

The bikers were rattled, and not very good shots, both shotguns came up, and both discharged both barrels, they started reloading.

The shotguns only hit one security light, there were three, plus the two spotlights, it was the 'spots' on Alex, he was still blinded, he had no chance of seeing the next trip wire, that one attached to the clothes lines, and linked to the Kennels. It ripped the blankets off the dogs cages and set them loose, four dark shadows came sliding across the ground so fast you only saw a fleeting shadow, but you heard the terrifying snarls as they tore forward in pairs.

Joey brought his gun up.Three 'spots' weren't heard over the snarling and shouts of scared men, the first two were wide of the mark, Joey was adjusting as he went, the third was on target.

Alex was half way through the throw, the arm was just above the shoulder and rising when the glass bottle disintegrated sending kerosene spraying over him and in a wide circle, then the lighted cloth made contact and ignited, engulfing his whole side in flames.

The screams didn't sound human! But Sandy knew they had to be, as soon as they started she hit the starter button as hard as she could, she didn't need to, but adrenaline kicked in and she couldn't help herself.

The 'Lannie' was already in four wheel drive, and in gear, she revved the engine let the clutch out and released the handbrake in one fluid motion, all four wheels spun as they took off, the two and a half liter straight four engine growling as the vehicle jumped forward.

The dogs were halfway across the front gravel already, Kevin had told them the dogs liked to work in 'tandem' with Jack always working with Rufus, Daniels working with Brutus, Jack was in the lead and launched himself at 'Scarface's' ankle, Scarface was turning and moving when Jack hit, he didn't penetrate the leather, but it was enough to throw him off balance, he took a swipe at the dog with the still unloaded gun, that's when Rufus flattened him with his weight, a hundred and twenty kilos of pissed off dog snarling right next to your ear pinning you to the ground basically saying."Go on, try it! I'm hungry and I'll have you for breakfast!" Scarface was winded anyway, Jack had let go the ankle, he moved round and bit down hard on the hand holding the shotgun.

That's when Joey figured out what the dogs were doing, one pair, Jack and Rufus, had gone for the guy on the left, Daniels and Brutus were heading for the guy on the right, just like they'd do if this was a flock of sheep with a couple of 'wayward' strays! Normally Rufus and Brutus would take care of the main flock, with Jack and Daniels chasing down the 'wayward'.

The other shotgun was reloaded and just coming up in Jack's direction when Daniels hit, Cairn terriers aren't the best jumpers, but he launched himself, even a little twenty pound dog makes a hell of an impact running at full speed, add to that razor sharp teeth aimed at the back of the knee and you get the picture.

The gun went up and off harmlessly shooting air as he crumpled squealing obscenities, he tried to bring the gun round to use as a club, that's when Brutus nearly took the arm off, both shotgunners were pinned.

The 'Lannie' flew out the garage, heading straight for the other three with the Molotovs, they hadn't lit them and were transfixed to the spot, plans unraveling by the second, seemingly at the last second Sandy recovered enough to turn hard left and floored the accelerator. All four wheels spun and spit gravel, something that's almost impossible to make a Landrover do, but she managed it, showering them with small but sharp stones as the 'Lannie' careered past. They dropped the Molotovs and ran for their bikes.

Peter was besides himself with rage, everything within him was telling him to 'hit 'back' at these bastards! The copper in him wanted to show restraint, but hell "Screw the restraint" he felt like screaming at himself.

They'd attacked his bloody family! They'd crossed a line that even the hardest criminals didn't usually cross!

Sandy swerved just as the shotgun went off, the women were keeping their heads low and doing what Sandy had told them, Jack, Kevin's dad was using his body as a human shield for them on the other side, he'd been doing the same but something had snapped. "Sod this for a lark!" He screamed, he shot bolt upright and reached for the shotgun.

The gun was in a weapons rack on the internal bulkhead behind the driver and passenger, Peter lunged for the weapon, turning and kicking the back door open he started screaming, "Slow down, Sandy slow down, let me at the bastards!"

Sandy got a fleeting glance in. "What the hell, Dad NO!" She saw him about to leap out, Jack lunged and grabbed him. "What the hell do you think you're doing? You'll get yourself killed" she'd turned back as the Land Rover picked up speed again.

"Joey's back there in his own," he shouted, "he needs help"

"The hell he does!" Sandy shouted back, "you'll get yourself killed!"

"But there are six of 'em!"

"Look" Sandy stopped the vehicle, they were at the end of the track, a mettled road crossed their path, "help is on the way, but Joey's more than capable of handling those arseholes!" Even she was surprised at her own language.

"How do you bloody well know that?" He demanded. "What aren't you telling me?"

"I've seen him handle much worse if you must know, besides, his help's here" she pointed to two shadowy figures approaching from the road.

"Who? What the hell is going on?" Peter demanded.

"Remember I said Joey said he was ex Army? Well, meet most of the rest of his unit" Sandy replied.

"Trust you bloody two to go causing trouble!" one of the two figures spoke, you could hear the amusement in the voice, "Joey taking care of business then is he?"

"Can't you tell by the screams and explosions?" Sandy shot back, "Dad," she turned and faced her mother and father, "There's a few things Joey and I haven't told you yet!"

Chapter 17

Three of them got away, at least they thought they thought so, as they sped down the drive, throttles open as wide as they could and 'going for it'. By the time they got close to the gate they were touching sixty or so miles an hour, "Screw this" they were all thinking, "Let's get the hell out of here" the lead biker, a heavyset knucklehead with the skull and crossbones and an inset Swastika on the skull stitched to the back of his jacket, screamed at anyone who was listening, not that anyone could hear, they were travelling too fast and 'crapping their pants' too much to bother trying.

Smithy had been busy, as soon as the gang had gone in he'd pulled a small axe out and chopped a medium sized tree down, not enough to cause a problem, but just enough to cause panic on a bike, behind the tree he placed a pretty decent sized log, if they hit that they were in trouble!

The bikes came roaring down the drive, they saw the tree, but were too scared and had no chance of stopping, one tried to swerve round it, hit a ditch and the guy went flying over the handlebars, literally thrown upside down into the trees, eventually crashing unconscious, only the ww2 German helmet saving his life.

Biker two couldn't stop in time, he hit the log at the other side totally wrecking the bike and thrown over it landing in a heap four feet further down the track.

Biker three saw what happened, managed to stop his bike, realized there was no way for the bike to get out, dismounted and set off running. Smithy was laughing too hard to even try to run after him, besides, that was the plan, let one get away and spread the word about the terrors facing anyone who meddled with them!

Down by the house Joey was taking stock of the situation, Alex was still screaming as Joey doused the flames, he wasn't gentle. "Shut the hell up" he shouted as he gave the guy a good hard kick between the legs. "Piece of shit SHUT IT NOW!" Alex started whimpering.

Looking at the situation, the dogs had both of the other two under control, they just sat there, Rufus sat on top of one, snout literally millimetres from the guy's face, growling, almost daring the guy to try something so he could enjoy himself inflicting pain on the 'piece of meat'. Brutus was doing the same, growling and staring. The two little dogs tails were going like crazy, clearly delighted at the chase and the result, they hovered near the hands that had held weapons, but keeping an eye on the other hands that the big dogs couldn't see!

"Over on your stomach NOW!" he shouted at Alex, and without waiting for a reply he grabbed his shoulder and started manhandling him, Alex started screaming in pain. "SHUT IT" Joey screamed back, "It's only a burn, you'll bloody well live, which is more than you planned for us you piece of shit!" as soon as he was on his stomach Joey grabbed his hands and roughly pulled them down behind his back, then taking a huge garden tie that he'd found in the shed he found in the shed he secured his hands there. Next he took out a pillowcase from his pocket and pulled it over Alex's face. "Man you're bloody ugly" he shouted, "that's an improvement" he stood back "On your feet" he spoke quietly next, Alex took a moment to respond, so Joey kicked him in the ribs, hard "MOVE IT"

As soon as he was on his feet Joey marched him off, he had no idea where he was going or what the hell was happening, he just knew this was one scary dude, he'd never had any arrest like it, and he'd had a few of those!

Just as they entered the shed, Joey turned and called, "Jack, Daniels, Come!" the two little dogs responded instantly, scampering after him like two small children running to their newest toy. He thrust Alex down with his back to the wall, "One move" he said, "and the dogs will rip your limbs off, do I make myself clear?" he spoke slowly, deliberately with malice dripping from every word, he could see Alex was literally 'crapping his pants'

Ten minutes later all three bikers were in the shed, Brutus and Rufus looked a little disappointed they hadn't been able to take more meat off them, but Joey'd given the dogs some food as reward, even though they still stood guard, the bikers heard the dogs chewing on meat, but had no idea if it was a piece of meat or one of their own!

"Take the next left" Hene said as they came round the bend, he and Sam were on State highway three just as it left the small Hamlet about twenty klicks south of Te Kuiti, they were up in the 'sheep country' of the Southern Waikato, that meant snow capped mountains and deep valleys.

"You sure you've got the right place?" Sam sounded unsure; she was a 'city girl'. She could cope with anything the city could throw at her, but out here, in the 'middle of nowhere' who knows what could be lurking around?

"Yes sarge" Hene replied slightly sarcastically, she glanced over and saw the smile on his face, he wasn't looking at her, he was concentrating on the map, Hene seemed 'at home' here, though he wasn't from round these parts, he just seemed to know his way round the bush, he'd spent the whole trip pointing out a 'type of bush here' or a 'bird' that she couldn't really see anyway, but that hadn't stopped him explaining about some of the creatures on the trip, it was enjoyable, but they were there for business, and she kept that in mind.

"Are they expecting us?" Hene asked as they turned onto one of the smaller roads.

"I tried a couple of times to get through!" She said, "all I got was the lines were down!"

"Kind of a long way to come Sarge" he replied just that little bit concerned, "not knowing if they're going to be here"

"Not really" she replied, "The cycling victim's family own the farm, and the funeral's tomorrow, they won't be far away, besides you heard the hospital, someone's been to visit the woman every day, and stayed most of the day!"

"The hospital confirmed the address?"

"Yep" she replied, "and they said there's someone by the phone all the time, they also confirmed the phone number too, before you ask!" She glanced over at the young cop, he was preoccupied with the map.

They'd used Google maps to find the place, and get the directions, so it'd just been a case of 'follow instructions' though they were a bit outdated as some of the roads they were told to take were closed off for building a bypass for a couple of the small towns.

"The driveway should be a couple of hundred yards up this track" Hene pointed to a mettled road going off to the right, there was a small wood down about a hundred or so yards down the road, he thought he saw a dirt track leading off, "just by the wood!" He pointed in the general direction.

"That must be the house then?" Sam half stated and half asked no one in particular, "over there, past the gully, see it?"

"Yep" Hene replied, "pull over and I'll get the gate"

A small ditch separated the road from a typical farmers fence, with livestock on the other side the chances were the fence was electrified, not that there would be much current running through, just enough to remind the animals not to wander too near.

Hene jumped out of the car and began navigating the cattle grid when a northern English voice spoke. "I wouldn't touch that gate mate, if we're you!"

He was half way through reaching for it, he half turned, and as he did the hand dropped slightly, just brushing the top of the gate. The pain was excruciating! It felt like someone wrenched the arm out of the socket at the same time as kicking him hard in the ribs, he flew back and almost fell into the cattle grid, " SHIT THAT HURT!" He screamed holding his side's, truth was he didn't know which hurt the most!

"Told you dumbass!" the voice came back, "typical idiot won't bloody well listen!"

"You could have given me more warning" he was still holding his side, "who the hell are you anyway?"

The 'figure' had stepped out into the clear now, Hene could see he was tall, probably a shade under six feet, white, spoke with a northern English accent, probably 'Geordie' but he wasn't that good placing English accents. The guy was filthy and scruffy with a couple of days stubble, but otherwise looked fit, he was suspicious, why was this guy here?

"Let's just say I'm a 'friend of a friend' who needs a bit of help shall we!" The man said. "And he doesn't want any more 'unannounced visitors', so no one gets past without telling me who they are, RIGHT! Now, again who are you?" He stood on the other side of the gate, looking directly at Hene.

Sam got out of the car, she'd seen and heard what was going on, it didn't make sense, but then again, nothing about this case made any bloody sense! "What's going on?" She demanded flashing the warrant card, "Sergeant Samantha Hughes, Auckland serious crimes unit," she identified herself, "and this is Officer Hene Kingi, Thames police" she nodded in Hene's direction, "now what the hell's going on?"

"Hold up a moment" Smithy replied, he turned, took a small walkie-talkie from his belt, it was a hand held Motorola VHF with a range of about two miles, Hene had seen them used on farms before, Smithy spoke into it, they didn't hear what he said, but it was obvious he was happy with the reply.

The conversation took about fifteen seconds, then he replaced the radio before reaching for the gate that was when they noticed he was wearing heavy rubber gloves, the electricity didn't bother him, "take your vehicle" he said to them as he pointed to the car, "Joey and Sandy will explain what you need to know"

It took a couple of seconds for things to register, "move your arses then!" Smithy gave them a verbal prod.

As soon as they were through the gate they saw the first glimpse of the carnage that awaited them. Two big motorbikes on their sides, the front forks and tyres mangled, headlights smashed, the damage that happens when you hit something at speed!

"Ouch," Sam spoke first, "hope they were wearing crash helmets!" It was probably one of the dumbest things to say, but it just came out without much thought.

"We know who came off second best!" Hene replied. "Normally I'd be looking for the tree, this time it might not have been one!"

"Yeah," Sam agreed, "pretty scary dude, wouldn't like to meet him on a dark night, would you?" She glanced over at Hene; he was thinking, "penny for them?" She asked.

"Eh, err what?" He snapped back to reality.

"Penny for your thoughts" she said again.

"Just wondering," he began, "who the bloody hell these people are? And what the heck they're doing here?" They carried on up the drive, past four more bikes, this time they were in much better working order, but no sign of the riders, in fact no sign of anyone, it was too quiet for comfort, then they saw the scorch marks on the ground.

"OHH Shit!" It was Hene broke the silence as they stepped out of the car, the scorch mark was in the middle of the drive and was pretty strange as there were only stones there, pebbles to be more precise, and they were the wrong colour! They should have been an off white, but were a dirty brown instead, a sure sign of high temperature and an accelerant, then there was the broken glass, it was everywhere! "What the?" he didn't finish the question.

"I think we're about to find out!" Sam cut him off "They're coming" it was almost like a warning, and both of them were bloody uneasy, Sam had pepper spray in her bag, she slowly began reaching for it, trying not to look too obvious, Hene wasn't carrying any weapons, except a small can of pepper spray on his belt, he unclipped the holster 'just in case'

"Hello Officer Kingi" the figure, a slight female form came out of the main house, "So sorry to meet up again like this," Sandy walked towards them, she held out her hands in welcome, something they weren't expecting, "and you must be Sergeant Hughes right?" she turned and addressed Sam directly, "sorry about all this, but we had some unwelcome visitors last night!" she gestured to the marks on the ground, and the bikes without riders, "but we'll get onto that later, I'm just about to make coffee for the boys, would you like some?" she started leading them back to the house.

Not sure what to do, or how to react, Sam found herself accepting the offer of coffee and cake, Hene was a little wary, but Sandy seemed friendly enough. "What happened here? If you don't mind me asking?" he began.

"Some visitors showed up!" Sandy began as they entered the kitchen.

Joey was there in the kitchen waiting for the kettle to boil, he'd already got the bodum coffee pot out, he was pouring the first coffees, "Sorry folks, but I'm taking these to the lads." He had a flask for one and the other was in a big ceramic mug, he headed outside.

"As I was saying some pretty unwelcome visitors showed up" Sandy began again, she cleaned the bodum out and set it up again with fresh ground coffee, "Apparently when we had the 'accident' the other week we saw something we weren't meant to see!"

"We're talking about the accident in which Mr Cavell was killed right?" Sam asked the question.

"I am" Sandy replied, "we knew something strange was going on, and this pretty much proves it!"

"Hang on, back up a bit!" Sam cut in, "he may have met you then, but I'm here for another reason I'm here about"

"A break in at Mr Cavell's apartment" Sandy cut her off. "You found the details about the break in, realized it was the owner of the car and who was killed in the accident, worked out we were there and came to see if we could shed any light on the matter right?"

It's downright annoying when you have your 'thunder' stolen like that! Sam did her best to try and hide her annoyance, but it still showed through some, "What do you know about it?"

The coffee was ready, Sandy poured them each a cup and cut a slice of cake, neither of them saw her take two very tiny objects, no bigger than a grain of rice and inserted one into each piece of cake; she was banking on them being hungry. "I could tell you it's because we watch the news!" She replied. "But I'd be lying, so I'll cut straight to it as I'm pretty sure you suspect anyway, it was Joey placed the call alerting the Police, that was after he'd disarmed the thugs!"

They both nearly dropped their coffees, they sat there in stunned silence for a good five seconds, Sandy had just admitted to being at the scene of the break-in, or at least telling them that Joey was there! That meant things just got a whole lot more weird than they already were, and that was something they didn't expect!

Sam was very slow and deliberate when she spoke next, "care to explain?" she asked.

"Gladly" Sandy replied, "but before I do I've got something to tell you, on your own government's orders, not one word can be recorded!"

"Yeah right" Hene replied, "but I'm sorry, but we need to take the information down!"

"No, she's right" a voice came from the back of the room, Joey had come back, "however I didn't think you'd believe us, so if you'd follow me I'll let you hear for yourself" he pointed to the living room.

There were three laptops set up on a desk in the corner, two were facing outwards, towards two chairs and the other seemed to be doing its own thing, but had a couple of mobile phones attached to it.

"What's going on here?" Sam asked about the mobiles, wary and her hand hovering over the pepper spray.

"All in good time" Joey replied, "and relax with the spray" he moved the mouse that was between the two other laptops, they both came to life, there were people sat in conference rooms in both of them, one, an older man was in a room where it was either in a building with no windows or it was night, the other was a woman in her early fifties in a room with daylight, Sam recognized her straight away, and did not like where this was going one little bit!

It was the woman spoke up, "Hello Sergeant, sorry for all the 'skullduggery' but we had no idea you'd pick up on the trail"

Chapter 18

Leaving Pio Pio heading north there's a sweeping right hand bend and a long straight stretch. As you come round the bend a ditch begins on the right that runs the whole length of it, nearly two miles, broken only where a dirt track comes out from a disused airfield.with only a line of trees on the left hand side running the whole length pretty much blocks any view.

It was beginning to go dark when Sam and Hene began the trip back; their heads were 'spinning' with all the information, stuff they could tell nobody, not even Sam's boss!

"How'd we know it's legit?" Hene asked, he was confused and wary.

"Remember the woman in the conference room, at the other end of wherever the laptop was connected to?"

"Yeah, she was strange"

Sam took a moment to formulate her reply, "I've come across her before, in an official capacity"

"So" Hene asked, "who is she?"

"I don't know her name, only her code, 'Mildred'" she replied, "She's the head honcho at SIS"

"Where?" Hene wasn't convinced. He had no idea who Sam was talking about.

"SIS" she replied, "The Secret Intelligence Service, New Zealand's equivalent to the CIA or M.I.6"

"Holy!" Hene stopped himself just short of swearing, "and we just walked right into one of their ops?"

it was half statement, half question, and even he wasn't sure which.

"They're not supposed to be running stuff inside New Zealand, but I guess no one told them that!" Sam came back, "that's why we didn't pick up on it, but yeah, handle this wrong and we're in the crapper, and I mean big time."

The sun was just sitting on the tops of the hills to their left, the sky beginning to turn from the blue with clouds high in the western sky to the deeper blue and crimson of fading light. Shadows were starting to grow, but between concentrating on the road, trying to figure a way forward and sorting out how the hell any report was going to be coherent without saying anything of substance she was not watching 'the peripheral'

Hene had offered to drive, but he's a 'rookie' and Sam loved getting behind the wheel, she'd 'pulled rank' and insisted on driving.,

"Not sure what to make of it!" Hene was shaking his head, "what do you think?"

"Truth?" She asked, "I haven't a bloody clue!"

They drove on in silence for a couple of seconds, "one thing is for sure though, these folks play by a whole different set of rules." She added, "and I don't particularly want to find them out the 'hard way' know what I mean?" she chanced a glance over at the rookie.

"I think they're making them up as they go!" Hene replied sounding almost envious, "then again he began, he didn't have time to finish.

From out of nowhere a black shadow came at them from Hene's side, slamming into them with enough force to push them off the road.

The airbags deployed almost instantly, they were the only things that prevented them getting seriously hurt.

The brunt of the impact wasn't on the passenger door, but just a little forward, ripping the front left wing clean off the car, twisting the axle and shattering the engine mounts, the safety cage however mostly held firm with only slight buckling round the doors.

Sam had caught a glance as she turned to look at Hene, not enough to prevent it, but enough to react instinctively. Pulling the wheel hard right and hitting the brakes as hard as she could, she grabbed the handbrake and pulled as hard as she could, the car brakes screamed in protest as it slewed towards the ditch, but better that than into the front end of the monster that just hit them!

They hit the ditch with a thud, Hene's side airbags had already deployed, now both sets of front ones did with a force that threw them back into their seats. Both were knocked out.

The vehicle had only hit with enough force to get the car into the ditch, it stayed on the road. The front 'cow catcher' bars preventing any major damage.

"Get them both" the driver, a short wiry man, almost devoid of emotion spoke to the men with him, "our bosses want them."

The other three were out of the vehicle and making their way to the car. The driver was easy, her side wasn't impact damaged, so the door still opened, she didn't look seriously hurt, just a few quick cuts with a hunting knife and the airbags were ripped out, she was free.

One of them put her over his shoulder and carried her 'like a sack of spuds' to the waiting vehicle. The other guy wasn't injured, not too seriously anyway, not that they cared, the bosses wanted them to talk, then they'd be 'shark bait' so injuries weren't much of a concern, just as long as they can talk!

None of them liked the idea, they didn't like cops, but murder was different, once the cops realized two of their own were gone there'd be no safe place to hide! None of them were squeamish, but it just didn't seem right, big Jake had sort of said so.

"If you don't want the same," 'the leader replied, he wa a stone cold killer, small, wiry type of disposition with a pockmarked face that gave the impression of fish scales, hence the name 'fish face' that they'd already begun calling him behind his back.

"Who the hell is this creep?" Henry asked under his breath.

"One stone cold son of a bitch killer!" Jake whispered back as they manhandled first Sam then Hene out of the car, "pity these poor sods!"

"Know exactly what you mean." Henry spoke quietly, "but I really don't want to join 'em, so let's get on with it and keep our traps shut!" He grabbed Hene and begun binding the hands, as soon as they'd secured them he tied the feet, Hene was just starting to come round when 'fish face' walked up to him, he had a syringe, "This'll keep them quiet" he spoke more to himself as he took the syringe, he injected the syringe into his arm, Hene went out like a light.

Two minutes later both of them were in the back of the big vehicle, it was a Dodge pickup, a two ton behemoth, late eighties model. They threw them onto the truck bed without bothering to be too gentle.

'Fish face' climbed behind the wheel, "you" he pointed to Jake, "in with me, you other two, on the back, let's move!" His eastern accent seemingly adding authority, he slapped the side of the vehicle, "come on MOVE!"

As soon as they were either in or on the vehicle he turned the key, put it into gear and pulled away taking care not to spray the gravel, all that draws attention, it was second nature.

As soon as Sam and Hene left both Joey and Sandy made their way back to the garage, they'd been careful not to show the two cops what or who was back there. The last thing they'd need was to be arrested for kidnapping.

The garage was slightly separate to the house, which was good as a military interrogation is a lot rougher than a 'civvie' one, even when the cops being 'brutal' it's still pretty tame compared to the military one.

The bikers all had pillowcases over their heads, the eyes had been 'taped' shut as well. The two worst injured were laid out flat, not daring to move, knowing movement means a beating, painful and severe, screams could be heard when that happened, even that was part of the technique.

"You'll get nothing from me prick!" Scarface had shouted at one point.

A crack across the back with something long, flexible but hard had shut him up. "I don't want anything from you YET!" A voice spoke quietly and menacingly into his ear, then the tone rose to a shout. "I'LL TELL YOU WHEN TO SPEAK!"

Twenty four hours, that's how long even the hardest of men can expect to last before breaking under a military interrogation, some do last longer, but getting the 'intel' quickly is the order, after twenty four hours you can expect it to be useless anyway, and just as many die before that twenty four hours are up.

They weren't planning on extracting information from the bikers, they already had all they needed, but they were still going to make these clowns 'sorry they were ever born!'

Sandy had taken their phones and 'cloned' their hard drives, every call, every text, email, every message was now M.I.6' and S.I.S's

Sandy was busy on the computer when the Skype screens came alive.

"Sandy, get the team together," it was 'Mildred' from the New Zealand Secret Intelligence Service or 'S.I.S' "We've got an urgent development needs immediate action!"

Chapter 19

The 'airfield' was little more than a flat farmer's field with a couple of sheds on it, without the sign proudly proclaiming it was an 'airfield' they wouldn't have known.

The helicopter, mid sized seven seater, was waiting, engine burning fuel, blades turning as the big Dodge pulled up just outside the rotor disk. 'Fish face' saw the pilot give a 'thumbs up' as the vehicle stopped, they were good to enter the disk.

Two shadows came out from the helicopter, they ran to the front of the Dodge and started manhandling the two extremely reluctant passengers, a quick pistol whipping for each one soon cured any resistance.

"You three take the truck and dump it!" 'he' gave orders to the three accomplices, "then disappear, and I mean disappear!"

They didn't need to be told twice, the three of them were in the vehicle and ready to scream out of there as soon as the V6 engine would take them, and Henry was just about to ram her into Gear when 'Fish face' spoke one last time to them.

"Don't be so bloody stupid as to try and keep the truck!" he was heading for the truck, "Cops will be looking for anything to lead them to it, AND BLOODY WELL SLOW DOWN!!!"

The other two had manhandled the two cops into the back of the helicopter, within minutes they were up and away.

"So" Jacko was summing up what they'd just heard from 'Mildred' and trying to draw up some sort of plan, "we knew they'd make a play for someone, just didn't expect it quite so damn well fast!"

"True" Mildred was still on the computer screen, "but everything's in play now, and we've just got to run with the 'hand' we've been dealt!"

"Any idea when they were taken?" Joey asked. He was angry, he'd thought that they had a little while at least.

"No" Mildred replied, "We only picked up the emergency call when the car was found, that was fifteen minutes ago, and before you ask, it was just north of Pio Pio. About fifteen klicks from you folks!"

"Jeez, that bloody close!" Smithy turned to Joey, "You really must have pissed 'em off!" every one of the team actually 'cracked' a smile at that.

"Any way we can track them?" Mildred asked hoping for some good news, "what about the trackers we gave you?"

"For some strange reason" Sandy had a half smile, "I fed them to the two cops, in the refreshments we gave 'em" there were a few comments, "what?" she demanded, "are you saying my cooking's that bad it's got bloody lumps in?" she half swung for Joey with a tea towel she was holding.

"Ow" Joey yelped, "I wouldn't dream of it!" he protested, then turning to the screen he carried on "You've got the frequencies they transmit on, haven't you?"

"Just telling my people to turn them on" Mildred was typing furiously on the keyboard in front of her, it took a moment before she started to reply, "Yep, we've got 'em. Moving northeast at, shoot that's fast!" she stopped for a moment and typed a few more strokes, then came back, "Confirmed, they're moving northeast at a speed of a hundred and sixty kilometres an hour, that's about a hundred and ten miles an hour, far too fast for anything on the road, They've got to be in the air!" She looked up from the computer screen, back to the camera.

"At the moment they're between Te Aroha and Paeroa in the Waikato, probably in a chopper! That's all we have at the moment"

"I'd guess it's a seven seater" Jacko interjected, "Pilot, whoever's in charge, the two cops and at least two muscle, with a seat spare for the equipment! And I'd say they're heading for somewhere deserted, probably an island off the coast!"

"I'm not going to ask how you might know that" Mildred came back, "Look, the earliest I can get any transport like that to you folks is three hours, when my team takes the people you already have off your hands, sorry about that!" she stopped there, then added, "I'm presuming you folks want to be the ones to finish the job?" She knew the answer, but had to ask,even if was only for the 'paperwork'.

"Wouldn't dream of it any other way" Jacko replied, he carried on "we've got a few things here to do, Joey and Sandy have a friend they need to 'invite to the party' if you know what we mean! Now you can try and stop us, or you can turn us loose on these pricks, but either way, we're going after them!"

"Figured you'd say that!" Mildred smiled, "Sir Mike warned me about this team!"

"Just make sure you send our Kit!" Mac spoke for the first time.

"All in hand Mac, all in hand, you'll have what you need in three hours," she reached for the off button, but before she pressed it she stopped for one last time, "Good hunting gentlemen!"

"It's going to be at least three hours before we're anywhere near ready to help 'em!" It was a statement more than anything else, one borne of sheer frustration, "but there's other stuff we can be doing" Jacko continued on, he turned and faced Joey, "I'd say you and Sandy need to go deal with that prick of a bent cop', I'll leave it to you how you interpret that!" He looked at the other two, they were eager just to start some preparation, any kind would do, and knowing that was being 'dealt with' was a start at least.

"The rest of us" Jacko went on, "Mildred's sending our 'kit' down, but we'll prep everything else, including likely places they're taking them."

"Killing house boss?" It was Mac asked the question.

"Expect so" Jacko replied. "We'll prepare for it, layout and everything!"

The 'Killing house' is a little corner at the SAS barracks in Hereford, they probably have one in every SAS barracks, but the Hereford one is the famous one, it's purpose is 'Hostage rescue' but not taking prisoners! All hostages rescued 'alive' but dead hostage takers, live hostage takers are extra paperwork, and the SAS hate paperwork.

Joey and Sandy both donned leathers, Kevin had a couple of sets for the work bikes they had on the farm, a couple of trials bikes, they'd already decided to take two of the road bikes, kind of "temporary loan on a permanent basis" as Joey called it.

"Which one you want?" He asked Sandy, "the Bonneville or the Commando?"

"What about the Harleys?" Sandy asked, she'd dreamt of riding a Harley Davidson, now they had the chance, she really wanted to take it!

"They're good cruisers" Joey replied, "but the Triumph and Norton are built for racing!"

"Okay" Sandy headed for the bikes, she straddled the Bonneville, reached down and turned the key, "I'll take Bonnie, you get Clyde" she looked over as she fastened the helmet, rocking the bike off the stand she pointed the bike towards the gate. "Ready?"

Joey couldn't help smiling, he was a bit disappointed, as he'd wanted the Bonneville, but a Norton Commando TT racer was a pretty good consolation, he straddled the bike smiling that only Sandy could come up with the names of two outlaws for the bikes, 'Bonnie' for the Bonneville, 'Clyde' for the Commando, it kind of fit them.

Last thing they did was plug in the phone chargers to the cigarette lighters and clip the phones into the brackets the bikes had fitted; next they put their earpieces on and turned on the Bluetooth.

"Scorpion four and five ready to roll" Joey spoke into the phone, it was like a complete transformation, out went the young kids, in came the professional team.

Both bikes roared to life, a final check of the lights and they were ready to roll, Joey flicked up the bike stand and turned the commando towards the road, taking a final look back at the team he flicked the visor down, "Let's roll" the bike roared to life as they set off, dirt and gravel spraying back as they tore down the road.

Chapter 20

The elevator door made a slight swishing sound as it opened, she stepped out into the cavernous place, artificial light kept everything 'as bright as daylight' but the reality was there was no natural light coming in.

She was on the fourth floor of a building that according to the plans only had three floors, mind you the people who 'owned' it didn't really own the building, they just rented it, and were too proud to say anything!

"Good to see you again Ma'am" a casually dressed man in his mid thirties approached holding out his hand for a handshake.

'Mildred' wasn't her real name, but it was the name everyone in the room, in fact almost everyone in the organization knew her by. It was the name on the door of her office, but it wasn't the name she was born with, or the name she was known by those few people she called friends. 'Mildred' was her "Call-sign", the name she'd chosen when she came into the world of 'shadows'.

"Good to see you too Mark, keeping you busy I see." She shook his hand, "Where are we up to?"

There were five people in the room; apart from 'Mark' they were all studying their computer screens. "Scorpions four and five just called in as rolling" Mark replied, "the rest are gearing up ready for the chopper!"

"Speaking of which" 'Mildred' asked, "Where are we with the helicopter?"

"First one's airborne now" Mark looked at his watch, "they'll be at the farm in just over an hour, second one will be on standby at Papakura, just in case it all turns to"

"Yes, I know" she sounded tense, "Hope for the best, prepare for the worst" is almost a 'mantra' the spy agencies live by. "Where are we with the rest of things?"

"Chambers in London's sent a list of accounts both here in New Zealand and Australia for us, we've notified the Aussies, they'll drain the accounts there when we give the go" Mark walked towards his desk at the far end of the room, "I'm just setting everything up so it's fully automated, and none get missed." he took his seat and started typing on the keyboard, "all set for when you're ready ma'am"

"Not yet," 'Mildred' replied, "We move too soon and they'll get wind of what we know! Where are we with tracking the two cops?"

"They're in a helicopter ma'am" another voice replied, it belonged to a youngish girl with long black hair and a nose ring. She was the youngest looking of the group, and seemingly the 'free spirit' with a semi gothic looks about her. "Travelling around one fifty kilometres an hour, they just left the coast, looks like they're headed for an island off the coast, either Whale Island or White Island, we're not sure yet"

"How long until you're sure?"

"They'll be over Whale Island in about ten minutes; if they put down we'll know from the GPS!"

"What about White Island?"

"That'll be another half hour flying time" the girl responded.

"Okay" Mildred looked round the room, "That means they'll have a half hour 'free time' with their prisoners! SHIT". She wasn't happy at all, turning back to the team, she spoke a little louder than intended, "where are we with Murray?"

"Scorpions four and five are on their way" another of the operators replied, he was slightly older, but not much, blonde hair and a ponytail were his distinguishing features, and a small goatee. It made him look like 'Buffalo Bill' the legendary figure from the Westerns; the team had given him the name 'Cody',

"I know that you imbecile!" She felt like shouting, but all that came out was, "I know, how long before they get there?"

"Judging by the speed they're travelling," 'Cody' came back, "I'd say about two hours, that is if Murray stays this side of the peninsula!"

"Is he..?"

"Mobile?" Cody finished the question off, "has been so far, he's in the squad car!"

"Okay," she was in thought, "What else have I missed?

"Jenny's been working on the list of phone numbers we got from the team" Mark pointed to the operator furthest away, a petite young one, she looked to be in her late twenties, or possibly early thirties, short brown hair and eyes.

"What's the story with those numbers?" she pointed to a screen that had just come alive, there were four lists on the screen, One in black, one in blue, one in green and a final one in red.

"I'm going through each number," Jenny began, "The ones in black are the ones I've still to categorize, or find out how they link in with the big picture!"

"Okay" Mildred came back, "Walk me through what you've got"

"The Green ones are the harmless" Jenny replied, "or at least as far as I can tell they're harmless, stuff like relatives wives, girlfriends etc. The blue are clearly in the organization, just not sure where they might sit as there's not really been the time to work out any type of structure"

"You've still got three 'red' numbers, what are they?"

"They're interesting" Jenny replied.

Mildred was about to rip into her verbally, but something told her to hear the girl out, "what do you mean by that?"

"It's the origin of the calls" Jenny replied totally missing the frustration in Mildred's voice, "Take this one here" she pointed to the first one on the list, "It's a Satellite phone, and it's at sea"

"What?" Mildred didn't like what she'd just heard. If they were heading out to sea then it's a whole different ball game, "What do you mean 'at sea'?"

"Well it was when it made the calls" Jenny replied, "it was off the Chatham Islands for one, and in the Hauraki gulf for the other! I'm working on what ships were in the area at the time!"

Mildred wheeled round and faced 'Mark' directly, "You knew about this?"

"Not until about two minutes before you got here" Mark replied, "that's what I meant about if it all turns to crap! I'm also working on finding out what 'assets' we can call up if we need them"

"What about the other numbers?" Mildred was still processing what she'd just heard, it wasn't liked, but at least this team was working on a backup plan to the backup plan.

"You're not going to like either of these." Jenny replied, "the first one's a frequency hopper, but it's the second one I'm worried about."

"Why the worry?"

"Boss" Mark cut in, "I think I recognise where it originated from, by the look of it, the call came from London, England"

"It gets worse" Jenny cut in, "The call came from inside M.I.6, at least that's what the GPS is telling me!"

"Any chance it was from the pavement outside the building?" Mildred really didn't like where this went, "GPS can only be accurate to within a hundred yards right?"

"The old GPS yeah" Jenny came back, "But not this one, it's down to within millimeters, they didn't use a company phone as far as I can tell, but a couple of 'burner' phones, and before you ask" she held her hand up, "It was encrypted and I'm working on cracking it!"

"A burner with encryption?" Mildred almost spat out, "that's a new one on me! What about the last one" she brought the conversation back.

"That's the curveball!" Jenny replied, "We only got about a tenth of a second transmission, so we weren't able to pinpoint any position, or even work out what was said! My guess is"

"It's a frequency hopper" Mildred cut her off, "They're supposed to be illegal, but if you've got one either end they're great as the FBI and ourselves can't work out what you're saying"

Back in the early 1990s Eriksson the Swedish telecommunications people developed a phone using technology that was invented by the British Military in the 1970s where the phone changes frequency twenty times in a second, each time the frequency is changed the phone transmits a signal telling the receiver what frequency to hop to, the transmission can only be picked up by the intended recipient thus making it impossible to listen in to the conversation, even when you're listening in across a 'broad band' you won't be able to listen in as there'd be too many other signals you'd pick up, thus the phone is literally 'unjammable'.

"So, what you're telling me," Mildred took the latest information in, "is we've got a Sat phone somewhere out at sea, and another unjammable phone 'out there' along with someone at M.I.6 involved, is that right?"

The whole team looked sheepish, no one likes to admit that despite their best efforts they just might have been outsmarted, Mark was the one who broke the silence, "That's not all, it seems the frequency hopper was the one that originated the call, that's why we picked it up, we don't know where they are, but we know they're the boss!"

"Who were they calling?"

"The Sat phone, who then called Murray and two other numbers, they're the ones with the notes beside them, we think one was to lay into Murray for the fiasco with the McLaren and the other was to order some goons into Cavell's apartment!"

"So we've got the other guy then?" Mildred asked.

"Yes, we confirmed that with the numbers the police were looking for, naturally they don't know that yet" Mark carried on, "Following on from that I've been looking at what assets we can call on if we need to launch an 'offshore' op"

"Please tell me you've got good news!" Mildred replied.

Mark took a moment to press a few keys on his computer, the large screen at the end of the room came to life with a map, there were a couple of dots on it. Mildred recognized the two islands they'd been talking about, but further northeast, a long way northeast was another dot.

"Her Majesty's New Zealand Ship Wellington's on her way back from fisheries patrol in the Kermadec Islands," Mark said, "She's about three hundred miles northeast of the Eastern Cape at the moment and doing twelve knots, going to full speed she can be within range of the RHIBs she carries within about three hours, that is if we need her!"

"What else does she carry?"

"Normally a sea sprite helicopter" Mark replied, "but hers was used in a sea rescue four hours ago, she's enroute to Gisborne and won't be back with the Wellington until at least tomorrow morning!" he pressed a few more keys, pulling up the full details of the Wellington's compliment and armaments, "she's got two RHIBs (Rigid Hull Inflatable Boat) both fitted with high performance outboards, they can hit sixty knots without breaking a sweat, and a range at that speed of about seventy miles, through the captain's likely to have a fit!" he half warned.

"Let him" she replied, "How many can they carry?"

"Each one takes six!" Mark replied relieved that they at least had the workings of a plan of nothing else, "that's one seaman to steer the boat and five operatives each, the RHIB can carry a medium machine gun, but that cuts the operators down to four each!"

"Sounds like a plan." She replied, "Get the captain on the line, and don't take any crap from him!"

Chapter 21

Traffic was pretty light for the time of day, they made good time, the only real problem was passing a couple of logging trucks coming from Tokoroa to Tauranga, then again they got a straight stretch and 'blew past' them as if they were standing.

Sandy could swear she heard the 'cat calls' as they flew past, her flame red hair streaming out from under the helmet, all they saw was a black streak with long red hair giving the impression of being 'on fire', she loved it.

Getting past the logging trucks was easy, but then they came up to a couple of 'boy racers'.
Joey didn't slow down and got past them with a few cuss words and the old 'finger' salute coming from the car, they moved to block Sandy, but she was ready and waiting working out the line they were going to take in the bend.

Halfway round the chance came, the bike was much quicker than any car. She waited until the right moment, dropped down a gear, let the clutch out and opened the throttle.

"Oh Shit!" Sandy had opened the throttle a bit too much, the bike reared up on one wheel, she pushed on the handlebars putting her weight on the front bars bringing the bike under control. The 'wheelie' was pretty spectacular, that was evidenced by the silence from the car, she was sure she heard a series of clunks as four jaws dropped to the car's floor, she also couldn't resist blowing them a kiss as she tore past!

"Hey, maniac!" She spoke into the mike, will you flipping well ease off?

Joey was having an absolute ball, he was loving every minute of it, despite the fact they were supposed to be on 'phase one' of the plan.

"Not a chance!" Joey replied, "sooner we get there, the sooner we prevent that prick Murray from causing problems!"

She didn't need to ask about any problems, Murray sent the bikers to the farm, surely the confirmation the job was done might even be overdue, 'he gets any idea it's gone wrong ' she thought, 'he's likely to bolt!'

They were just south of a Paeroa, a small town on the eastern edge of the Hauraki plains, Sandy didn't dare look at her speedometer, all she knew was they were doing well in excess of the speed limit, the guys working for 'Mildred' had seen to that.

"We get into Paeroa, hang a right at the main crossroads, head for Thames," she gave Joey the directions over their intercom; "he's on the road between Thames and Tauranga!"

"You're sure he's there?" Joey asked, if it didn't fire a projectile at high velocity he didn't really trust it, and that meant computers weren't high on the 'trust' list!

"About as sure as the GPS can be!" Sandy was truthful.

Every mobile phone, regardless of who manufactures it has one thing in common, they all have GPS chips in them.

A cheap 'burner' phone has the GPS on the sim card, take the simcard out and the phone can't be tracked, but it's also useless, that is until another sim card goes in. the trick is, if you know who was using the sim card, if they put it in another phone, and you're watching for it, you've got them again!

The more expensive phones have another GPS installed actually in the phone, that way if it's stolen, even with the sim card swapped out, the phone companies can still find it!

Murray had a 'burner', he'd turned the phone off, but neglected to take the sim card out, the GPS had been hacked by agents at 'GCSB' New Zealand's equivalent of the NSA, they passed the location on to Mildred's team who were 'live feeding' it to Sandy.

They slowed down as they came into Paeroa. "Take a left at the junction, then next right at the crossroads" Sandy called over their headsets.

"You said"

"I know," Sandy replied, "I forgot about the first junction" the first junction, a 'T' junction was coming up, both bikes indicated left and moved round the junction.

Paeroa is about twenty miles south of the Coromandel peninsula and the perfect place for a 'staging area'. The place where final preparations are made before doing what you need to do.

They found a small piece of ground just off the main highway; it was perfect for what they needed. Final checks were made, maps checked and everything confirmed, it was odd that Murray hadn't moved in a half hour, but other than that, 'it was all go'.

"How do you want to play this?" Sandy asked, she might be the senior rank of the two of them, but Joey had the experience, with regards to tactics, she'd learned to defer to him.

"Ever heard of a 'Tiger hunt?" He asked as he put the stand down, then slowly dismounted.

"You're not really talking of hunting the 'big cat' are you?" She followed suit, they disconnected their mike's, removed the helmets and went to the grass verge to sit a few moments.

"Nah" he chuckled, "it's an old tactic they used to use in World war two, the 'Tigers' were German Tiger tanks, damn near impossible to kill when they were in defensive positions, so old 'Blood and guts' Patton thought up a way of drawing them into the open to kill them"

"Okay!" Sandy held her hand up, "enough with the history lesson, what do you need from me?"
Sandy pulled a small computer tablet from her satchel on the back of the bike, she turned it on and booted the GPS location software up, it took a couple of seconds to come alive.

"Murray's here according to the GPS" he pointed to the glowing dot on the screen, "probably not easily visible from the road" he went on. "What I need you to do is ride down the road being your 'irresistiblc' self"

Sandy wanted to give him a good hard slap for that comment, but now wasn't the time or place, instead she settled for a look that had been known to strike fear into 'lesser mortals' and a semi serious punch on the arm, he winced, but continued on, "draw him out of whatever hole he's in," Joey went on. "Once we know he's chasing you, I'll close in from behind, and you'll turn to keep him busy while I close the trap!"

"Sounds simple enough?" Sandy said, there were a dozen things could go wrong, none of which they wanted to think too hard about, if they did then they'd make it up 'on the fly'.

"Piece of cake!" Joey assured her as he rose from the grass, "now let's get moving".

Chapter 22

"Here's the boxes of tricks you folks ordered" the young soldier gestured to the three boxes his men were manhandling out of the helicopter, there were three of them in the team, flown in with the 'kit' Jacko had told them they needed. "MP5s, two with grenade launchers, only smoke and flash bangs though, no high explosive" he looked almost apologetic.

"No worries," Jacko replied, it's those we need, how many mags for the '5's though?"

"Four each" the soldier replied, "plus three clips each extra for your sidearms"

"And the Sniper rifle?"

"We got two mags for it and an extra fifty rounds loose, though where you got the rifle from?"
"Don't ask," Smithy spoke up, he'd been relieved from guarding the bikers as soon as the stuff was in the farmhouse, "that way I don't have to lie!" He gave an 'innocent' look. It was clear these 'relief boys' weren't going to ask too many questions. "Probably just where the food is?" He thought, but didn't say.

"Your transport is still turning burning," the young soldier replied, Jacko figured he was probably a corporal. "The rest of our boys will be here in about an hour with our transport, you better get outta here boss!" It was the first time he'd even acknowledged any rank, "those Airforce wallahs don't like wasting their precious fuel!"

"Some things never change do they?" Jacko managed a smile; they all laughed a little, picked up the cases with the equipment in and headed for the aircraft.

"Body armour stowed behind the rear seats" the corporal in charge shouted after them, "and God help anyone who crosses you" he said to himself under his breath.

"The 'armour' was seven 'tactical' Kevlar jackets, five for the team and two for the two cops they were going to 'rescue' if that's what you could call it!

Conventional police 'vests' are good for stopping your average thug with a handgun, but anything more powerful than a handgun it won't stop, it will hold your insides together and stop the massive gaping hole it would cause, but you're going to be a few months in hospital, but even that's better than the alternative.

Bomb disposal people are encased in Kevlar to stop fragmentation damage, that stops anything, but it's too big and bulky

Hostage rescue teams use armour somewhere in between that's bolstered by heavy ceramic (Kevlar) plates in the right places, they're still heavy, weighing about fifteen to seventeen pounds each, but they'll stop all but the meanest badass bullets. Jacko figured the 'other guys' would be toting Uzis and Ingrams machine guns with maybe an AK47 or two, the AK47s they'll have to deal with, but the other stuff won't be a problem.

The 'transport' didn't have military markings, at first the thought did occur 'civvie chopper'? But one look inside dispensed with that idea.

The aircraft looked like a small to medium sized executive one from the outside, but outside looks can be deceiving.

There was easily room for eight fully armed men, plus any kit they might need, four 'eyes' in the roof specially for abseiling from the helicopter said this was not your average 'bird'.

As soon as they were in and the door slid shut the pilot increased the throttle and took off. "Where to captain?" He looked over his shoulder.

"We've only got the first RV at the moment," Jacko replied as he donned the headset he'd been offered, the other two found their headsets, put them on and logged in, "first RVs on the beach just south of a place called, oh hell, here it is!" He showed him the information, "can't get used to these strange names!"

The two pilots started laughing, Maori place names aren't easy to get the Western tongue around.

"No worries bro" the co-pilot replied, "we got this!" He took the map, spent all of ten seconds looking at what was written there then turned to the pilot. "Bearing of zero three zero degrees, height four fifty feet, that'll take us to the entrance of the Karangahake gorge, from there we'll cut through the gorge, it'll bring us out just south of where we need to be,"

"That's a bit too high" the pilot replied, make the height three hundred!"
At first Jacko thought they meant three hundred feet above the ground, it soon became apparent, they meant 'above sea level'.

Trees flew by less than twenty feet below, phone and power lines even closer. A couple of times the helicopter dived and went under them, they didn't slow down either, but the most worrying thing was the cattle running to get out of the way, then again, if they didn't it would be minced Beef for dinner, compliments of the rotor blades!

Jacko looked at his two comrades, he could feel the smile on his face, the warmth radiating out, it was more than reciprocated with both of them wearing grins a mile wide.

"Do we have to go this low?" Jacko was a bit surprised, but didn't want to sound alarmed, he got it wrong and the pilots misread that they'd got him worried.

"Unless you want to explain to Auckland air traffic control what we're doing!" The pilot replied, "I was told this was off the books!"

"It is!" Jacko replied, "okay, we get the message,"

The pilots were enjoying every second of the flight, it's not often they get to fly this low, and even more rare you get to 'put the wind up' the SAS!

Just then Jacko's headset came alive, an incoming call, it was Joey, "they should be mobile for the RV now" he thought as he answered the call.

"Boss, we've got a problem!" Joey came back over the radio. "Murray's gone"

'Shit' he thought, 'That's all we need, Murray on the run and giving the others the heads up they were coming' all he could say though was, "Roger that, anything else?"

"Yeah" Joey replied, "he's armed with a Glock 17 and an M4 Assault rifle"

New Zealand Police aren't normally armed, but some of the Highway patrol vehicles patrol remote areas, and they never know exactly what they'll come across, everything from a normal speeding motorist to a Bull out on the road and loose. To deal with the things they come across they carry 'lockboxes' with weapons in the back of the cars. Murray had his own Glock, but the car had an M4 assault rifle as well as sixty rounds of ammunition, that was missing.

Murray wasn't a 'happy camper'. That was putting it mildly! Something was amiss, the pricks he'd sent to deal with the 'dipsticks' causing all the problems should have called by now. The news should have been full of reports of a house fire, hopefully with bodies found in it (he could only hope) but nothing, Nada, zilch! Neither on the police radios or on the normal news stations.

He flicked through the radio stations again, to make sure, but nothing, that wasn't good. Then a call from the Chinese, "make sure there's a path clear for a cargo!" That's all he was told, that was even worse, if they are doing things then the whole lot could 'turn to crap' real quick!

His shift was traffic patrol today, the highway between Thames and Whangamata on the other side of the peninsula, 'should be pretty cruisy' he thought, 'give me time to think!'

There wasn't much need for 'thinking' really, he just wanted an excuse to run through his options again, there weren't that many!

'Why the hell?' he began the thought, "first the screw up with the car, then the bloody botched break in, why?"

The Triads can be pretty 'ham fired' at times, at least their 'soldiers' can, 'but those 'further up' the food chain are normally a bit smarter than that', at least that's what he'd thought. Evidently whatever was going on was serious enough it had even them 'spooked' and they were doing dumb things,

"Gonna get us all either killed, or a jail cell" he said to himself, 'time to cash up and leave the casino' was all he could think.

Just like a casino, there's a time when you know you should quit, that was now, some saw the stuff they did like an addiction, a need for the thrill, doing stuff that could go 'haywire' is what kept them going, sure the money was good, and he'd got a few neat toys, but for him, it was payback for all the times he'd been passed over, least that's what he told himself.

He knew this road 'like the back of his hand', every dip in the road, every camber and every farm building, more importantly, he knew what was in each of the buildings, and where the keys are!
Cruising down the highway, he found the spot he was looking for, a small rise with a farm entrance and just enough space to pull the 'cruiser' off the road, not quite hiding the vehicle, but just hidden enough that it wouldn't be seen until you were 'right on' it, ideal for the speed trap he was supposed to be doing.

Fifty yards down the track was an old looking barn, Murray knew it was padlocked, and the padlocks were pretty decent, there'd been a spate of farm equipment robberies in the area, but he knew where the keys were, it took him under a minute to find them, the farmer, a share-milker on the farm, and lived a few hundred yards from his shed, besides, they were on holiday down south at the moment.

The keys were right where they were supposed to be, it always amazed him just how trusting the rural folks were, the farmer had left the keys there for his 'relief' worker to use whatever they needed, but the relievers nearly always brought their own equipment, and this stuff was not going to be needed for a few weeks, and by then they'd all know what he did, not that he'd care, he'd be a couple of thousand miles away, and with a sizable 'retirement fund' with any luck.

The padlocks quickly clicked open, he swiftly opened the door and went inside.

There was a bike in the shed, just like he knew there would be, a Yamaha 200 trials bike, perfect for what he needed, the bike would blend in well both in the country and the town.

He'd carried a holdall with him; he set it down, unzipped the bag and began changing clothes.

Two minutes later all traces of 'Senior constable Murray' were in the bag, they'd soon be at the bottom of the Pacific, but not yet, he zipped the bag back up, slipped his arms through the handle so the bag was on his back, grabbed the bike and wheeled it out of the shed.

He could be at Auckland airport in just under two hours, Wellington in about six, 'not really an option' he thought, 'if the proverbial is going to hit the fan, it's going to be a lot faster than that!' he had another plan, much quicker, and avoiding any customs, especially with what he was taking from the back of the cruiser, besides, he wasn't leaving his boat behind.

"He should be just round this bend," Sandy shouted into the Mike, "drop back and wait for the siren!"

Joey throttled back as Sandy blew past him, red hair streaming out from under the helmet, "wish me luck" she shouted as she blew him a kiss, then turned, took hold if the handlebars and opened the throttle.

The bike responded like the racer it was, eager for the race and ready for the challenge.

Joey pulled up and waited as Sandy roared round the corner, she was well over the speed limit, nothing.

"Boss" it was Joey's voice on the line, he was talking to Jacko, but Mildred was 'patched in' through the network, "We've got a bit of a problem"

"Go ahead" Jacko replied, they were airborne, but still a good half hour away from the RV.

"Murray's done a runner, "Joey came back, "but that's not the problem!"

'Shit' was all she could think, 'if he's got word out, this is going to turn real bad, real soon!'

"Come again?" Jacko replied, "What's the real problem?"

The team in the control room were looking stunned. "Don't just bloody gawp!" Mildred spoke quietly, yet every word was heard by all, "find the swine, AND I MEAN NOW!!"

"The squad car had a lockbox boss" Joey came back on the line, "an M4 assault rifle and sixty rounds of ammo, he's taken them!"

Chapter 23

Pain, that's what she felt, coming from seemingly all over her body, but especially the back of her skull, 'Jesus, what, or rather who hit me?' she tried to open her eyes, everything still stayed black. She could see little pinpricks of light, and something moving really fast from right to left, seemingly dozens of times a second, like a really fast moving disc, rotor blades?

She felt the eyelids actually moving, it wasn't that they couldn't, there was something over them, but she was still too groggy to fully really realize what was going on, 'and what the hell is that drumming noise?'

At least it sounded like a drumming, but it was too regular to be anything but mechanical, "Hene?" She spoke quietly, Sam remembered Hene had been with her in the car, beyond that she had no idea what happened.

"Silence" a strange voice demanded, it sounded male, probably the wrong side of thirty, but the right side of forty, and it sounded foreign, but no idea where from.

She felt movement on her right, a very low voice talking in Maori, saying two simple words, "Kia Kaha!" repeated quietly a few times before something, probably a fist silenced him, she didn't hear any moans, just a stoic silence.

It was worth the risk just to acknowledge Hene, she turned slightly to her right and whispered, "Kia Koha". He'd told her to 'Stand tall' so she'd given the reply 'Stand strong' and that's what they'd do.

She didn't have to wait more than a second for the retaliation as a fist crashed into the side of her head, she didn't flinch, but it increased the headache she already had.

Actually, there were two parts of her body that didn't hurt, that's because they were numb. From what she felt of her shoulders, her arms were attached to the roof, probably using 'plasticuffs'. If that was the case then there'd be no way out yet, not that she'd even try, she had no idea where they were or which direction they were going in.

The country was just a blur, trees, houses, farms and even cars flew by as they raced for the RV point. Joey could have sworn he saw 'stunned mullet' looks on the face of at least one Porsche driver, mind you even he thought Sandy's flaming red hair streaming behind her was pretty spectacular, (he did have to admit to being 'just a little biased ' but it wasn't much 'honest').

Sandy was in the lead as they approached a sweeping left hand turn, she went wide in the approach, kissing the centre line just before leaning the bike and turning into the corner in a 'racing' stance, as soon as she was clear she opened the throttle and headed for the one lane bridge, there was a car coming the other way, and it had priority, but that didn't stop her gunning the engine, the car slammed the brakes on as she roared over the bridge, Joey was right on her 'tailpipe', all he heard was the screech of brakes and loud horn and a string of unintelligible abuse from the driver as they blew past.

"Twenty five minute trip, twenty minutes to do it in!" was their only thought as they pushed the bikes to their limits, or at least tried to, whatever they did the bikes seemed to roar their approval, it was if the caged beasts had finally been let loose, all Joey could think was, 'I gotta get one of these!'

Twenty minutes later they were pulling into the area when they saw the helicopter approaching from the south. Joey flipped the bike onto its stand, dismounted and ran holding his arms straight up, stopping after a few paces he brought both arms down pointing to where he wanted it to land.

Joey repeated the actions a few times as the chopper came round and lined up, Sandy came and stood beside him so that the pilot could see them both. As soon as the skids touched the sands, Joey gave a 'thumbs up' sign, it was a request to approach the helicopter, the pilot signalled back and they headed in, the rear door on the pilot's side slid open just as they reached the aircraft, they hopped in as the door slid shut.

The pilot didn't wait, as soon as the door was closed they were away, skinning across the top of the water at about fifteen feet, just enough to stay clear of the surf.

"Sorry boss" Joey spoke up as he strapped himself in, "Murray's done a runner, took some important kit with him too!"

"Never mind that" Jacko replied, as he pointed to the body armour, "We just got a location for the others, we'll deal with Murray later, this takes priority," he turned to Sandy and asked. "You know about a place called White Island?"

"Yeah" Sandy replied, "It's a rocky Island just off the coast, thirty miles or so from Whakatane, probably about sixty miles from here, is that where they are?"

"Looks like it" Jacko replied. By now both Joey and Sandy had their 'vests' and were reaching for their weapons, they'd found Joey a browning, Sandy was surprised and pleased to see a Makarov for her, she'd gotten to like the compact Russian weapon. "I've had the weapons adjusted for you both, as much as we could anyway" he carried on speaking as they turned the weapons over in their hands, they felt good, and familiar, "anyway back to the point" Jacko went on, "It looks like the helicopter landed at the southern end of the Island!"

"Makes sense" Sandy replied, she prodded Joey for the tablet he was carrying, it took her a couple of seconds to access a file, "Here's a map of the island from Google earth!" she tapped the tablet, "the Island used to be a Sulfur mine back in the early twentieth century, the original mine was on the west, but the volcano erupted and wiped the settlement out back around 1910, when they went back to the island they built the miners huts on the south side, but the mine itself is still on the western side!" she pointed to the two. "If they're on the southern end then they'll be either in or near the old huts, but they could have people on the west as well!"

As soon as they got the weapons the first thing both Joey and Sandy did was strip them down to their component parts, check and make sure they were spotlessly clean, properly oiled and then slowly, almost lovingly re-assembled them, adjusting things as they went.

Even though Smithy and Mac had spent most of the flight cleaning and checking the weapons, neither of them felt put out by it. They had fully expected them to do it, in fact they'd have been worried if they didn't, every soldier, no matter who they are, takes care of their own weapon; Your mates can only do so much for you, they can make sure the basics work, but the 'fine tuning' is all up to you. They were all pleased that Sandy had taken the lessons on board, she didn't even look around, as if to try and work out what was expected, she just knew what was needed.

Sandy reached for the switch on her headset, it put her in direct contact with the pilot, "Head along the coast as far as Opotiki, then turn north for thirty five miles then" she began.

"Then come in from the east?" the pilot asked.

"Yeah" she replied, "that should prevent them seeing or hearing our approach, land us on the eastern side and make the same way out, re-fuel at Whakatane and wait to hear from us!"

"The eastern side?" the copilot was puzzled, "that's a hell of a"

"Hell of a climb were you going to say?" they could hear the laughter in her voice, "Don't worry, these guys are bloody mountain goats! It's not going to be an issue!"

Chapter 24

The sun had just disappeared over the horizon when they got first sight of the Island, the pilots had stayed out of sight 'at the first' pass and now it was looming up straight ahead.

"Will ya look at that!" Mac was looking off to the right as they approached, the sky was a deep blue, and getting darker almost by the minute, except for on their right where there was a steady stream of what looked like steam, so thick it looked just like white smoke coming off the mountain that was at the northern end of the island. "And what a bloody smell!" he was trying to hold his nose.

Imagine the smell of rotten eggs, then intensify it a hundred fold, and add a burning sensation on the back of the throat, that's what White Island smells like! Not dangerous for short term exposure as in a couple of days, or even months, but any longer and you're going to have some serious health consequences.

Sandy looked up, saw Mac's face, and turned to the pilot who was also looking round and smiled, the copilot was also smiling, though he was concentrating on the flying, being a 'local boy' he couldn't help smiling at the faces they were all pulling, he knew it was partly letting off tension, but also partly trying to get used to the totally alien environment that was below them, it literally was like Mars, and quite a few movies had portrayed it as Mars!

"If New Zealand is the bottom of the earth" Joey began, "this must be where the farts come out!" the whole team erupted in laughter.

At three miles east to west, and four miles north to south the island is almost perfectly circular, apart from a small, mile wide and long peninsula at the southern end, the peninsular being where the volcano once erupted and pushed a sort of plain out towards the mainland thirty or so miles away.

Rising straight out of the water to a height of around a hundred feet, without even one tree or so much as a plant on the island. The plateau was only a hundred feet above sea level, but the volcano itself rose several hundred feet more, and not one plant lived there.

That was the southern end of the island, the peninsula that formed a plain, the north started with a steep incline that suddenly stopped in what looked like a razor sharp ridge ringing the volcanic crater, the crater was the source of the 'steam' and while it was partly water, it the very high sulfur dioxide content gave it the foul smelling.

"Two minutes to landfall" the pilot called out, he slowed the machine down as they got ready.

Smithy took up his position at the right hand side of the helicopter, he took out his night vision gear, put the helmet on activated the night vision, everything turned green. "All good this side boss"

Mac did the same for the other side, they were scanning, making sure no one had seen their approach, last thing they needed was to get so close and screw it up now, "all good here too".

The pilot brought the aircraft in close, so close Joey was sure he could see the rotors clipping the rocks, at least that's what he thought he saw.

"Last checks" Jacko knew he didn't really need to give the order, they'd all checked, double checked and triple checked their equipment, "Sound off"

Each member of the team was responsible for their part of the team's setup, each one had a task to perform, and the team could only function when each member of the team was doing that job. Jacko, as the commander would be the one making the decisions, or at least having the final say in how things went, Mac was the team medic, and anyone who got injured, or when they got the hostages out, they'd be his responsibility, Smithy was the team sniper, with the sharpest eyes, his job was making sure they got to the 'staging point' without any hassle, or eliminating anyone who might give them that hassle long before they realized what was going on.

Joey was the explosives expert, his job was making sure that they had 'all the tricks' they needed to make it happen, any special stuff needed to 'even the score' that was Joey's job, he had one other job too, keeping the intelligence officer with the team alive, it was a job he relished as Sandy was their intelligence officer, and she'd proved just how much an asset to the team she was in Iran!

Each one checked off every piece of equipment they had, special attention was paid to the headsets and the radios fitted into them, they even checked the radios as much as they could, it didn't matter how many times they'd already checked it, they just did it. Finally they all looked up and it was Joey said "All ready boss!"

The pilot brought the helicopter to the hover about four feet from the surf, Smithy launched out first and sprinted up the beach, as soon as he was by the rocks he took up a defensive position, next was Mac, then Jacko, fourth was Sandy, and last, watching everyone's backs was Joey.

As soon as Joey was in the crouch just clear of the rotors he turned to the helicopter and gave the pilot the 'thumbs up' sign, the pilots acknowledged with 'thumbs up' turned the helicopter rose about ten feet and headed out to sea, within seconds the silence descended.

Smithy and Mac had their night vision visors activated, as soon as they were on the ground the others did the same, but they waited a good ten minutes before doing anything.

The most dangerous time in any operation is right after the 'insertion'. You think you've not been observed, but you can't be totally sure, so many ops have gone 'tits up' simply because someone saw something, but wasn't sure so they were taking a second look when the team, confident they hadn't been seen broke cover, if only they'd waited an extra five minutes, they'd have seen the hazard and thing would have been different, this team wasn't taking the chance.

Jacko reached for the throat mike's pressel, flicking the switch he spoke into the mike, "Scorpion team to control, insertion complete, heading for Sierra Pappa"

'Sierra Pappa' was their staging point, from there the team would have a view of the whole of the Island, that is all except for the very northern points beyond the rim of the volcano, they'd be able to see how many 'targets' they faced (from this point on everyone on the island, with the exception of the team and the two they came to rescue was a target!) and where they were.

"Scorpion team, this is control" the voice came back, it was 'Mildred's', "Roger that, we have updates, check your intel links, timetable moved to ASAP, out!"

Chapter 25

The hoods were still on, but the change in pitch from the engines told her they were coming in to land, the smell of salt in the air suggested it was either on or near the coast, but the foul smell of rotten eggs was so bad it was almost choking.

"What the hell is that?" she thought to herself, "It's absolutely disgusting!". She was trying hard not to retch up, partly through fear it might cause a reprisal. It never occurred to her it could actually be a natural smell.

"White Island" she heard Hene whisper next to her, at least that's what she thought she heard him say, "Only one place in the"

"Silence" there was a shout above the drum of the rotors, and a sickening thud that she could only guess what happened, Hene's silence seemed to indicate she'd guessed right, he's been either clubbed or pistol whipped and knocked senseless.

"You'll get chance to talk soon" the voice they'd heard earlier giving the commands spoke up, "then you'll be begging us to listen, and spare you" there was almost an amused note to the voice, as if he'd found something funny to say.

Right there and then she knew she had a choice, she could let the fear take hold, panic and give them exactly what they wanted within a few minutes, it would be over quickly after that, with a nine millimeter bullet to the brain, or she could fight back, and do it by not even thinking about what was going on! Literally by 'going to her safe place'

Sam's 'safe place' was the old movies, not the fifties and sixties movies, but the old Laurel and Hardy movies, the classics, and right now she had a picture of Ollie Hardy sat in a pile of dung with Stan beside him saying, "Well, that's another fine mess you've gotten me in!"

She started to laugh, she had no idea why, it didn't make sense, but she just couldn't help herself, she 'saw' with her mind's eye the confusion on the faces of her captors, looking just the way Stan Laurel used to look when Ollie said those words, that made her laugh even more, even though the hood was still there, you can't stop the imagination from seeing things, even if they aren't really there! She saw the look of consternation and bewilderment on their faces, or at least the imagined look, and it felt good, knowing she was 'sticking it to them' telling them "Go screw yourselves!" They were going to make a fight of it, and to hell with the consequences.

Hene had been fighting his own demons, he'd been trying hard to 'hold it together' thinking he had to for Sam, he was dazed from the pistol whipping, which made the laughter sound even stranger, but dammit, he just didn't 'give a toss' anymore! He was going to make it as hard as he could and to hell with the consequences, they were going to fight back with the only weapon they had, he reverted to chanting a prayer in Maori.

There was a slight bump, and a change in pitch of the rotors, next hands were reaching across them and unclipping harnesses, a pair of hands reached up and cut the plasticuffs that had been attached to the roof, their hands were numb, but that didn't stop Hene from launching out at the nearest one, knocking him off his feet, he tried to run, but the boot laces were tied together and he sprawled on the earth, two kicks came in, one from either side.

"Try anything like that again" a voice spoke, it was a Kiwi one, "and I'll gladly do you here and now!"

"And you won't get what you want!" Hene shot back as another kick came in, he stopped struggling, but he'd shown there was plenty of 'fight' still left in him.

Two others were on top of him now, one of them grabbed his hands and wrenched them back, behind his back, plasticuffs were put back on and pulled tight, next they grabbed the cuffs and used them to lift him, nearly breaking his arms in the process.

Sam heard it all, she wasn't scared, neither of them were, they were in that 'zone' when you know bad stuff is going to happen, you can't stop it, but you're gonna take as many of them down with you as you really can, no matter what happens, kind of the "We're outnumbered two to one, we're outgunned and totally surrounded, GOOD I've got them right where I want them!"

They were more careful taking Sam out, they grabbed hold of her hands before they cut the 'cuffs' off, and as soon as she was out of the aircraft they wrenched her to the same position as Hene As soon as they had that one each grabbed the plasticuffs and started dragging them off backwards.

The pace was fast and more than once one of them tripped, their captors didn't slow down, they just dragged them along until they could find their feet, and then kept dragging them until finally a voice said, "In here!" they were thrown forward into a heap, then silence.

"Leave them there for a few hours" fish told the others, "the sun and thirst should soften them up" he wasn't interested in their comfort so much as 'getting the job done' and a bit of heat stroke followed by cold temperatures coupled with a healthy dose of fear worked wonders in that area. Their paymasters wanted to know what the police knew, and they wanted the information fast.

"Where the hell is he?" Mildred was getting desperate, the team were just about at the island and there was still no word on where Murray had disappeared to!

"Boss" it was Cody called out, "think I might have something" he shouted out, "Patching it through to you now"

"Don't bother" she sprinted over to his terminal, grabbed the spare headset, utter into his machine and looked at the screen. "Talk!"

He moved the mouse, he had and audio file open, "this just came in on the sat phone we're monitoring, it's not a number we've seen before, but it's definitely a burner, and voice recognition says ninety five percent sure it's Murray!"

"Finally some good news, where is he?"

"Still getting the final details, but it looks like he's about twenty nautical miles north of Tauranga, possibly heading northeast"

"Let me know when you've got all the information, especially the kind of boat he's on"

"I'm already checking out whether he's stolen the boat or what" Cody worked the keyboard, his fingers moving at almost blinding speed, "I should have you an answer in the next couple of minutes"

Mildred couldn't wait for the answer, she was pacing up and down the room, another voice came on the line. "Boss, I've got something you're not gonna like, we've got another, I think it's a Gremlin inbound to the island"

A 'Gremlin' is an unidentified call sign, but where a "Bogey is one you're really unsure of, a 'Gremlin' is one you're pretty sure is a hostile, on the island, it was possible they were tourists, but highly unlikely, much more likely to be hostiles.

"What? Where from?" She shouted as she headed for the one who spoke, it was one of the girls.

"Just came up on radar, about fifty miles north of the island, Judging by speed and direction, they'll be there in less than an hour!"

"SHIT" she almost screamed, "where'd it bloody well come from?"

There was only one place it could have come from, a ship, or something like that, "mule ship?" She didn't wait for an answer, "where's the Wellington?".

Her Majesty's New Zealand Ship Wellington, a fast offshore patrol craft complete with crew of thirty or more, two RHIB craft for interception was racing towards the area, they'd thought she probably wouldn't be needed, how wrong could they be?

"She's at flank speed, heading for the area," ponytail said, "but still a good two hours away!"

It was if everything was slipping away, all the best laid plans, the 'contingencies' and possible variations just slipping down that proverbial 'gurgler' that seems to appear when things turn to custard!

But they weren't going down without a fight! She had to find a way of distracting whoever was 'pulling the strings' long enough for the team to get there, at the moment the other chopper would be there before they could strike, that couldn't happen.

"Get me Chambers on the line." Mildred shouted as she headed for her own desk, "then I want the AOS squad leaders for Auckland, Wellington, Christchurch and anywhere else that's got one!" She took a breath, then continued in a much softer, but more determined tone. "Let's get these pricks back on the defensive, and keep 'em there!"

Chapter 26

London was the first to feel it, without warning, a couple of large accounts 'zeroed out', no explanation was given, the previous night they'd had large sums in, by morning there was nothing, and no trace of where it went!

"What do you mean, there's no sodding money?" He screamed down the phone at the hapless call centre operator, "I flaming well checked last night, there was a couple of million there, easily enough to cover the cost of the house purchase, what the hell happened?"

"According to our records sir" the centre operator, a young lady with a Middle Eastern accent began, "you with"

"I know what I did and didn't withdraw you bloody idiot!" The client was almost apoplectic, "and I didn't withdraw any money from that account! Now, because of a screw up, I've got a major property deal in bloody limbo" they couldn't see him and that was probably good as they heard an almighty crash, he'd smashed something, the operator was so glad she was somewhere else.

Pretty soon it was the same all over the globe, tens of millions of dollars disappearing without a trace.

"What do you mean disappearing?" He tried speaking above the sound of the rotors, "how?"

"If I knew that" the voice on the other line cut him off, it was speaking English, but with a heavy Eastern accent, not quite Asian, but not European either, kind of a blend of the two. "Now get back to the computers and work out what's going on! And I want an answer within the hour, are we clear?"

"What about Chen?" he asked, the Chinese guy on the ship was responsible for the financials, surely it was him should be chasing this up.

"Chen's an idiot" the voice came back, "It's his screw up that caused this, I want someone I can trust not to screw up dealing with this, now get moving!"

"Yes sir" he signalled the pilot for a 'turnaround', interrogating the two police officers would have to wait, not that they were going anywhere, the Island was closed to the public, there was no escape.

"Sir" the comms officer, a young sub lieutenant looked up from her console, "I've got the director on the 'line' sir"

They'd been half expecting this kind of call, still, it didn't sit well, he jumped out of the command chair, leaning over he picked up what looked like a typical phone, waited a couple of seconds, as soon as a voice came on the line he spoke, "sorry to disturb you sir, we've got the spooks on the line," a couple of seconds later he replaced the handset, looked up towards the comms officer and said, "put her through."

As soon as Mildred came on the comlink he began, "Lieutenant commander" he was about to identify himself.

"I'm aware who you are Lieutenant Commander," Mildred cut him off, she knew it would appear rude, but really didn't give a damn, "the situation's changed a bit since we last spoke."

"The Captain's on his way ma'am"

"That's fine" Mildred carried on, "you can 'fill him in' but meanwhile, we've got a situation developing, and we need your help!"

The captain arrived within seconds of Mildred starting, there wasn't a need to go back over anything, they both knew something was up, they just didn't know what.

"Captain" Mildred continued, "the situation's now gone critical, there's been a few developments, and we need you for an interception"

That didn't sound good, it never does. They did 'interceptions' all the time, but the 'word' usually came down through 'defense' channels, this one, it was leapfrogging just about every link in the 'chain of command'

"Roger that, send us the details" the captain radioed back, "we'll check the details with Devenport and"

"There's not going to be time for all the details captain," she cut him off, "We're sending them all the information as we speak, but this needs to happen ASAP, and a word of warning, it's a 'hostile' interception, consider them armed and extremely dangerous!"

As soon as the words were out the first officer activated the ship's intercom, while the captain was talking with Mildred, he mobilized the ship's company. "This is the first officer, ship's company to general quarters, repeat ship's company to general quarters, this is not a drill, weapons officer to the bridge, RHIB crews to the captain's wardroom!"

As soon as he finished he flicked the intercom onto the 'Engine room', the Chief engineer came on the line, a gruff Aussie complete with the Aussie twang that made it sound as if he was speaking through his nose, "Chief Smith 'ere boss, what's yer problem?"

"Chief" the captain came on the line, "what's the top speed we can maintain?"

"Twenty two knots if you want to keep 'er even" the chief replied, "but if you want a burst of speed, we can do twenty five, maybe twenty seven knots until she 'redlines' then back 'er off to the twenty two!"

"How long can we keep the 'burst' up?"

"Dunno boss" he replied truthfully, "I know we can do it, probably about half an hour, then back her off, before we blow the turbines!"

"Okay, do that" the captain gave the order, "but keep an eye on those turbines"

"Don't worry boss" the chief engineer sounded happy, like a kid let loose in the cookie shop, he'd been wanting to push these engines, just to see what the 'protector class' was capable of, "I won't let you break MY boat!"

They were both amused at the chief's 'possessiveness', but neither said anything, it was good to know the crew looked after the ship that way. As soon as he'd finished with the chief, he looked up, "number one, you brief the RHIB crews, they'll be at the extreme of their range, with only each other for backup, I'm ordering the weapons techs to fit the fifty calibers and five hundred rounds each"

"I'll get the crews briefed and kitted up sir"

"We'll be launching them in two hours,"

"Sir" the first officer stopped, "it sounds like a pretty dicey situation, is there any chance of support from anywhere else?" He felt bloody awkward, in fact almost cowardly asking, but he knew it's the first question the teams will ask, no one wants to walk into a 'shitstorm' like they were going into without at least knowing they had some backup, even if it was only 'token'.

"Apparently" the captain looked nervous, he was fidgeting with his top pocket, where he used to keep his cigarettes, he'd only stopped smoking a couple of weeks ago, he really felt the urge, "there's an SAS team on White Island, apparently these drug dealers have got some hostages there," he turned and looked at his 'number one' as the first officer or 'exec' is known a " they'll give assistance as soon as they've 'neutralized' those on the island, whatever the hell that means"

Sometimes it's just better not to ask those kind of questions, you really might not like the answer, they decided this wasn't the time to ask.

Chapter 27

"Update!" Mildred demanded, almost shouting as she came round the banks of computers, it'd only been fifteen minutes since the last 'update' but she'd had to go onto the secure line with London, and things change fast.

"Scorpion team are at the staging area" ponytail called out, "they're doing a 'recce' as we speak."

"We sent them all the latest?" It was a question more than a statement, everyone knew it didn't matter how much information they had, nothing was going to happen until the team were confident they had whatever they needed, and every one of the 'enemy' were accounted for. The only time that might change was when either the team were confident of the situation, or the enemy started shooting hostages, then all bets were off!

"What about the rest?" She positioned herself so she could see the large screen that dominated the main wall. "What's the Wellington's situation?"

"She's made good headway" Mark replied, he'd been the one watching her.

"She's just a hundred and twenty miles from our mystery guest, and making a shade over twenty six knots" he sounded puzzled.

"What's the problem?" Mildred picked up on the puzzlement, if her team was worried, then she was!

"Oh probably nothing really" Mark began a reply, "just the books says the 'protector' class is only capable of twenty two!"

Mildred actually smiled, "you should know not to believe everything in government papers, especially when it comes to 'specs', but make sure you adjust everything to read what we want it to!"

Mark smiled back, slightly embarrassed, he should have known that was the case, you never tell your enemy exactly what your kit can do, only what you think they want to hear, and they usually want to hear their stuff is better! It's the spy's job to find out if that's true!

"How long before they launch the RHIBs?"

"Skipper says just over an hour and a half," it was Cody spoke this time, "and before you ask," he went on, "it'll take them forty five minutes to reach the target."

"Going like two bats of hell" Mildred muttered quietly, not quietly enough though.

"When the day is done, and the sun goes down, I'll be going like a bat out of Hell. What we pay the big bucks for isn't it Ma'am" Cody couldn't resist the quote and comment. She let it slide, they were all feeling the stress, a bit of humor never went amiss.

"What's the range on those things?" She asked curious, fifty or so miles from the target seemed a bit far, for such a small boat that is!

"One thing you'll realize boss" Cody cut in, "call those boats 'small' to any of their crews, and they damn well skin you alive!" he was concentrating on his computer screen, but still half watching her. "I did once, I was in a Navy bar in Davenport, believe me, it was a bad move!"

"They may be only about twenty five feet long, but the aluminum hull fixed to the inflatable sides gives it a stability most bigger ships can't match, then throw in two three hundred horsepower outboards and you've got a boat that can 'go like the bloody clappers' in a serious sea storm, clip on the fifty Cal's, and I'm beginning to feel sorry for the other poor sods on the other end!"

The 'RHIBs full name is Rigid Hull Inflatable Boat, they were first designed in the 1960s by the British Royal National Lifeboat Institute (RNLI) a volunteer lifeguard institute that has a kind of quasi government standing as an unofficial Coastguard. They're built for rough seas, and long range, it's when they come into their own.

The Irish Sea and the English Channel are some of the roughest stretches of water on earth, so when they decided to build a lifeboat that could actually get out to a shipwreck they had to be tough and fast. Someone at some point had the idea of getting an aluminium hull for strength, sticking two inflatable sides on it, to prevent water filling it in heavy seas and sticking a huge outboard motor on the back. The result, spectacular! A boat that can go anywhere, racing in at nearly sixty knots (seventy five miles an hour), do a three sixty degree turn in their own length (twenty five feet) and make her crew of very experienced seamen very 'green at the gills'.

As soon as they saw it, the British and US Navies said "We want them!" and pretty soon every navy in the world had them,

The Wellington had two, both twenty five foot long, with gun mounts and two three hundred horsepower outboard motors that powered them along at nearly sixty knots (officially fifty five knots) and were perfect for the rough seas they were in, not only that but they had the agility of a ballerina on steroids and pack a punch.

"I take it you've seen them in action then?"

"Hey, after an insult like I gave them" Cody replied, "Punishment was going out on harbour patrol the next day, man I was as sick as a dog after the fifth pirouette! And scared shitless when we left the water for the tenth time as we were going full bore in fifteen foot waves! Hell, even the bloody ferry wasn't running that day, but the bloody Navy insisted it was 'perfect for training'" he waved the index and second finger of each hand in a gesture that said he was quoting 'verbatim'.

"So getting the Navy to the scene isn't going to be a problem then!" It was a statement. "All we can do is wait until the team are ready"

Sam hadn't heard a thing for the last hour, they'd been dragged out of the helicopter, literally by the scruff of their necks, she figured they'd been dragged about a hundred yards, then she'd heard the aircraft take off again. No one had spoken, no one had said a thing, yet she knew they were there, she could hear a couple of them walking around, it was as if they were waiting for orders.

"Still with me Sam?" it was Hene who'd broken the silence, a couple of minutes after the aircraft had taken off, he'd tried to whisper to her, all he got was a kick in the ribs.

She managed to cough, not that she needed to, but as an acknowledgement she was still here, still alive, and while she wasn't saying anything, she was finding where the boundaries were.

Was there any hope of getting out? She had to think that there was, but reality was it didn't look too good. Apparently these bozos thought that Sam and Hene knew something about how much the police knew about their operation, 'they must be worried' she thought to herself.

Most people would think they'd be scared in situations like that, truth is you just don't know what you'll be! The most timid person can suddenly become as stubborn as a mule for no other reason than yes, they're scared, but they're also pissed off and just decide 'screw this, I'm giving these pricks nothing'

Others, those whom you'd think would be tough and hard men or women, can end up giving everything up within minutes 'hoping to live'. Somehow, they just knew, if they did that' they weren't going to make it out alive, they had to 'hang in there' and believe that someone might come in time!

"Listen up folks" Jacko spoke into the headsets, they were in the Staging point, Joey, Mac and Sandy were in a defensive position watching the side approaches while Smithy and Jacko had been watching the front. "Looks like they've got two camps here" He carried on, "One to the South, that's where the hostages look to be, they've got two guarding them directly and three more patrolling where the huts are"

"They're in the huts Sandy cut in, "That's where the GPS trackers put them." We've got ten huts altogether, probably with booby traps in"

"That's why you and Joey get the good jobs" Jacko replied, "Smithy. You'll make sure they get a 'clean approach' the come and assist us right?"

"I take it we've got the fun bit then boss" Mac chirped in, "Joey gets to rescue the hostages and play the hero, while we do the real work and take out the rest of the cutthroats and pirates here!" they all gave a little chuckle as Mac wasn't so far from the truth.

"Yeah" Jacko sighed as he came round to that point, "Shit, no one expected they'd have a bleedin' warehouse here!"

The 'other camp' was on the Western side of the Island, only about four hundred yards away, but totally different to the Southern side.

The original settlement had been on the Western side, back in the nineteenth century, but an eruption took the whole lot out, and no one was ever found from the eruption, however, when the companies came back, they kept the mine on the western side and built fresh huts on the southern side, the result was that the miners lived in the south, but every morning they'd take a boat over to work the mine in the west, eventually someone put a small path in, but it was perfect for storing the contraband as tourists came to the huts.

The mine was 'off limits' and supposedly sealed, but no one questioned tour operators going out there, and while the tourists were looking around, someone was picking up the 'other supplies delivered by ship, then they flew back to the mainland none the wiser for sitting on a couple of hundred grand worth of cocaine or heroin!

"So far we've counted fifteen" Smithy cut in, "But there could be more, and they're well armed, looks like they've got Uzis and the like, I even saw a couple of AKs"

"What's the intel on these people?" Joey asked, Sandy hadn't said anything, but maybe Jacko had been briefed.

"Nada" Jacko replied, "All we know is they've got three Asians in jail in Auckland and a bunch of bikers in jail somewhere else, no idea who these might be, but best guess is Triads, and that means anything from street thugs to SF guys on the payroll!"

"You really know how to make a guy's day don't you boss?" Joey joked back, they were all tense, black humour works wonders in situations like this for relieving the tension.

"A man of your skills Joey?" Jacko was almost laughing, "only three guards, and two more in the 'zone', should be a breeze!"

"Thanks for the vote of confidence boss" Joey half joked back. SAS trained for this sort of stuff, but in a normal 'breach' there'd be a whole team going through the door, in this one, there'd be just him and Sandy, and they weren't totally sure what was on the other side.

"Joey" it was Smithy spoke next, "those goons on the outside are doing an unpredictable pattern, looks like they know what they're doing that way, and they seem on edge if you know what I mean, like they're expecting someone?" The last part was part question, like there was something they might not have been told.

"Maybe I can explain that," Sandy chipped in, she'd been quiet up until now, "about a half hour ago they picked up another helicopter inbound, so Mildred got London to start the Bank jobs, the chopper turned back and headed out to Sea, we think they've got a boat out there"

"Anyone looking for it?" Jacko asked.

"HMNZS Wellington, she's returning from the Kermadec islands, she's bearing down on the area with a couple of RHIBs, we don't think it's a trawler, maybe a container ship, big enough for a helicopter to land on".

"Who's giving the signal to kick off here boss?" Joey brought the discussion back to the 'here and now' with a practical question.

"You will, when you take down the two bozos in with the hostages" Jacko replied, we move out as soon as we're done here, but give us an hour and a half for setup!"

"Okay, probably take us at least that to get past the three stooges, should be a good timeframe boss!"

"Then let's get started"

Chapter 28

Smithy was the first to move out, everyone else stayed where they were until he called in. "Three, in position, looks clear."

Next went Jacko and Mac, they had the furthest to go, and the longest to wait at the other end. Joey and Sandy had orders to give them fifteen minutes, then begin their approach, from that point on, in theory at least, everything should 'just flow', it never does, but it should.

The first part was pretty easy, they were moving across solid rock, moving silently across the rock wasn't hard, it isn't if you know what you're doing, and experience had taught them well.

Joey led the way, walking at first in a semi crouch, something soldiers call a 'monkey run' for its similarity to the way Gorillas and Chimpanzees run using their knuckles on their hands as well as the feet.

They'd strapped the rifles over their backs, muzzles facing down. Using this method they were able to move faster than a normal walk, but slower than a run, more importantly they kept low, blending in with the rocks around them. Joey was using his arms as they went to feel for any nasty surprises like trip wires, he didn't expect any, but that didn't stop him checking.

Trip wires can come in all ways, from the elaborate wire with explosives attached to the simple piece of number eight wire with a coke can filled with pebbles, an effective 'early warning device'.

They were wearing night vision visors which take the available starlight, by magnifying it a hundredfold you get enough to see most objects, they appear in a green haze, good for aiming and taking a shot, but not enough for the little things, it's always the little things that trip you up.

The first hundred yards they covered in about five minutes, stopping every ten to twenty paces to wait and listen.

"Ouch" Sandy whispered, "caught my bloody knuckles"

"You alright?" Joey stopped and turned around concerned.

"Yeah" Sandy sounded sheepish, "just clunked my bloody knuckles on a rock, that's all"

"Careful" Joey mockingly advised, "rocks are harder than knuckles" he chuckled.

"Watch it buster" Sandy retorted, "I've got a nine millimeter, and right now I'm happy to use it!" she joked back.

"And knuckles too sore to use it!" Joey joked, "seriously though, be careful, last thing we need is one of us getting incapacitated!"

They stopped, turned their night vision visors off, lifted them and checked her hand while their eyes came back to normal, it took fifteen minutes, the glove had taken the brunt of the scrape.

There was a good reason for deactivating the night vision, they're great for getting you where you want to go without being seen, but as soon as a firefight starts they aren't just useless, they're downright dangerous.

Night vision gear takes the minutest amount of light and magnifies it at least a hundredfold. Do that to just a match as it's struck and the guy wearing the night vision gear will be blinded momentarily! It'll literally take about fifteen minutes for the sight to come back. Now put that in the middle of a firefight with muzzle flashes and explosions going off and you've got a recipe for disaster, and total blindness with people running everywhere, blind as bats and straight into the line of fire, that's why the night vision gear comes off before the fight starts.

It takes about fifteen to twenty minutes for the Mark 1 Human eyeball to adjust to low light, when it does, it's not as great as the night vision gear, but good enough to aim a weapon in a firefight and make sure you take the target out, Joey and Sandy had a trick or two up their sleeves, an old WW2 trick a mentor of Joey's once taught him, he went to work.

Taking a piece of chalk out of his pack Joey reached over and touched the muzzle of Sandy's weapon with it, literally just by the front sight, he lightly coated the front sight in chalk.

"What the?" Sandy began.

"Take a look down the sight" Joey urged her, "an old trick from a Commando I once knew."

Sandy did, she looked down the barrel, it was faint, but there was no mistaking she could see the sight! "Well, I'll be"

"No you won't" Joey shot back, "This'll keep us alive, not send us there!" He did the same to his own weapon, only when he was satisfied did he put the chalk away and call Smithy.

"Three, this is four" Joey clicked the radio on. " We're in position, can see one bogey, where are the other two?"

"Three here," Smithy came on, "ones in the southern building, the others patrolling the other side, you're good to go"

"Roger that" Joey clicked off, He left his weapon with Sandy and drew out his commando knife. Moving stealthly he left Sandy's position and worked his way round behind the sentry, it took about two minutes.

Sandy took her MP5 back and took up the ready position, she had a 'bead' on the sentry who was coming their way, just in case things turned to custard.

"RHIB crews are ready boss" the NCO in charge, a 'leading hand' with the insignia indicating 'combat specialist'. He looked only slightly older than a teenager but he was in charge, and giving the orders, turning to the rest of his crew he switched channels on his radio and spoke to every man and woman in each boat, "final harness check folks, make sure you're secured to the deck of your boat!"

Each one was wearing a lifejacket, that was mandatory, each was also a good swimmer, but that isn't going to save you when you're tossed out of the boat like a piece of flotsam! Preventing that were two rugged canvas ties attached to the deck by sturdy metal clips, and at the other end two 'quick release' clips with adjustable pins. The idea was safety, not comfort, and everyone swore by them, the last thing you want is to be plucking some idiot out of the water while some lunatic Somali pirates are taking pot shots at you!

Four half inch steel cables held the boats to two winch arms each, two cables per arm, the outers attached to one side and 'inners' to the other.

"Lifting" they heard the operator's voice in their headsets, "clear, extending" was the next.

As soon as they were clear the side the operator began their descent. "Set your engine to one third speed, he gave the command to the other helmsman."

Each boat had a crew of six, the 'helmsman' had the wheel, she was the most experienced, then the gunner on the fifty cal. The 'boss' was part of the boarding party along with three others, usually one of which is the medic and another the linguist. They worked in silence, only speaking when spoken to, each one thinking through what they were about to attempt.

No one on the boats thought it strange that they had an officer on the landing party, but they weren't the ones in charge on the boats, yes they ran the 'operation' but they didn't know the 'kit' like the men and women operating it did, it was the person who knew the boats best who was in charge.

Launching a boat is enough of a challenge, it's got its dangers under the most ideal conditions, that was, broad daylight, light wind, perfect weather and good visibility with the ship stationary. They had none of the above!

There was moonlight, but also rough seas, visibility wasn't great, and their ship was motoring along at eighteen knots. The captain had ordered the slowdown even though it meant they'd take that much longer to get there.

"You don't even get this kind of crap facing pirates" he heard the helm mutter, she'd done two tours with the Te KAHA in 'pirate alley' as the horn of Africa, off the Somali coast was known.

"Keep your eye on the gauges" he shot back, looking round he saw they were in the water, clicking the radio onto the ship frequency he called, "boat in the water, release the cables?"

"Go for release" the winch operator replied.

He signalled the men nearest the cables, as soon as he got the 'thumbs up' from all four he called back, "cables released, boat is free"

"Roger, and good hunting"

Turning to the helm, he gave the order, "peel off, full throttle, as soon as we clear the ship set course two three zero."

"Peeling off," helm replied, they felt the surge as the twin three hundred horsepower outboards roared to life, the force pushing them back on their feet, everyone was strapped in, but that didn't stop them grabbing hold and hanging on 'for dear life', less than fifteen seconds elapsed before the helm shouted above the deafening noise, "course two three zero laid in skipper"

A quick glance round confirmed the other boat wasn't far behind. Flicking to the bridge frequency he gave the call, "Commencing the hunt."

As soon as Joey'd given his rifle to Sandy he slowly and silently drew his dagger out, Sandy actually did a bit of a double take, 'How the hell?' she thought. 'Maybe Jacko and Mac?' Joey wasn't going to be telling, right now it was better than using a silencer.

The sentry was about fifteen feet away, he couldn't see them, they were in a ditch, Sandy was watching every move, even the slightest hint he saw them and she'd open fire, he didn't. He stopped, looking around he reached down into the jacket pocket, took out a pack of cigarettes, took one out, returned the pack to his pocket, reaching for his lighter he started sauntering off as he took the lighter out and lit the cigarette, it reminded her of a condemned man before a firing squad (like in the TV adverts she used to watch as a kid) taking his last cigarette, savouring one of earth's last pleasures before going to meet his maker, and that's exactly what was happening.

As soon as he started to saunter off, Joey rose to a crouch, he waited a few seconds to make sure he wasn't heard, then slowly began the advance.

Sandy kept the rifle trained on the sentry the whole time, she was literally covering Joey if anything went wrong, if it did then they'd only get one chance before all hell broke loose.

The sentry kept on his saunter, Joey's moves were fluid, almost graceful, (if death can be delivered with 'grace' that is) and quick, neither the sentry or Sandy heard anything, one second he was enjoying the cigarette, the next there was a hand over his mouth and something sharp going into the back of his neck, at the base of the skull, the next second all feeling below that point ceased.

He tried to reach up and beat whoever it was doing this, but his arms refused to move, he tried screaming in his mother tongue, but the voice box refused to co-operate, the bowels relaxed, as well as the intestines, he could smell the foul smell of faeces and urine, but couldn't feel a thing, it's a horrible feeling knowing you've crapped your pants yet can't feel anything! He didn't even feel the legs buckle under himself, only that he was prone on the floor and unable to move, that's when he realized that the lungs weren't functional, he was dying and there was nothing he could do about it.

Joey withdrew the dagger as he dragged the guard to the nearest hut, out of view of any others that might pass. Then, pressing the com he spoke softly "Clear"

As soon as she heard the words she was on her feet, ready to sprint for Joey's position.

"Stealth, not speed!" Joey's whisper was almost a hiss, it also felt a bit like a rebuke, or maybe she was feeling dumb for not thinking of it herself. "Too much haste will get us killed" Joey went on, "noise is the critical thing, as in none at all"

Sandy didn't reply, it felt like a rebuke, but she knew Joey, and she knew that was the last thing he was thinking of, she took the magazine off his rifle, cocked it and passed it to him, showing him the empty chamber, even then, in the middle of a combat situation safety was paramount, as soon as he saw it, he took the rifle, replaced the mag, cocked the weapon, checked the safety was where he wanted it, clipped the mag back on and slung the rifle over his head and shoulder.

"Look at this!" Joey whispered as he removed the 'vest' from the now dead sentry, "police issue by the looks, but not New Zealand police!"

"Let me have a look" Sandy held out her hand, Joey passed the jacket over, "you're right." She said, "look here" she pointed to the Kevlar plate, "it's the wrong size for here, looks more like those the cops in the US use!"

There are different types of 'bullet proof vest' on the market, from the basic one that'll protect you from a knife and some small arms, right through to the serious ones that'll stop just about anything (but still give you seriously cracked ribs)

A US police issue 'vest' is in the middle, and pretty much means 'shoot for the torso' (as most cops are trained for) is a waste of time as all but the most high powered rifles will just 'bounce off' and they'll be up returning fire before you're aware of it.

"Scorpion team, this is four" Joey clicked his radio on, they were supposed to be on radio silence, but this was important, "be aware, bandits are wearing US police issue vests,"

"Roger that" Jacko replied for the rest of the team, "we're in position"

"Roger that" Sandy cut in, "Showtime in five"

Chapter 29

"What the hell's going on?" Fish face asked angrily as he burst into the lounge that doubled as the control centre for the ship, he wasn't happy at all, but he wasn't normally one to show his emotions. "Emotions in my line of work" he often told his clients when they commented about his manner, "get you killed!"

"Sir" the young man in the room, Fish face figured him for an accountant type, someone used to being 'behind a desk, crunching the numbers' in some grey building in any city in the world, not here, on on board a ship in the middle of only the almighty knows where. He looked nervous, unsure of either himself or the surroundings, either way, it was obvious, he was uncomfortable, and in a role he didn't relish, well tough 'He'll get used to it' he thought.

"We've had strange things happening with the accounts, money disappearing, and I can't find where it's going!" he sounded almost apologetic, "and"

"You got me called back for THAT?" fish face cut him off, "Like I can do anything about that?" he turned and headed back for the door.

"No sir" the accountant replied, "Least it wasn't me," he stopped momentarily, it was obvious he was afraid where this was going, then again, changing an assassin's plans can shorten your life expectancy significantly, even if they weren't known for showing anger. "It was Mr Chen, he reported it, not me" he pointed to the door to the private suite at the back.

Drug smuggling is a lucrative but risky business. Every time a border is crossed, a search can be made, any suspicion and the authorities come down 'like a ton of bricks' ripping everything apart, like Rottweilers on a scent, they work through until they find what they're looking for. Cruise ships, Merchant ships, even fishing trawlers get the treatment, only two kinds don't, Warships and Superyachts!

Warships and police don't normally get searched, but the most you'll get through their procedures is a few hundred grams. A Superyacht is a different story, stop one of those and its owner might just be on their way to lunch with your boss's boss and you're suddenly 'unemployable'. That's what Chen and his people counted on!

Where they got the boat, you just didn't ask, one thing was certain, it wasn't by legal means, not that anyone was concerned, it did a job, and that's all they needed.

At the back of the lounge was a big mahogany door, the dark brown of the wood blending in with the dark coloured carpets, he reached for the door and opened it.

The door swung open noiselessly. Chen was more 'slumped' in the chair than sat, feet stretched out in the large Teak desk, a relic from the ship's previous owner. Fishface didn't know or care what happened to them.

"You no knock?" Chen blurted out as he moved forward, "it polite to knock you know!"

Fishface didn't care much for Chen, he wasn't the boss, just an average 'thug' in a suit, probably slightly more of a brain than the others here, but in the end, just a 'thug in a suit' working as a drug mule taking all the risks, for very little of the reward.

"Only when I need to!" Fishface replied, "your boss sent for me remember, and now I've got come come back again, and clean up your mess! Your boss isn't happy at all."

"It not matter" Chen replied.

There was a tumbler by his right hand, it was full almost to the brim with a yellow transparent liquid, 'probably Scotch' fishface thought, 'idiot's drunk' he continued the thought. "How come?"

"Email" Chen replied almost shouting and waving a piece of paper about, "you see" he slapped the paper down in front of them both, "we been robbed!"

He knew about the account hacking, "I'm an assassin" fishface replied, "not a banker, what's it to do with me?" He took the paper and read it, it wasn't good.

"Cops know nothing!" Chen stated, "we kill them then leave, time for Australia delivery, boss say!"

"I was on my way to do that" Fishface replied, in a very low but threatening tone."after I'd questioned them!" He reminded the thug. "That is what your bosses wanted me to come back for, isn't it?" Malice dripping from every word.

"I know" Chen screamed as he shot to his feet, "but all change now, we have new," he stopped for a moment, struggling with the English, "how you say, instructions?" It was half question, half statement. He thrust the email towards Fishface, it said. "London advised you're compromised, get rid of cops and move on"

"I already gave order" Chen brought them back to reality, "My men, they do it, then helicopter pick them up, they feed bodies to sharks, then come back to boat and we outta here!"

"And I stay onboard until we get to Australia" Fishface sounded almost resigned to his fate, two days with these idiots.

The two guards didn't give a damn about their 'charges'. To them, they were just two pieces of meat, waiting for the slaughter, once they'd got what they needed, they'd be dispatched, the guards themselves were getting tired, so they'd probably do it quickly, so they could get some sleep afterwards.

The prisoners were trying to put on a brave face, the brown one, the man, he was saying something over and over to himself, and possibly to the woman, but it wasn't in English, and she wasn't saying anything back, 'If they want to dream of escape' he thought, 'let 'em, there's nowhere to go, and besides it'll feel that much better when we crush their spirits right at the end'

The prisoners were kneeling, hands tied in front of them, at times he made them put their hands behind their heads, but always kneeling, they'd been like that for hours, probably lost all feeling in their lower legs.

He took out his hip flask, it didn't have alcohol in it, just juice, but slowly he unscrewed the cap, making sure the prisoners saw him, the girl was licking her lips, they hadn't drunk anything for at least five hours, 'she must be thirsty' he thought of the fun he'd normally have with a prisoner like that, but orders had been 'they're not to be touched!' Ah well, at least he can fantasize.

The phone took him out of his daydream, at first he forgot he had the phone, then finally clicking he opened it and began to speak.

"Shut up and listen" the voice was Chen's, "New orders, Helicopter on way for you, kill the prisoners, dump the bodies with the sharks and get back here, ALL OF YOU" the phone went dead.

He looked over at the other guard, nodded and both of them drew their pistols, walking up to the prisoners he spoke in very broken English. "Time over, lights out time". He cocked the pistol and put it to the man's head. That's when his world disappeared in a blinding flash.

"We go in five" Joey said as he clicked the radio off, just then he heard a phone ring, "SHIT, what the F" was his first reaction, he spun around to look at Sandy, she was almost as shocked as him.

'I'm not that stupid' was her thought, just then they saw the guard reach for his phone, 'That's not good' was the first reaction.

Joey threw himself against the wall, at the side of the door, she could see he was preparing himself mentally for the next task, running through all the possibilities in his head, all the angles and outcomes, everything from both of them killed to a clean 'take down'.

Joey reached down and took out what looked like a cardboard cylinder, she knew it immediately and got ready, this wasn't going to be pleasant, but at least they knew what was coming.

How do you get the advantage when the enemy are holding hostages and are seconds away from killing them? Answer, you disorient them for a couple of seconds, and that's what the 'cardboard cylinder' was designed for.

SAS refuse to use blank ammunition, even on exercise, actually they almost never use blanks as they believe that the only way to know what it's like in a real situation is to use the 'real deal', but then again, I did say 'almost' as there's one toy they love, the 'thunderflash' or 'flashbang' s they call it, but to them it's not used as a 'blank' but a distraction.

The thunderflash or 'flashbang' is a 'mock grenade' in that it creates the same big bang as a grenade, and a bright light, just like a grenade, but none of the shrapnel, and when it goes off, it leaves you wondering which bloody way is up for about fifteen seconds.

The SAS first used them in Mogadishu in the late seventies when they helped the Germans take down a bunch of hijackers who'd got a planeload of hostages, all the hijackers died, and none of the hostages.

Got a room with a bunch of terrorists holding hostages, chuck in a couple of thunderflashes (or the bigger version that the SAS like to use, called the flashbang), wait for them to go off, then walk in and shoot the guy waving his gun in the air, it's that simple.

"Two flashbangs" Joey whispered as Sandy reached for hers, Joey peeked round the corner, the thugs were drawing their pistols and cocking them, Hene looked up, Joey wasn't sure if he'd seen Joey, 'just have to hope he realizes what to do' he thought. "On three, one, two, three".

Both of them struck the fuses, leaned in just far enough, threw the flashbangs in and got the hell out of the way. Both had their pistols drawn and cocked. Two almighty bangs nearly deafened them, then both were leaping round the corner, Hene had screamed just before the bangs went off, he'd thrown himself onto Sam who was kicking at anything, mostly Hene.

Three shots, each from the Browning and Makarov and both guards were down, the holes in their chests and foreheads quite neat and small, but the exit wounds as big as tennis balls. Joey advanced on both of them and checked the job. Next he was on the radio. "Scorpion team, this is four, two bandits down, hostages secured, GO GO GO!"

Chapter 30

Jacko heard Joey's first call, that was good, he and Mac were plotting the positions of each of the others, they had five of them worked out when all hell broke out to the south, followed almost instantly by his phone vibrating and Joey screaming, "Scorpion team this is four, two bandits down, hostages rescued. GO GO GO"

'Shit Joey,' he thought, 'give us all a bloody heart attack will ya?' as he cocked the HK, he didn't bother with the phone, it was obvious what the message was,"Mac, pick your targets" he didn't really need that, but needed the extra moment to think, "Smithy, two hundred yards north, bit of a fuel dump and generator"

"Got it boss, incendiary, watch your vision" Smithy sounded all business, "go to starscope"

Both Jacko and Mac had been using infrared or 'thermal imaging' as it was called, that works off heat output, everything produces a certain amount of heat, picking up variations in heat output can identify what you're looking at, only problem is if you start a fire, it'll only pick up the heat from the fire, even if you're not looking in that direction, all you'll see is the heat of the fire.

Starlight takes the light of the stars, heat doesn't affect it, as long as they weren't looking directly at the fire, they should be able to function, for the guys in the camp however it would be a different story!

"Roger, switching to starlight"

The explosion was impressive, Smithy's first shot, a tracer, took out a half full barrel, passing clean through the top half, the heat from the bullet warming the vapour to combustion point, causing expansion and more vapour to ignite, the fireball was about five feet across, engulfing two more barrels that went off a few seconds later, their fireballs were just as impressive, one barrel was launched a couple of hundred feet into the air, then came crashing down onto the main camp setting the tents alight.

Two were killed instantly, they'd been unfortunate enough to be filling the generator up, a couple of others got sprayed with burning fuel, their screams were almost inhuman, the others were motionless, pinned to the spot by the horrible situation, that is until they started dropping as they were shot!

The firefight, if you can call it that, lasted less than a minute. In that minute six went down and stayed that way. Three others, not knowing where they were 'taking fire' from, or how many there were, threw down their weapons, knelt down, placed their hands behind their heads and prayed their enemy would see their surrender.

"Ceasefire" Jacko called into the radio, "Smithy, you reckon it's for real?" He asked wanting to know what the sniper saw.

"Yeah boss," Smithy replied, "I think a couple hoofed it out at the start, didn't get chance to take 'em all, but at least one's got a leg wound, these guys lost the will!"

"Roger" Jacko replied, "Mac, you're with me, Smithy, cover us" both Jacko and Mac checked their weapons, making sure there was one in the breach, safety off, finger on the trigger guard, not the trigger. "STAY DOWN" they screamed in unison as they moved forward weapons trained, waiting for the slightest twitch.

As soon as Joey clicked the radio off, he reached up and unclipped the backpack he was carrying, it wasn't a 'backpack' proper, but two full sets of body armour, rolled up so that he could carry them, Hene and Sam were still on the ground, but Sam had almost kicked Hene off, he was still dazed and and groaning from the kicking she'd given him, still not sure which way was up, let alone what time of day or night it was.

"STAY DOWN" Joey shouted as he unfurled the two suits and threw them down on top of the two, they covered all the important parts, "Stay under these until I tell you, They're Kevlar" and with that all wiggling stopped.

"Rooms clear" Sandy called in.

"Stay with them" Joey ordered as he headed for the west, "I'll deal with the other two"

"What the hell, what's going on?" Sandy recognized the voice, it was Sam, she wasn't moving, but at least she was coherent.

"Sugar!" Hene was trying not to swear for some reason, probably some misguided sense of not wanting to swear in front of a female, "My head hurts, what the hell hit me?"

"Actually" Sandy was half smiling, "It's more like what, or rather whom did you hit, I think you headbutted the ground as you went down!"

"Yeah, but what the hell's happening?"

"We're the good guys" Sandy replied, "Come to rescue you, now stay down while we finish the job!"

Just as she said that all hell broke out further up, it was Jacko and the rest of the team doing their thing, it lasted less than a minute, then they heard screaming.

About a minute later they heard two more shots, in quick succession, Joey's voice came on the radio, "Boss, one more coming your way, he got away!"

"No worries, I got him," Smithy came on the line, he's raising his weapon, going to try his luck, the sniper rifle boomed. "Target down boss"

"He still alive?" Jacko asked.

"I know these guys are pretty brainless" Smithy quipped, "So maybe, but minus his brain as I blew it out!"

Joey headed back into the room, "It's okay now" he said as he peeled the suits off the two cops, "Put these on though, there's still a few of the gangsters out there!"

Hene looked at the suits, they were like none he'd ever seen before, a normal police one finishes at the waist and is held together by velcro, these you actually slid over your body and the fastened round the crotch, as in underneath! "What are these, some kind of secret armour?"

"Pretty close" Joey replied, "These are special tactical body armour suits, for when you're going into a real shit fight and got no idea where the bad boys are coming from." he turned and checked their armour as the donned it, "You know, just like now"

"And you're supposed to be 'just insurance people'?" it was more an insult than anything, like saying "Don't insult my intelligence again" and it was from Sam.

"That part was sort of true" Sandy spoke up, "we were doing a favor for the insurance company, and checking something fishy out"

"Besides, we did 'ensure' you stayed alive didn't we?" Joey added cheekily, neither of them got the humour.

"And who did the asking? Or maybe I shouldn't be told"

"Hey" Joey chipped in, "we got you into this mess, we're getting you out, but for your information, right at this moment we're seconded to your SIS now get a move on, we've got work to do!"

They were both moving slowly, mainly because being sat so long in the position they'd been in, they'd lost all sensation of feeling in the extremities, it was returning, but slowly. Hene couldn't resist one more question, "And I suppose you've got the SAS for support right?"

"Actually" it was Sandy replied, Joey was busy outside checking the perimeter, "Joey is SAS, or at least he was until a couple of weeks ago, and so were the guys over there, who just took the rest of the goons out!". That solved it, there were no more questions.

It was two minutes before they were ready, before both Joey and Sandy were satisfied the suits were fitting properly and it was safe to move them. "How'd you find us by the way?" Sam asked.

"Tracker device" Joey replied, "Minute enough that you ate them in the cakes you ate at the farmhouse!"

"You mean you Damn well set us up!" she blurted out.

"We knew Cavell's killers would make a move, they couldn't get us, they didn't know that though and we'd taken the family out of the picture, they had to try something, but no, we didn't actually think it would be you, it was just Sandy's 'woman's intuition thing', and I'm glad she ran with the idea" Joey replied, "I think you should be too, we didn't use you, you weren't in the picture until you showed up! I'm thinking they took you by mistake, thinking you were us!"

"Joey," Jacko came over the network they were using, "you've got friendlies inbound south of you, ten minutes, it's the '60' with the local armed offenders squad, bring 'em and whichever pilot volunteers for some fun ASAP"

"Roger that boss" Joey replied.

"We've got more bandits headed our way," Jacko went on, "make sure the friendlies follow your lead, we should have the bandits dealt with by the time you get here!"

"What about the chopper boss? We need it?"

"No, but we'll need the pilot though, I'll explain when you get here" Jacko cut out.

Joey was confused, he'd thought the plan was for them to go and 'assist' taking down the ship, for that they needed the chopper, now Jacko was saying no to the chopper, and he'd explain 'When they got there'. 'Situation normal, hair brained scheme in the works' he thought, 'I'd bet a million quid on it, if I had it that is'

Even Jacko wasn't totally sure they could pull it off! A great con if they could, and it just might give them advantage they needed, but the risks?

The other chopper was almost on them, coming in to land, expecting to pick up their people,'straight in and out'. The 'boys' had other plans.

"Ready boys, here they come" Jacko spoke softly into the radio. He raised his arms and turned the torches on, effectively telling the pilot where to land, they wouldn't wait for shutdown.

The aircraft banked and came in, turning on the landing lights at the last minute, the pilot saw nothing strange, he kept coming in, the skids gently gently settled on the sand, as soon as it was down Jacko gave one 'blink' of the right hand torch, a signal asking the pilot if they can approach.

Mac and Smithy were both ready, Mac would go left, Smithy right, Jacko got the pilot.

The landing light blinked the 'ok' "Let's go boys" Jacko whispered into the mike. The pilot was expecting them to be carrying weapons, so he thought nothing of armed men approaching, that was a mistake.

"We're here to, WHAT THE HELL?" he was staring down the barrel of a Glock 17, he slowly raised his hands.

"Shut up and shift your arse out of the plane, MOVE" Jacko snarled, swinging the door wide open he hit the release on the pilot's five point harness, grabbing the man, hurled him out of the seat, onto the sand, "on your feet". He hauled him up and began frogmarching him to the front of the helicopter. Mac and Smithy had flung the back doors open, no one was there, but that didn't stop a thorough search, eventually Mac reported in.

"All clear boss, where's Joey?"

The blades had stopped, the pilot having put the brake on just before his nasty surprise, but the engine was still turning over as Joey and the rest approached, there were seven from the AoS and the pilot, then there were the two cops, finally Sandy was bringing up the rear.

"Boss" Joey began the introductions, "this is Senior Sergeant"

"No time for that" Jacko cut him off, looking down the line he shouted, "where's the pilot?"

"Here," a voice came back, a youngish looking officer stepped forward, "flight lieutenant Carol"

"We'll do intros later" Jacko steamrollered her, "can you fly this thing?"

'Carol' looked the big oaf in the eye, she was about four inches shorter than him, but the tone of voice said it all. "No, I just volunteered to piss you off" she pushed him out of the way, grabbing the door handle, she climbed up onto the fuselage and into the cockpit, "of course I bloody well can, I take it you want me to take you boys somewhere right?" She reached up to release the brake, the rotors slowly began turning, she looked back down in them, "well come on then, get your arse into gear."

There aren't many people can silence Jacko, but she did, if only for a few seconds. "Guess that's not going to be a problem then, I'll explain where we're going in a min"

"No need," she cut him off, "machines got a Doppler navigation system, I'll just punch up the last set of coordinates, there we are, thirty six miles out to Sea right?"

"I've no idea?" Jacko replied truthfully, "suppose it's not safe to ask how you landing on a ship, maybe as small as a superyacht?"

"No worries," she broke a smile, "done a few hair raising ones in my time, mostly oil rigs, but we'll be fine."

"Good," he turned to the rest of the team, "climb on board, hey wait a minute," he went to physically restrain Hene and Sam, "not you two!"

The female cop had a fat lip, her left eye was half closed, she was moving with difficulty, there's no way she was ready for what they were about to do, she just stopped, looked at Jacko and said, "don't even think of trying to stop me soldier boy!"

The acid in the comment was so potent, all five of them winced, unsure of what might come next.

"We came here to rescue you," Jacko replied, "I'm not putting you back in harm's way again, especially in the condition you're in!"

"I'm going with, that's final" Sam replied and started to climb in, Jacko blocked her path, "out of my way soldier, or I'll tie myself to the bloody skids!" She actually got a length of nylon rope out and began wrapping it round the struts.

"I'm with her" Hene spoke up, he was doing the same.

"Boss" it was Sandy broke the impasse, "we might actually need them anyway, S.I.S want this by the book, that ship's in a marine sanctuary administered by New

Zealand, we need a cop presence for any arrests and the like"

"We'll have the Navy for that"

"They only get to take pictures, they've no power of arrest, that is until the ship is in international waters!" Sam cut in, "you need us two cops."

Momentarily he was flummoxed, but it seemed the rest of the team were reasonably okay with the idea, not that it made it any easier to handle, after all they had been originally tasked with getting these folks back, not putting them in any more danger.

"The flight will give me time to check their injuries." it was Mac spoke up, "and besides, they'll be encased in Kevlar, they'll be virtually bullet proof!"

That much was true, the Kevlar 'vests' were much more than just a normal vest, they stretch all the way down from the neck, protecting all the vital organs, even the ones in the groin, going half way down the thighs, they protect even the femoral artery most of the way, with Kevlar most of the way down, and where the Kevlar isn't (in the legs) you've got a 'compression suit' that helps hold anything in if you do get hit.

Bullets might not penetrate the suit, but they still hurt big time, and something like a round from an AK47 from as far away as two hundred yards will still break bones, with the sheer force it hits you with, but that's so much better than the alternative, a body bag!

"Okay" Jacko finally relented, "You're on the chopper, but no all clear from Mac and you stay there, UNDERSTAND?"

Neither replied, they just smiled and climbed on board. Jacko turned and was about to finish briefing the Sergeant from the AoS.

"I've already got my orders Sir" the Sergeant cut him off, "Hold the perimeter until the others from the Regiment get here, they'll do the search of the Island, only after that's done can I call the drugs squad in to sort the rest of the bloody mess out, by the way, How much do you think we're talking about, just out of curiosity?"

Jacko jumped into the chopper, he started sliding the door shut, but stopped half way through, he paused for a moment then said, "I think you're gonna need a forklift to get it out, they were doing stuff on an industrial scale, using this place to resupply the whole South Pacific, and I mean Aussie as well!" with that he slid the door closed and gave the thumbs up to Carol.

As soon as the Sergeant was clear they were up and away.

Chapter 31

"We're enroute to the second target now." Sandy had Mildred on the Sat Phone, "Should be there in about twenty minutes!"

"Thanks for the update, I've got the RHIBs on the radio at the moment, texting you the frequency now, any luck with entry?" Mildred asked, the one part of the plan that still needed a lot of work was how the heck they were going to get onto whatever ship was out there, the support vessel, so far, the only plan they'd come up with was using the firepower of the RHIBs and literally blasting their way in, but that ran the risk of sinking the ship and losing any intel they might gain, not to mention the possible loss of life to the Navy and themselves, no one gave a damn about the other guys, they got what they deserved as far as Jacko and the team were concerned!

"Yeah" Sandy began, she looked around the cabin slowly, "About that, we've got a bit of a plan forming here, we're in the chopper we captured on the beach, that's why we needed the pilot!"

"That figures" they actually heard Mildred laugh, "That's why I got you Carol! She been stroppy with you yet?"

"Let's just say one officer with his tail between his legs" Sandy replied, half joking, "Guess she's good for the job then?"

"Carol's a reservist, flies commercial choppers for the oil rigs out of New Plymouth normally, she was in the area doing some work for me, she's used to landing the dam things on a postage stamp, and in a full fledged cyclone if she has to!" the translation really was that Mildred had expected this might be a possibility and had her pilot ready 'just in case', "She's perfect for it"

"That's good," Sandy came back, "We're going for a Trojan horse approach, have the RHIBs stay within a couple of hundred yards, but out of sight, have them ready to move as soon as we say so!"

"I take it you want their frequency?"

"Would be easier, if we were in the driving seat." This point was delicate, no one really likes to 'hand over control' of any operation, and one this huge was going to either make or break a lot of careers tonight, the slightest thing going wrong could end up with them all getting the sack, if not going to prison for attacking an innocent ship, not that anyone believed their target, not for one second.

"Okay" Mildred took a moment to reply, "I'm sending them right now, I've put both in, one for the RHIBs and one for the Wellington, as soon as your helo drops you off, I want it outta there, preferably with those two coppers on, got it!"

"Ship's on the horizon" Carol came over the intercom, "RHIBs are trailing it, couple of hundred meters astern, as ordered"

"Okay, listen up folks" Jacko turned and faced everyone, except Carol who concentrated on flying, she was keeping low, "we've no idea if we've been 'rumbled' and frankly I couldn't care less, here's what we're gonna do." he pointed to Mac and Smithy, "you're with me, as we planned, we go first and secure the deck, next is Joey and Hene." He turned to the two men.

Both of them were busy with Hene's pistol, they'd managed to 'relieve one of the live prisoners of a few weapons, Hene and Sam both had Glocks, with a couple of 'clips' each, Joey was taking him through some of the safety precautions. Here had baulked at first, that was until Joey asked if he'd ever used the pistol to kill anyone, that got his attention.

They both stopped and looked up, Joey spoke up for the two of them.

"We're next" Joey began, "soon as you're clear, you clear a way for Sandy and Sam, all the way to the bridge cum comm center".

"And we'll be right on their heels" Sandy added, "we need to get in there before too much gets wiped from hard drives!"

"Shit, guys we've got a problem." Carol came over the intercom, "they just called us".

"Well reply then!" Jacko replied.

"In case you didn't notice" Carol shot back, "their boy, was a boy, last time I checked my voice was a bit too high, besides, I noticed he had an accent!"

"We're only what, A hundred fifty yards? Soon as we cross the stern, come hard right, broadside on," turning to the team he saw Joey and Sandy, both in the middle, MP5s at the ready, "suppression fire as soon as the doors are open"

The chopper came in low and fast, they could see men running, weapons coming out, no one was firing, but a couple were looking like it could erupt any second. As soon as the chopper cleared the stern Carol threw a hard to starboard, at the same time Mac threw the door open, both he and Smithy were out and running.

Sandy saw one from the boat bring his weapon up, it was an Uzzi, she let off a short burst, it caught him clean in the chest, he went down, two more were coming, raising their weapons, they hadn't seen Smithy, he poleaxed the first with his pistol, the second got an almighty kick in the groin, both were down, next Jacko was on top of them, plasticuffs were put on and they were bundled to the side, Jacko removed both their weapons.

"You two next" Joey shouted at Hene and Sam, they were trying real hard to keep up with things, but this team worked so radically different to anything they were used to, "Head for the door" he pointed to the door about ten feet outside the disc of the blades. There were a couple of cylinders there, "We'll be right there"

All four of them leapt from the chopper, as soon as they were clear Carol pulled hard on the collective, put the nose down and flew off like a screaming banshee, creating as much panic among the boat's inhabitants as she could, ten seconds later she was hitting a hundred and fifty knots calling out for a bearing to the Wellington.

"Smithy, cover us, we'll get the RHIBs in" Jacko called out, he and Mac worked their way to the stern and signalled the two boats, they heard the roar of the huge outboards as the two boats came to life, two ropes came hurling over the back of the boat, Mac grabbed one, Jacko the other and both found a secure point to tie the boats to, next came rope ladders that were also secured, then came the Navy, each one ready for whatever was coming their way.

The door was locked, that didn't stop Joey, one flying drop kick and the door gave way, they were in the corridor, Joey in the lead, MP5 slung over his back and the Browning at the ready, "Hene," Joey called out, "You watch our backs, anything that doesn't identify either Army or Navy, waste it!"

"What?" Hene started to protest, "What about?"

"Don't bloody argue, just damn well do it! We'll worry about the niceties later, GOT IT?"

"Just do as he says" Sam chipped in, figuring it might get taken better if it was coming from a fellow police officer.

They moved quickly, not worrying too much about stealth, Joey leading, next was Sandy, then Sam and finally Hene, checking their rear.

The corridor had a left turn, Joey halted, glancing furtively round the corner he saw a set of steps with a guard at the bottom, he had an Uzi, and he looked nervous.

Joey reached down into one of the pouches on his belt, he took out his silencer, put it on the end of the barrel, pushed and turned, the familiar sound of the bayonet connection clicking into place.

"ARMY, DROP YOUR WEAPON!" Joey demanded as he pivoted round challenging the guard, either the guard didn't hear, chose not to hear or simply thought 'screw you' and started to bring his weapon to bear. The outcome was two shots in quick succession, one to the left knee and one to the right shoulder, the weapon fell to the floor as he slumped, his cries of agony drowned out by the shouting and occasional gunfire outside.

"First team" the lieutenant in charge of the boarding party ordered, "take the port side, use extreme prejudice if you have to, second team, you get starboard, move out!"

"Lieutenant" Jacko spoke loudly and forcefully to the young officer, "I've got four of my folks heading for the bridge, there's likely to be some carnage in their wake, tell your men not to engage them, just make contact!"

The officer looked dubious, he knew the SF team was here, and they were supposed to be 'assisting' but the idea of 'carnage in their wake' didn't sit well, he'd be the one explaining to the brass if anything or anyone fouled up, "Listen up teams, we've got an SAS team already either on the bridge or on their way" he radioed in, "take care to ID yourselves, out." He let go the mike, "care to explain that mate?" He had no idea whom he was talking with, or their rank.

"It's Captain, and no, not really" Jacko replied, "now you go with the portside team, I'll go with the starboard, our medic will treat any wounded back here," he pointed to Mac,"and the corporal will take care of prisoners" Smithy said nothing, but wasn't happy.

Smugglers and drug dealers aren't well disciplined normally, these weren't an exception, sure, they were loud, and aggressive, but put them up against a well trained, well disciplined unit determined to win and there's only going to be one outcome. Within minutes they realized the fight could only end one of two ways.

First, even if they do beat the boarding party off, somewhere 'out there' is a warship just waiting to blow them clean out of the water, and they probably wouldn't hesitate.

Secondly, they could surrender and take their chances with whatever prison system they end up in. The second option seemed much more attractive, especially as most of them would still be 'upright, and sucking air,' that was definitely a bonus.

A couple of the Asians, knowing what awaited them tried to fight on, but they were no match for the Navy, within minutes the ship was going silent, even the engines had been cut back.

The door was locked, they could hear voices on the other side, the sound of panic, frantic voices shouting and cursing in at least a couple of languages, at least that's what it sounded like to Joey, he couldn't tell which one's, but there was no mistaking the tone.

They were on the top deck, at the stern, the stairs that lead them were just to the left, Sam and Hene were still on them, Sam was half way up and Hene at the bottom, watching their backs. Joey snaked his way across to the right hand side of the door, he indicated to Sandy they needed the lock pick, she had a small rucksack with her 'bag of tricks' in, she took it off, set the pack down and found what she needed.

The lock wasn't anything special, just a standard mortice and tenon lock, Sandy only took a few seconds, then she gave Joey the 'thumbs up', he hand signalled her to move away.

Work with someone for long enough and you begin to understand how they think, she knew Joey was thinking they had no idea what was behind the door. Yes it lead into the lounge, the main control for the ship, but what was waiting on the other side?

The one thing she'd learned with the team was 'always expect the unexpected' it was just a hazard of their occupation, or as Joey would say, "it goes with the territory."

"What the hell's the holdup?" Sam asked, unsure of the situation.

"Booby traps" Sandy replied, "you wouldn't want to walk through a door with a claymore waiting on the other side, or a machine gun!"

"Oh" there wasn't much to say really, "sorry I asked" Sam felt sheepish something she probably should have known.

"Joey's ex bomb disposal" Sandy went on, "to him, it's second nature," she shifted slightly, "you and me however, we'd never think of it, and head straight into the trap"

Just then the mike came alive. "Joey, Jacko here, sitrep now!" It was more a demand than a question.

Sandy noticed Joey had moved, he wasn't in the 'ready' position with back against the wall, he'd lowered himself down and was lying prone on the floor, he was at an angle, it took her a moment to realize he'd moved so he presented the smallest target and maximum Kevlar protection, he was gently pushing the door open, checking for nasty surprises.

Thunder broke out, continuous rumbling as the wall and door seemed to explode at waist height, two machine guns were blasting anything along the wall.

The door was far enough ajar for his needs, he still had the Browning in his left hand, he waved it to tell them "get ready." Sandy couldn't really believe it, the wall was being torn apart by machine gun fire, and Joey was as calm as ever, preparing to retaliate with stun grenades!

Laying the Browning down, he reached back and found the last 'flasbang' keying his mike, he whispered. "Just about to breach boss, stay out of the lounge, they've got a couple of AKs in there, stand by" he pulled the pin, released the handle and rolled the cylinder forward round the door.

As soon as he let go, he rolled back behind the door and held up his hands. "On three close the eyes and cover the ears!" He counted down using hand signals.

There was brilliant white light, they saw it even through closed eyes, followed by a deafening bang.

Joey was up and through the door, he saw two with AK 47s.

"ARMY, WEAPONS DOWN!" He shouted, the two were trying to swap magazines, they'd used a whole magazine each on the wall, they started bringing up their weapons.

Joey saw it, the Browning came up and barked twice, the first guy went down with two in the chest, that's when he heard another shot fired, then a second.

He was thrown across the room, it felt like he'd been kicked in the chest, he could hardly breathe.

Sandy burst into the room, she took out the second one, but that's when they realized he wasn't the danger, she didn't see it at first, it was only when Joey knocked her flying as he was knocked over by the force of the two rounds hitting him they became even aware of any danger.

Fishface knew what was going to happen as soon as he saw the cylinder, he'd made a grab for the table and tried to upturn it, but it was bolted to the floor, he threw himself behind a chair just as the flashbang went off.

His 'cat like' reflexes saved him, he came back up, a Beretta 9mm in hand, with one fluid motion he took aim and squeezed off two shots, the first guy, Joey, went sprawling, next he followed through to the second target.

Sam saw it happen, she saw it through the holes in the wall that the bullets had made, she saw the two shots, saw him line up his next target. Training kicked in.

There wasn't time to warn, it would be over in a nanosecond, Sam's police training 'kicked' in, seemingly from nowhere, she'd done these in training, but never in real life before, still, it was like a 'second nature' to her, no thinking, just following through. She had the Glock, flicking the safety to auto she flung herself through the door, not sure how many rounds she still had in the clip, she let them all off in the general direction of the shooter. Glass

Seven rounds left the chamber, but three found their mark, all three to the chest, Fishface wasn't getting up from that.Glass disintegrated as the other four hit various panels, shattering and spraying everything with broken glass.

Chen saw the door move at the beginning, he saw the two guards 'spray and pray' the walls and he ran. As soon as he was through the door he heard shouting on his right, so he headed for the left side, he threw the briefcase he'd been stuffing money into down the ladder and grabbed hold, sliding down the ladder he was working out how to get away when a hand came up from behind and yanked him off the ladder. He was forced back, tripping and ending up on his back staring down the barrel of an Steyr AUG less than an inch from his face and an extremely pissed off Naval rating.

"Move and I'll blow your sodding head off!" the rating was screaming, even with his limited English, Chen understood the situation perfectly, he stayed as still as a stone.

"On yer back" the rating screamed as he grabbed Chen and began to roll him over, the muzzle never more than two inches from his face, "arms out, spread yer legs" another rating took up a position behind them, covering the first one as he began a physical and none too gentle search or 'pat down,' finally, when he was satisfied the rating grabbed both arms and wrenched them down and behind him, taking the plasticuffs from his belt, he put them on and made sure they were uncomfortably tight, but not too tight to totally cut off circulation, it was over.

"Captain" the young Naval officer called into the radio, "we got him, rest of the teams are reporting the ship secure." Jacko could hear the relief in his voice.

"Thank you Lieutenant, and tell your men, bloody good work" Jacko replied.

Hene got into the room after the gunfight, just in time to see Fishface go down, he'd made it to him just in time to see the light of life go out of his eyes, he wasn't sure if he wanted to try and save him, part of him said he should, but another part said, "after all the pain and misery this one's caused, the world might be a better place without him!"

That's what he felt, but inside there was that little struggle that a fundamentally good person has when even the most awful and evil meet their demise, a sadness that it came to this, fighting with the thought of 'good riddance', he was glad that he didn't have to make a choice as the light went out before he could do anything.

"Don't bother with him" a female voice came from behind, it was Sam's, "go check on our own people." It was almost an order, he began to look around.

Joey was rubbing his chest, it felt like he'd been kicked by a mule, "Shit, that hurt" he mumbled as he slowly rose to a sitting position, "I forgot how much it hurts"

"You mean this isn't the first time?" both Sam and Hene asked the question, they were cops, but they only trained for this, reality was quite different.

"Wish I could say it was" Joey replied with a rueful smile, "Hazard of my job"

"Remind me never to apply" Hene shot back, they stopped for a moment in stunned silence, then slowly Sandy began to laugh, followed by Joey, but he didn't laugh much as it hurt to try too much. "Hell, I must've cracked a rib or something!"

"Bloody typical" Mac came through the corridor, the same way they'd come in, "give him a bit of an audience, and he'll make a bloody show, get all the sympathy, especially from the women, eh Joey?"

Joey couldn't help laughing, even though it hurt, "you taught me well Mac!" He reached out for the big Scot to give him a hand, "come on, let's go see what we've found."

Chapter 32

"Boss" the radio came to life, it was one of the Navy ratings calling the Lieutenant, "We're down in the stern compartment, you better come take a look"

"On our way" the officer replied, he turned to Jacko, "Maybe you'd better come too"

Jacko was half in the bridge and half in the lounge area, Mac was still checking Joey's injury,'Nothing but a bruise" was the only comment he'd made, the Kevlar had saved his life, but that wasn't new territory for them, "Joey, let's go take a look, you too Mac" he turned to Sandy, there's the laptops there, see what you can retrieve,"

"Will do" she turned to Sam, "any good with computers?" she asked as she set the first one back on the table, it didn't look too banged up.

"Not bad" Sam replied, but are you sure they're going to work?"

Sandy was reaching into the backpack, she pulled out a small device, that sort of looked like a smartphone with a few leads attached, "Won't matter really, all I need is the hard drive to be intact, and a power supply, this little device will do the rest!" she plugged it into one of the ports on the laptop, next she turned the machine on, "looks like the battery still has juice in it, she was basically bypassing the motherboard and using the machine's own battery supply to read the files on the hard drive. Next she took the tablet they'd been using and connected it to the device, that allowed her to open and look at any file they wanted to.

Jacko was still in the doorway, "Hene, you come with us, I've got a feeling the police are going to want to know all about what's there!" They left the bridge.

The stern compartment is where the billionaire toys are normally kept, you know, the Ferrari they use to drive, the Jet Skis and anything else they take along for the ride. It was a huge compartment, big enough to be a small warehouse, and that's exactly what it had been turned into.

Five pallets of what looked like hessian sacks lined the walls, two of the pallets were eight layers high, and covered with shrink wrap, only on close inspection did you see the 'sacks' themselves were packed with 'bricks' of various kinds, some looked like bricks of white powder, some were a slightly different colour, but there was no mistaking the substances, Heroin and Cocaine and literally tons on if!

"Holy….." Jacko blurted out as they walked into the room, "Jeez, How much?"

"At a guess sir" the rating who'd made the call replied, "about a ton and a half of the Heroin, and nearly a ton of Cocaine, but that's not all, step this way" he showed them to another compartment, "This is the crystal meth!" there were two more pallets, "and next door is the lab, they're making and supplying from the ship." he let that sink in before continuing, "We've got the precursor material in another compartment"

"How many compartments altogether?" the Lieutenant finally recovered enough to ask a question, this was easily going to be the biggest drug bust certainly in New Zealand.

"Four sir" the rating replied, "last one's where they kept the weapons and the safe with the money in!"

They were just coming to terms with the magnitude of the bust when Jacko and Joey's earpieces came to life, it was Sandy, "Jacko, something you'll need to see, bring Joey, and Hene"

They were there in double time, "What you got for us?" Jacko demanded as they came through the door.

Sandy took a small thumb drive and gave it to him, "Guard this with your life boss, our lives might just depend on it!" the last time she'd looked this serious they were about to storm the fortress at Alamut.

Jacko took the drive, unclipped his breast pocket and slid the drive in, clipping the pocket shut again he asked, "what exactly is it?"

Sandy looked him directly in the eye, she motioned for Joey to close the door, Joey did, Hene had crossed the room and closed the other door as best he could, Mac was treating wounded and Smithy was dealing with the prisoners they'd taken as the Navy boys and girls were still doing their search. As soon as the doors were closed she spoke in a voice so low it was almost a whisper, "It's got the reason we had to get out of London boss! Not the name exactly, but the first clue that'll lead us to"

"Cut the cloak and dagger Sandy, just come straight out and tell us" Jacko demanded.

"Okay" Sandy replied, "it's got a phone number there, someone from that number was making a call, it's also got the location and time, they were making it to the Satphone here by the way"

"And?"

"And it was coming" she replied, "from inside M.I.6 headquarters. Third floor!"

If you enjoyed this story, then read on.

This is an excerpt from next novel in the series.

Scorpion's Vengeance
Scorpion's Vengeance

Chapter 1

Location	**London**
Time	**Tuesday 05.30 (local time)**

There was a slight chill in the air as she stepped out of the apartment block, there was a noticeable trail from the moisture she exhaled, the temperature was in single digits, and probably near to zero celsius. Not surprising considering it was autumn, and winter was closing in.

The first thing she noticed outside, (apart from the cold that is) was the traffic, pretty steady at this time in the morning, any later and it would be its usual diabolical situation, it made her glad that the 'tube' (as Londoners affectionately call the London underground rail network) got her to within a few minutes walk of work.

It also meant that instead of having a horrible commute of at least an hour by car, all she had to do was walk to the local 'tube station' at the 'Elephant and Castle' jump on the Northern line and ten minutes later she'd be right outside the Bank of England in one of the world's greatest financial hubs.

But the really great part about the place was, just a short jog from home was some of London's best attractions. Walk out of the apartment, take a right on

Brook-street, and you're right outside the Imperial war museum, with the massive fourteen-inch guns from the front turret of HMS Warspite, one of Britain's last Battleships to be decommissioned after the second world war on full display.

Turn right onto Kennington road and first left onto Horse-ferry road and Lambeth Palace is right there, the official residence of the Archbishop of Canterbury, and a medieval palace in its own right. Head across the bridge and you're right there, in the seat of power, Westminster Palace, better known as the House of Commons, and the House of Lords, Parliament, and all within a short jog of her place.

There were a few cars about, but most of the traffic was commercial, trying to make their final deliveries before the six am deadline when delivery trucks need to be out of the urban centres, so as to give room for those crazy enough to try getting to work by car, not that there are many of them in London, 'congestion' charges make sure of that either only those who live within the limits drive their cars around, or those addicted to their cars and willing to pay the exorbitant charges for using it, the tube is much easier, and safer.

She stopped for a moment, adjusting her beanie, checked her ponytail, no need to hide any keys, the apartment had one of the latest locks with a four-digit keypad system, unbreakable, then again the four-digit code she'd programmed would have been easy to break, it was her birthday, easy to remember and easy for anyone who knew Jane to break into the apartment, if they knew her date of birth that is!

As soon as everything was ready, everything checked and working, she was off, a morning jog, she was planning to start gently as there were a few main streets to cross, and the last couple of years the local council had been converting the pedestrian underpasses to cycleways, meaning at this time of the morning, she could be dealing with a few maniacal cyclists hell-bent on running anything in their path down.

After the run it would be a shower, breakfast, and into work by 8 am, that was the plan, the same every morning, she had no idea the change that was going to happen.

At the end of Hercules street she 'hung a right' and started picking up the pace, next stop would be Lambeth bridge, just alongside Lambeth Palace.

It always puzzled Jane, She worked in the financial world, and was used to opulence, or wealth, but wasn't the church founded by a poor son of a carpenter? And didn't he teach "The love of money is the root of all evil?" Yet here was a huge Palace, all for the use of one man! Just didn't make sense to her really, in some ways' she was a traditional 'C of E' as they said in Britain for the Anglican church, but in other ways, she didn't really have too many beliefs, apart from the need to be a basically 'good' person, yet the church seemed to 'float' its own rules, teaching poverty for its members, but wealth for its hierarchy!

Crossing Lambeth bridge, she turned right, but not the hard right that would take her along the river, and started her run in earnest. Sycamore trees lined the right-hand side of the road, they'd lost about half their leaves so far, a street sweeper was slowly making its way down the opposite side of the street, clearing away the foliage before 'the powers that be' surfaced and took charge of the country for the morning, this was the time when only the lowly paid would be working.

About half a mile further up she took a right, the house of Lords on her left, the imposing tower where Big Ben rang out was on the other side of the building.

Most tourists think of Big Ben, the most iconic landmark in London as the big clock tower you see on just about every postcard from London, but Big Ben actually is the massive bell inside the tower, and at thirteen tons, it lives up to the name! The tower has another name, the Elizabeth Tower, named after the present Queen, and in honour of her Diamond Jubilee celebrations.

Reaching the Thames, she turned right again and was just hitting her stride something caught her eye, something floating in the river.

"What the?" was her first thought, "What is that?" she stopped to take a closer look, "Oh my God" she screamed as the thing turned over, slowly, seemingly reluctantly as if it didn't want to reveal itself, but now there was no doubt as the gruesome thing stared back through lifeless eyes.

Chapter 2

Location   Bay of Plenty off the coast of New Zealand

Time.   Monday 0500 (local time) and 12 hours ahead of London.

"You are aware" Jacko shouted into the headset, "the mission is over, you are aware of that aren't you?" he tapped Carol, the pilot on the shoulder as he spoke.

They were at fifty feet, touching two hundred miles an hour, and heading for the coastline. No navigation lights

"Sorry Captain" Carol almost laughed, "in case you didn't know, you're not supposed to be here, that means I've got to get you outta here with no one knowing you were ever around, get my drift?" she had a cheeky grin.

'Black ops' or Covert Ops aren't just about getting in without your enemy knowing you're coming, they're just as much about getting out again without anyone knowing you've been there! Literally 'keep 'em guessing' and that means the 'exfil' can be just as hairy as the 'infill' and Carol was loving every second of it, it's not often she got to push her 'cab' to its limit (and we'll beyond what the manufacturer said it could do).

Jacko turned back, the rest of the team were busy, Mac, Smithy and Joey all had their weapons stripped, and were busy cleaning them, Sandy was poring over the laptop, checking files, from the look on her face, he wasn't even sure it'd registered that they were airborne. Sam and Hene were at the back, slightly dazed look on their faces, 'with what they've just been through, no wonder' he thought to himself. He was surprised and encouraged how well they were holding things together.

He keyed his mike again. "How far to our destination?"

"Fifteen minutes until we're over land" Carol replied, "then about forty minutes"

"Bird off the Starboard" The co-pilot spoke the warning, the set of navigation lights seemed to be heading straight for them and coming in really fast. "Closing fast, break right, BREAK RIGHT" the second command was almost a shout as Carol yanked the controls hard right, all Jacko saw was sky as the aircraft went into the steep turn.

"What the" Mac's reaction was instinctive, he grabbed for the bulkhead, not really necessary as they were all strapped firmly in, "what the hell boss? I'm looking at the bloody ocean!"

"Thank your lucky stars you can still see it, and aren't in the bloody stuff" Carol cut in, she glanced at the co-pilot, "thanks for that"

"Eagle one, this is eagles nest" they all heard the call, it couldn't be a good thing, 'Eagle's nest' was where 'Mildred' was, someone was changing things, and that was never good.

"One go ahead" Carol replied on the radio.

"Go to channel one"

Everyone was listening, they were still working through cleaning the weapons, but there was a sense of urgency, Carol had told them at the start that channel one was the scrambler channel, "You know, just in case" she'd said. Now, whoever it was wanted to speak to them without even the professional 'snoops' listening in, that was reserved for only the most important. It didn't bode well for whatever they had to say.

The co-pilot reached out with his left hand, turning a dial on the central console they heard nothing at first, then a voice came on the line, they'd heard it once before, at the start of the op, but five of the seven recognised it straight away.

"Captain, I presume you can all hear me?" the voice asked, it was female, and from the sound, she was an older middle-aged woman, one used to being in charge.

"Yes ma'am" Jacko replied, "We're all here"

"Good" the voice came back, "then I don't have to waste my time repeating myself, sorry about this, but a formal debrief isn't going to happen at this stage"

'Shit' no one said the word, but that's exactly what everyone was thinking, whatever was going on meant that this op wasn't over, but what the hell can be next?

"We've got so much information" the voice went on, "it's going to take months to put everything together, but some of what we got we've got to get our arses into gear and move on it, and I mean now!"

"Figured that," Joey thought he whispered it, but the 'voice' heard it and cut him off.

"Glad you're with us Mr Metcalfe, how's the wound?"

"The jacket took the bullets" Jacko silenced Joey with a glare and a finger over his lips, "Just a couple of bruises, that's all, besides, where there's no sense, there's no feeling right Joey?" he joked, it brought smiles from the rest of them, even Joey enjoyed the joke.

"Glad to hear it" Mildred's voice came back, "we're going to need every one of you in this, and that includes the two police with you!" she didn't refer to Sam and Hene by name, she didn't know their names, but that didn't matter.

Sam and Hene had been sat trying to comprehend what they'd just been through, Police training prepares you for a lot, but what they'd just done was in a different league. Yes they'd used firearms, and there'd been times when Sam had drawn hers in the line of duty, but this had been a full-fledged firefight where they'd been shooting to kill with every shot, and the team had been absolutely ruthless, but what had thrown them was the fact that none of the team seemed too concerned they'd just been in a life or death firefight. The voice mentioning them snapped them back to reality.

"As I said" the voice went on, "we've got to get your arses into gear, otherwise we'll lose the momentum, at the moment, we've got an enemy that's wounded, but from what we can make out, they're a long way from being finished, and if we don't move fast, they're likely to strike back and do it hard!"

"Roger that ma'am" Jacko cut back in, "what do you need from us?"

"I'm going to need you to deliver a message for me" the voice came back, the helicopter had turned nearly ninety degrees and was heading straight for the Coromandel Peninsula, it was going to be an interesting flight. "The two police, with you, Sam and Hene isn't it?"

"Yes," both of them confirmed.

"You're still officially with the police" the voice replied, "but as of this moment, you work directly with me, a new task force that the Prime Minister will set up as soon as I've put the paper on their desk, and yes, they've already agreed to it, you'll be working for me on the legal side of things here in New Zealand, at least that's what the papers will say, reality is you'll be running 'backup' for the team, and just about anything else I can think of"

Sam and Hene just looked at each other, Sam was a good cop, even got noticed by her bosses, but this was way beyond even her paygrade, whoever it was, clearly had some pull!

And that phrase "that's what the papers will say" kind of bothered her, made it sound like there was more to things than even Mildred was letting on.

"As for the rest of you" the voice went on, Jacko and Mac, a vehicle's waiting on the tarmac for you, it'll take you to a waiting C130 that'll fly you back to Aussie as soon as you're aboard, from there, you'll board a flight to London, papers and passports will be given you when you get to Sydney, Should take you about twenty-four hours all told"

Silence, no one knew what to think, clearly, something was going on, "Might I ask why?" it was Mac asked the question, no one liked the sound of what was going on.

It took a few moments for the voice to reply, "We need to get the information to Sir Michael, but can't use the normal channels"

"We've got a leak to haven't we?" it was Sandy who cut in, "Not just a mole, but one that could blow the whole thing, isn't that right?"

"Whoever it was," the voice came back, "fed your names and details to the ship, that means the whole organization knows who's hunting them! And as far as I know, only three people knew whom you were, all three can be accounted for, and they didn't pass the information, so it has to be someone working in the secure comms networks!"

"Holy crap" Joey let out a few more choice words as well, "that means every"

"Every signal we sent, every word we reported back, all got given to them, not only that, but every detail about us, they have, and they probably know that we know!"

"Hence the 'old school' face to face" the voice came back, "and that's where you come in Captain"

The rest of the flight went off without a hitch, better yet, no one needed a 'puke bag' despite seemingly Carol's best efforts, she was quietly impressed at the way the team handled themselves.

They approached the coast with little let up from the pilot, there was a trust there, very few pilots could pull off the kind of flying she'd done on the 'intercept', she'd got them there without the enemy having a clue.

Contrary to what the movies say, no helicopter has a 'stealth mode!' Sure, some have noise suppression technology on the engines, but the 'dead giveaway' is the 'thwack' the rotor blades make as they move forward. The rotors, when they're moving forward are actually travelling at twice the speed of the aircraft, that means two hundred miles an hour, the blades are doing four hundred. Anything going through the air at four hundred miles an hour makes a hell of a noise!

There are only two things can help reduce that noise, terrain and wind, sound carries 'on the wind' so come in 'upwind' of the location and they aren't going to hear you, throw in some terrain blocking the way, and they've got no chance of spotting you.

"Two minutes," Carol turned and gave Jacko a smile. Everyone began re-assembling their weapons, Smithy was first to finish.

He could see landing lights, from the 'black' all around, it looked like they were in the middle of nowhere, that's exactly where they were.

Ten minutes later, they were on the ground, Carol didn't even bother shutting the aircraft down, she just turned slightly in their direction, keyed the mike and smiled, "Boss girl wants to see you, off you go!"

Somehow, it felt like being dragged into a school principal's office for some event you were involved in, but not responsible for! They were in the middle of nowhere, by the lack of even starlight near to where the horizon should be, they were in a clearing, and from the smell, it was a pine forest, but other than a small building they'd caught a glimpse of, there wasn't anything, not even transport waiting for them.

'All will be revealed' he thought to himself, but what came out was, "Okay folks, let's move".

The doors slid open, Mac and Joey were first out, Mac ran from the right-hand side, heading for the 'two o'clock' position, Joey went from the left to the ten o'clock, both stopped just outside the rotor disk and went down, into a kneeling position, ready to return fire if it turned to crap and was an ambush, Smithy, Sandy and Jacko watched, covering, weapons at the ready, fingers on the trigger, safeties on, even though it was supposed to be a 'safe' area, it paid to be cautious.

Next was Sandy, she joined Joey's side of the aircraft, but a good ten feet further away, close enough to be seen, but too far away to be 'taken out' by any incoming fire. Next was Jacko followed by Smithy, as team Sniper, Smithy often got the job of covering everyone else's arse in a firefight, he was nearly always last to move.

As soon as Smithy was clear of the disk, Jacko turned and gave her the 'thumbs up' sign, he heard the whine increase as Carol brought her up to 'lift-off speed', the aircraft lifted off smoothly, the nose dipped slightly as she used the rate of climb to increase her speed leaving the clearing, no lights came on as she left.

The light was just starting to filter over the eastern horizon as the world began to wake up, it was waking up to a very different situation. The light was starting to show, just as noise from the engines on the aircraft faded.

The most vulnerable time for any military unit is just before the dawn, that's when the men and women who've worked all night keeping the unit safe are tired and ready for rest, but the new men and women, those just coming on duty, aren't fully 'up with the play' and literally 'half asleep', it's the time when the soldier needs to be at their most vigilant, everyone on the team knew it, and all were watching, waiting, relaxed yet ready.

Silence, at least that's what it seemed like, just the noise of the wind gently blowing through the trees, the smell of fresh pine was strong, but there was another smell too, faint, but unmistakable to the trained, the smell of human habitation.

Everyone stayed totally still if there was anyone to meet them, it was up to them to show themselves, even the slightest move from the team could result in disaster, too many ops had failed because of bad discipline at the end during the 'exfil'. They knew they were being watched, it didn't matter the damage they'd just inflicted on the drug operation, with the SAS, everything you do is analysed by someone.

The darkness of the night gave way to the dimness of the dawn.

A light came on in the building they'd seen on the way in, it wasn't a huge place, actually looked more like a forest hut than anything else, but that was strange as there weren't any roads or even tracks around as far as they could see, and there's no way Carol would have landed them near to any inhabited huts, whoever it was, had a bloody good place to hide.

"Captain Jackson" The female in the group spoke up as they got about twenty feet from the team, "Glad to make your acquaintance" she held out a hand, "You can call me Mildred"

Hope you're enjoying the first couple of chapters of the new 'Scorpion Team' novel called "Scorpion's Vengeance' also available on Kindle and Amazon. It's a great read.

Before you go

Other books by the author.
Scorpion one series

- **Sting of the Scorpion**

MI6 have a problem. A missing agent, kidnapped and taken to hostile territory for interrogation.

Only one option is open and that's a high risk rescue operation over two hundred miles into hostile territory with no support, a 'do or die mission' where the stakes are high

- **Scorpion's Vengeance**

A body in the Thames, a city in turmoil and a traitor at the heart of British Intelligence. The two agents that might have the answers have 'gone off the grid'

Thirty-six hours ago Joey Metcalfe and Sandy Little were twelve thousand miles away with the rest of Scorpion Team on an 'Op' tracking down leads that might lead them to the identity of the traitor, but that was thirty-six hours ago, a lot has happened since then. They have gone 'off grid' along with the rest of

A quick word before you go

First of all let me say I hope you enjoyed the novel, though I'd say you probably did by the fact you're still here reading, and that means I have a small favour to ask of you.

See, Amazon loves to know how much people enjoyed (or didn't) enjoy the books they bought through them, and probably on the next screen they're going to ask you if you did. Replying is pretty easy, they give you a star rating system where the star on the left hand side gives the book '1' star (Kinda okay) but move over to the right and you give the book '5' stars (Really good)

I'd really appreciate it if you took the time to tell them how many stars the books deserves, and also leave a little comment saying what you liked, or didn't like about the book, for me this is important as I can look over them from time to time (without knowing who wrote what) and can see what people are enjoying, and what I can work on doing better.

One last thing
If you would like to recieve more of this kind of novel then you can join me through the following link
lawrence'sletters@wordress.com
You'll get regular information from me about future releases along with a weekly post keeping you up to date.

Thanks again for your time.

Lawrence

Printed in Great Britain
by Amazon